# BENEATH THE ASHES

# Jane Isaac

Legend Press Ltd, 107-111 Fleet Street, London, EC4A 2AB
info@legend-paperbooks.co.uk | www.legendpress.co.uk

Contents © Jane Isaac 2016
The right of the above author to be identified as the author of this work has
been asserted in accordance with the Copyright, Designs and Patents Act
1988. British Library Cataloguing in Publication Data available.

Print ISBN 978-1-7850794-7-4
Ebook ISBN 978-1-7850794-8-1
Set in Times. Printed in the United Kingdom by CPI Group (UK) Ltd.
Cover design by Simon Levy www.simonlevyassociates.co.uk

**Jane Isaac** studied creative writing with the Writers Bureau and the London School of Journalism. Jane's short stories have appeared in several crime fiction anthologies. Her debut novel, *An Unfamiliar Murder*, was published in the US in 2012, and was followed by two novels with Legend Press: *The Truth Will Out* in 2014, and *Before It's Too Late* in 2015.

Jane lives in rural Northamptonshire with her husband, daughter and dog, Bollo.

Visit Jane at
janeisaac.co.uk
or on Twitter
@JaneIsaacAuthor

*To Dad and Lynne*

# Prologue

The cool air nipped at her ankles as she climbed out of the car. She turned on her heels 360 degrees. The sun was dipping into the field behind, a thin glimmer on the horizon. A crescent moon stared down, vying for superiority in the silvery sky.

Police sirens screamed in the distance.

The car door slammed as she moved away. A rustle above followed, as a bird was disturbed on its roost. She paused again, glanced around. The air was still and clean, and completely empty.

The sirens hitched up a decibel. They were getting closer.

Salty tears streaked her cheeks. She started up the lane, the handle of the knife gripped firmly in her hand. The light became painted with brushstrokes of charcoal as the trees met in the middle, fingers of branches entwining to form a natural tunnel. She'd been here so many times in the past. Watching. Waiting. Hoping to catch a glimpse of *them*.

In the daytime this area was frequented by dog walkers; golfers heading for the nearby course; families with blankets and picnic baskets sat in the churchyard in summer; kids playing football on the uneven ground out front, using jumpers as makeshift goalposts. The thought raised a fresh tear to her eye. Memories that might have been.

The latch on the gate was stiff. She had to wrench it hard to lift it. Leaving the gate hanging on its hinges, she moved into the churchyard.

The sirens grew louder, piercing the air around her. But she didn't look back.

Edges of grass poked through the gaps in her sandals, spiking her feet as she strode across. She caught her foot on a clod of hard mud, wobbled slightly and continued around the back of the church, to where the earth rose into soft peaks and mounds, pulling down protectively on the fresh graves.

Something stirred in the bushes to her side. She turned. Squinted in the semi-darkness. All was quiet.

She stared back down the hill. Then side to side. Empty.

The sirens were replaced by a rumble of engines, the squeaking of brakes.

Another glance down the hill. Desperately searching. She bit her lip.

The sound of car doors banging, voices shouting.

She looked around once again. More urgently this time.

Finally she found it. The grave was overgrown, the flowers old and wilted, but the gold writing stood out. Pounding footsteps grew closer, gaining momentum. The gate creaked.

She stroked the marble, dropped to her knees, pointed the knife at the centre of her stomach and let out an almighty wail.

# Chapter **One**

## One Week Earlier

Dappled rays of sunshine picked through the gaps in the trees overhead as Inspector Will Jackman turned off the A46 and navigated the back lanes of the Warwickshire countryside. He wound down his window. The rich early morning breeze was infused with a pungent mixture of smoke and fresh dew. Relishing the emptiness of the roads, he coursed around the twists and turns smoothly, slowing at intervals to pass through the picture-book villages, stone houses and thatched cottages that lined his route.

He braked to overtake a horse rider on the outskirts of Ardens Grafton, passed the sign that read *Access to Exhall Village only*, rounded a bend and dropped down the hill before making a sharp left. The aroma of smoke was stronger in the valley, blanketing the surrounding fields with a murky haze as he faced the gentle easterly wind. In the distance, grey tufts hovered above a brick-built barn like hefty clouds in the clear blue sky. He grew nearer, closed the window and parked up on the verge at the end of a line of cars gathered behind two fire engines that blocked the track.

Jackman opened the boot and wrestled with the zip on his holdall. He retrieved a set of coveralls and scanned the surrounding countryside as he pulled them on. It flattened out into the heart of the valley here, the low fields edged by a dense line of trees and bushes that framed the landscape, obscuring them from view of the nearby villages. Cherwell Hamlet, a gathering of four old farm workers' cottages, was dotted about a quarter of a mile in the distance. He zipped up, locked the car and was holding up his warrant card to the uniformed officer on the cordon when he heard the low hum of an engine, wheels crunching over the uneven ground. He turned as a door clicked open.

"Morning, sir." Sergeant Annie Davies climbed out of a car and bustled over, beaming a greeting.

Jackman waved at John, her husband, and watched as he drove the car back down the lane. "Chauffeur service this morning, I see," he said. "All right for some."

"It's the only way we can get the baby to sleep."

Jackman allowed himself a wry smile. "Still teething?"

"It's ridiculous, we're sleeping in shifts. And John's away on a training course tonight." She shoved her sunglasses up onto her head, pushing back wisps of black curls that had escaped from her ponytail and were now flying about in the breeze.

They headed down the track towards a barn, located just off the pathway. Fire officers huddled in groups, some packing away equipment, others meticulously checking the surrounding area. White-suited CSIs wandered in and out of the barn with briefcases. A man and woman in blue coveralls stood beside the entrance with their backs to them, discussing some sheets of paper attached to a clipboard. The woman turned as they approached, leaving her colleague to peel off and assist another fire officer struggling to wind up the final hose. Her mouth stretched into a smile that exposed a perfect set of white teeth. "Will, it's good to see you again."

"Sara." Jackman smiled. "Didn't realise we were on your watch." He extended a hand, which she grabbed and shook heartily, before he introduced her to Davies.

"Our daughters used to go to the same athletics club," Sara said to Davies, grinning from ear to ear. "Inspector Jackman here used to race with them."

"I bet." Davies raised a brow.

"Is Celia still running?" Sara asked.

"Not seriously. She's down in Southampton, studying marine biology. How's Martha?"

"Microbiology at Sheffield. All work, no play. Or that's what she tells me."

Jackman nodded knowingly and turned towards the barn. "What do we have?"

"We received a call from a resident at Cherwell Hamlet," Sara paused briefly to tilt her head towards the cottages on the horizon, "about 2am. A Mrs Buckton. Says she was woken by the smell of smoke. She looked out of the window, identified the source of the fire and called us straight away." Davies produced a notebook from the inside of her jacket and began scribbling down the details as Sara continued. "We arrived within twenty minutes. It took a while to get it under control, looks like it was encouraged by the use of an accelerant."

"We're pretty sure it's arson?"

Sara nodded. "Looks that way. There are a few cars in these barns. A couple of our officers found a petrol cap discarded in the hedge across the way. The doors at both ends of the barn were locked when we arrived and there's a timber inner structure. We made access about half past four when we could be sure it was structurally safe. The body was found beneath some fallen debris."

They followed her past the front entrance, down the side of the barn and through a pair of double doors at the rear. Damp soot covered every inch of brick and tinged the floor giving the appearance of entering a dark cave. As they skirted around three burnt-out vehicles, Sara pointed out where a petrol cap had been removed.

They moved on, making their way across to the far corner where a man in white coveralls was on his knees, examining something. The edge of a familiar smell caught Jackman's nostrils. He inhaled deeply, trying to pick through the smoke, but couldn't place it.

"Morning, Mac," Jackman said as they grew closer.

Doctor Mackenzie Oliver glanced up sideways, nudged his glasses up his nose with the back of his wrist and nodded at them. "How are you?"

"Good, thanks. You got here quick."

"Well, it's my neck of the woods, isn't it?" A thick Glaswegian accent coated his words. He sat back on his heels and turned to face them giving Jackman a clear view of the charred remains of a body on the floor. It was laid out flat on its front, arms wrapped around the head, obscuring the face.

Jackman bent down, leant in closer. From the size of the torso he guessed it was a fully grown adult, although there wasn't anything to indicate sex or age. He turned and looked up at the fire officer. "You haven't moved it?"

Sara shook her head. "Not apart from removing the boards on top."

Jackman looked back at the pathologist. "Any early thoughts?"

Mac sighed. "By the shape of the pelvis and ribcage I can tell you it's an adult male. It looks as though he was either knocked out, or maybe even killed first and planted here afterwards."

"What makes you say that?"

"Look at where he's positioned." Mac pointed towards the door. "If he was still alive and died from the fire or smoke, we'd expect to find him at the door, as though he was clambering to get out. Can't see any obvious cause of death. I'll know more when I get him on the table of course."

Jackman stood. A water droplet dripped down and landed on his shoulder as he turned full circle. The body was located a few metres in from the front entrance. An area at the corner contained an array of metal shelving, melted into uneven shapes – the remains of an office or a workshop perhaps. He wound round and his eyes rested on the shells of three vehicles parked at the far end. They were pretty much burnt-out, although from the curved bumpers and long bonnets,

12

Jackman could see they were some sort of vintage cars. He nodded towards them. "Any chance the fire may have started in one of those? An electrical problem maybe?"

"Unlikely," Sara said. "Their fuel would certainly have bolstered the strength of the fire though."

"Seems a big barn for a few cars. Nothing else in here?"

"Not at the moment. Usually we might expect hay or straw at this time of year, but they tend to float up with the smoke in fragments and we haven't seen any evidence of that. There's a generator out the back too."

The doors at the far end of the barn were flung open and Jackman could just about make out the corner of a generator outside. He turned to Davies, "Get someone to walk the perimeter of the barn outside, will you? We need to check all possible access points."

As he stared at the rear entrance, two CSIs shuffled through. One carried what looked like a stretcher, the other a green body bag. Mac waved them over.

Jackman frowned, "You're using a stretcher?"

Mac nodded. "He's fragile. I need to keep him as intact as possible."

Jackman watched as they hooked gloved hands around the shell of the charred remains. The body appeared to be stiff, the right arm glued to the side of the head on one side. A CSI with a camera stepped forward and clicked, recording every movement. They gently transferred it across to the stretcher. More flashes. They were almost there, rising to a standing position when one of the men slipped his footing. He lost balance, tripping backwards, placing his arms out to save the fall, letting go of the cadaver as he did so. It juddered slightly. There was a moment when Jackman thought it might fall apart. To their astonishment it rolled over to reveal the remains of a pair of jeans, a dark shirt, the clear skin of the insides of forearms and a face which, although singed and blistered around the hair line, was completely visible, the right side pressed against the arm.

Mac rushed forward. Once he was satisfied the victim was stable, he looked up at their surprised faces. "It's a common misconception that people are burnt to a cinder during fire. Often they curl up to protect themselves, or limbs that aren't exposed are protected like the skin on the insides of arms, or stomachs."

"The flames will rise too, go above low objects or just catch the top of them," Sara said. "The timber that fell from the roof would have probably protected him somewhat."

"At least it'll make it easier to identify the body," Jackman said.

The fresh breeze provided a welcome respite as they exited the barn. Sara was just handing over details of the person who reported the fire to Davies when Jackman saw one of the CSIs approach. Something about the set-up bothered him. And there was that smell again. He gave him a quick smile. "Could you make sure you check the generator for fingerprints?" he asked. The CSI nodded, moved on.

They bade their goodbyes to Sara and started back to Jackman's Saab. "Who owns this barn?" he asked Davies.

"Not sure." She pointed in a north easterly direction towards the road. "Nearest farm is the Lawton's if memory serves me right."

"We need to pay them a visit."

# Chapter **Two**

The floor felt hard beneath her face. And wet. Nancy opened her eyes. Blinked several times. Sunlight stretched in spiked lines across the floor. A pain seared through her head. She lay there motionless for a moment, her eyes squinted, waiting for the pain to abate. She could feel fluid. No. She was lying in fluid.

She wriggled to release her arms, flinched at the pain that speared her right knee as she drew it forward and pushed herself into a seated position. A strange metallic smell filled the air. She opened her eyes as wide as she could. The light didn't feel so blinding this time and eventually they found focus. But the pain behind them remained.

A tiny pool of blood on the floor caught her eye and instinctively she lifted her hand to the left side of her head. It felt crusty, the blood already clotted. She moved her hand to her mouth and wiped, looking down, expecting to see more blood, but there was only spittle, the remnants of her own saliva.

Last night's black dress clung to her thighs. How long had she been lying there? Another pain shot through her head as she forced her body into a standing position. A wave of nausea followed and she swayed, clutched the kitchen side for a moment. *Big, deep breaths, in and out*. Eventually the room stopped spinning enough for her to look around.

Nancy recognised the pine cupboards of Evan's kitchen. A single wine glass sat next to the sink. She tried to think back but her thoughts were caught in a haze. She closed her eyes. She was in the kitchen laughing, a glass of wine in her hand. She snapped her eyes open, looked back at the floor. A pair of black stilettoes were sprawled across the tiles. Green wellingtons sat beside the door, encrusted with mud, beside shards of broken glass. Nancy looked up to see the window pane in the back door broken. Splinters of glass littered the floor. She stared at it a moment, puzzled. Where was Evan?

A flashback. The oak beams and low lighting of The Fish pub. Sitting opposite Evan, a yellow napkin on her lap. Oversized wine glasses clinking across the table. She remembered eating steak, later wobbling out into the night air. Blurred images of a pub car park. The drone of Evan's truck.

She moved gingerly. More dizziness, less prominent this time. She waited for it to pass, stepped out of the kitchen into the hallway and halted, listening for the sound of the television, Evan's music, the dogs in the garden. Nothing.

"Evan?"

The call was enough to start the dogs barking in the kennel outside. She hesitated. They needed to be let out. But first she needed to find Evan.

Nancy moved across the parquet flooring in the hallway and into the sitting room. The floral curtains sat open. A messy array of cushions were squished into the back of the sofa. A quick peek into the dining room revealed it was also empty. The dogs were still barking as she climbed the stairs slowly, dragging her fingers on the varnished banisters. She glanced out of the window to the truck in the drive, then headed for Evan's bedroom at the back of the house. The duvet was pulled across, the pillows plumped up. She sat down on the edge of the bed, ruffling the duvet as she did so, and inhaled. But there was none of the fresh, sporty shower gel Evan always used. She searched for a pile of clothes, his shoes. Nothing. "Evan?"

Her voice was drowned out by the dogs. It didn't make

sense. She grabbed her phone from the bedside table, dialled his number and tapped her foot with each ring. Until it switched to voicemail.

A floorboard squeaked beneath her step as she reached the bathroom. Finally the dogs had hushed. She looked in the mirror and started. A dark bruise hung over her left eye with a rich red slice through the middle. It stung like hell and looked like it needed a stitch. Several strands of hair were caught up in the congealed blood and she flinched as she tried to pull them free. Weariness wrapped itself around her.

*A head injury. Don't sleep. Need to see a doctor.* The floor reached up to her, inviting her to rest. Just for a minute. She resisted for the shortest of seconds, before she felt every ounce of energy trickle out of her legs, forcing her down. For a while she felt as though she was floating. *Focus. My name is Nancy Faraday. I'm in the farmhouse where Evan is living.* But even as the words drifted into the ether, two questions rang out in her mind. *How did I end up on the floor? And where in the hell is Evan?*

\*\*\*

"It was the smell that got me first. My nose seems to be drawn to the smell of smoke."

Davies smiled politely at Sheila Buckton. They'd been seated at the round pine table in the centre of her tiny kitchen for over half an hour. Sheila inhaled deeply and straightened her back. This was clearly one of the most exciting events to touch her life for some time and she was not about to rush her account.

The room was situated at the front of the cottage, one of a bank of four that comprised Cherwell Hamlet and overlooked open countryside. Jackman glanced fleetingly at the dregs of tea in the bottom of his mug and stared out of the closed latticed window. He could see the barn in the distance.

"And what time was this?" Davies asked.

Sheila leant back in her chair and folded her hands across her stomach. "Around 2am. I always wake around that time. Usually get up and make a cup of tea."

The sound of a cat meowing filled the room. Sheila rose and opened the side door. She was a tall woman and thick set. A tabby slunk in and wound itself around her ankles. "Hello, Tilly," she said. She bent down and picked her up, crossing back to the chair. The cat purred loudly as she placed it on her lap.

Jackman shot Davies a look. She tilted her head in an effort to get Sheila's attention. "What happened then?"

Sheila scratched the back of the cat's head. "Well, my bedroom is above here at the front. The smell of smoke was so strong I thought it came from one of the neighbouring cottages at first. Jumped up with a real start, I did. But as soon as I got to the window I could see the flames, burning like a towering inferno. Took the fire engines a while to get there too—"

"Did you see anything else?" Jackman asked.

She glanced across, clearly annoyed at his interruption. "What do you mean?"

"Did any vehicles pass through along the road out front?"

She shook her head. "Not that I remember. Until the fire engines arrived." Her eyes grew wide. "Do you think it was started on purpose?"

Jackman ignored her question. He'd already spoken to the press office and arranged to give a statement to the media later that morning, releasing information about the body found in the barn and appealing for witnesses. He could only begin to imagine the look on Sheila's face when she discovered that gem of information. "Does anyone else live here with you?" he asked.

"No. I've been divorced for over thirty years. Used to live near my son in Stratford. Moved here," she glanced at the window a moment, then back at Jackman, "almost nine years ago now. When I heard it had come up for rent I couldn't resist. Such a beautiful location."

"What about your neighbours?"

"Ray and Jenny next door are a week into their Greek holiday. Then there's Kris and Tim at number three and old Jim on the end."

"Do you know which farm owns the barn?"

"Of course, it's Upton Grange Farm. Owned by Ronnie and Janine Lawton, although they're away at the moment. Touring Australia. He's not a real farmer, not like they were when I was a kid. Hearts not in it." She gave a disapproving headshake. "Our local farmer would never have left the business to go gallivanting around the other side of the world for a year."

Jackman sighed inwardly and glanced back out of the window. The view of the barn across the fields was fairly good from here. Good enough to witness comings and goings. Especially if you had nothing better to do.

"Who is managing the farm for them while they are away?" Davies asked.

"I've heard he goes by the name of Evan Baker. Worked on the farm a couple of years, but I've rarely seen him since the Lawtons have been away. Got some strange habits though."

"What do you mean?"

"Most of the fields are full of rapeseed this season." She gave a dismissive sniff. "Does wonders for my hay fever. And he seems set on doing his work after dark."

"Harvesting?"

"All of it. Lights and machinery going on until the wee small hours. It's a disgrace."

# Chapter **Three**

The sound of a shrill bark woke Nancy. She peeled her eyelids back, surprised to find herself curled up on the bath mat. She slowly sat forward, rubbed her forehead, caught the edge of some dried blood and winced.

The mat wrinkled as she pulled her feet from beneath her. They were cold and rubbery where the circulation had been cut off. "Evan?" she called out.

Nothing. She waited a while, called again. *Where was he?*

Nancy stood slowly, holding the edge of the sink to steady herself. The gash above her eye had puckered up like a pair of red-painted lips. Crusted blood ran down her cheek and into her left ear. Her lip was split in the middle.

She slid back the mirrored door of the medicine cabinet and looked inside. A couple of blister packs of paracetamol and a box of plasters filled the bottom shelf. A tub of Nivea and a pot of cotton wool buds sat above, next to a bottle of shaving foam. She closed the door, pulled some toilet paper off the roll, ran it under the tap and started to clean her face. The blood had scabbed over and had to be peeled off in places, like a plaster from her skin, but eventually it came away. She tried to clean the cut, but gave up when the pain was too intense, instead arranging her blonde hair across to the side to cover it. It needed stitches. She moved into the bedroom and instinctively smoothed the creases in the duvet. Evan wouldn't like that. He moaned when she left her earrings on the side, or her clothes on the floor, even if they were in a neat pile. A pain rippled through her lower back as she stood.

An urgent scratching in the distance. The dogs. They must be clambering around, trying to get out of their kennel. She reached into the wardrobe, pulled one of Evan's fleeces around her shoulders and made for the stairs. The scratching was replaced by a chorus of barks as she reached the bottom. She moved across the quarry tiles in the kitchen, sidestepped the glass still scattered across the floor, and picked up Evan's wellingtons, shaking each one upside down to check for pieces of glass before shoving her feet into them.

The barking hiked up a notch. As she reached for the handle, another sound filled her ears. Knocking. Somebody was at the door.

*\*\*\**

Jackman lowered his fist, about to give up when the face of a young woman appeared around the side of house. Her hair was unkempt; she looked pale and tired.

He introduced them both. "We were looking for Mr and Mrs Lawton," he said.

"They're not here." The girl stepped closer as she spoke in a whisper.

"That looks sore," Davies said, glancing towards the wound on the woman's forehead.

The girl ignored her, shifting her eyes from one detective to another. "What's all this about?"

Jackman gave his kindest smile. "You are?"

"Nancy Faraday."

"And you live here too?"

Nancy shook her head. "No, I stayed with my boyfriend, Evan, last night." She paused for a minute, inhaled deeply. "He lives here."

Jackman glanced up at the double-fronted, red-brick house with large sash windows that looked out onto the long driveway. A wide lawn stretched around to the back of the house, giving the impression of large accompanying grounds. Nothing like the postage stamp gardens of some of the houses in Stratford town. He turned to face Nancy. "Is Evan home?"

"No."

"Where is he now?"

The woman's face looked bewildered. "I don't know."

Before Jackman could ask anything more, a loud howl rose from beyond. Almost immediately another joined in harmony. Nancy looked back. "I need to let the dogs out."

She gestured for them to follow her around the side of the house. Stray fragments of broken glass crunched beneath their feet as they walked past the back door. Davies looked askance at Jackman and raised a brow.

"What happened here?" Davies asked.

Nancy turned back, paused to look at the door and back up at them. "I don't know." She opened a gate, closed it behind her and approached a wooden kennel at the side of a paved patio area. As soon as the latch was opened, two spaniels leapt out. The dogs danced around her feet for a couple of seconds while she petted them, then raced off down the garden.

Jackman waited for her to return and close the gate behind her before he spoke again. "Have you had an accident here?"

Nancy placed her hand on the bridge of her nose and thought for a moment. She took a deep breath and looked back up at them. "The truth is I have absolutely no idea."

"Are you here on your own?" Davies said.

Nancy looked back at the door and appeared momentarily transfixed by the spikes of glass edging the frame. The morning sunlight bounced off them, a kaleidoscope of colours winking back. She swayed backwards.

"Careful," Davies said. They both rushed forward. Jackman threw out an arm. It didn't reach in time and Nancy collided with the brick wall. She winced, raised a hand to the

22

gash on her forehead, which had caught the brickwork and immediately opened. A line of red trickled down the side of her temple.

"I think we need to sit you down," Davies said. "Why don't you come and join me in the car?"

Davies placed her hand in the small of Nancy's back and guided her around the side of the house. Jackman waited until they were out of sight before he retrieved a pair of rubber gloves from his pocket, snapped them over his hands and moved into the house.

He pressed his hand to the cold kettle, glanced up at a key rack beside the back door where several sets of keys hung side by side. Jackman was aware that many burglars were after car keys these days – modern cars were so difficult to break into – but whoever had broken that glass was seemingly not interested in stealing cars. The room looked largely undisturbed apart from the shards of glass that littered the floor beside the door, and what looked like a few smears of blood on the tiles in the middle.

He walked through into an open hallway, past a long gilt-edged mirror and ducked his head around the first door he came to. It was a utility room. Several coats hung off a rack on the far wall, a door at the end was ajar revealing a toilet and hand basin. He withdrew and pushed open the next door with the tips of his fingers: a sitting room filled with the kind of furniture that looked both expensive and threadbare. Something in the corner of the next room caught his eye. He walked around the oversized dining room table to an oak cupboard in the corner. The door hung on its hinges to reveal another cupboard tucked inside. A gun cabinet. The metal was bent and mangled where the locks had been forced. The inside was empty.

Jackman climbed the stairs slowly and opened each of the doors in turn, counting five bedrooms and two bathrooms. Most of the bedrooms smelled musty; cobwebs hung from the ceilings and wound their way around the light fittings.

Apart from a few spots of red on the scrunched mat in one of the bathrooms, nothing looked awry.

Jackman paused at the rear landing window to glimpse the array of farm machinery arranged haphazardly in the back yard, then moved into the last bedroom. The air was fresher in here, largely thanks to a small window sitting ajar. A bath robe hung from the back of the door. Either the person using this room was obsessive in their tidiness or they rarely stayed here. He opened the wardrobe. Several pairs of trousers hung on rails at one end, a row of shirts next to them; jumpers and overalls were stacked neatly along the top.

He wandered over to the bedside table and picked up a framed photo of a couple, arm in arm. He recognised Nancy's long blonde hair, her petite frame, and peered closer at the man beside her. The man in the photograph had a rich head of blond hair, a wide smile, eyes lit up like fireworks. He couldn't be sure if it was the victim he saw in the barn earlier.

By the time he'd stepped over the glass and was back outside, the sun had disappeared, enveloped by more gathering clouds. He glanced at the broken pane in the back door as he removed his gloves and made a few quick calls, before he made his way back around to the front of the house.

\*\*\*

"How are you feeling?"

Seated in the back of the unmarked police car, Nancy stared up into the green eyes of the detective. He'd removed his jacket, pushed up the sleeves of the white shirt that stretched across his chest. His dark hair was in dire need of a cut and flopped down into his eyes, but there was a rugged handsomeness about his appearance. "I think I'm okay now," she said. "Just felt a bit dizzy back there."

A triangular washing line was perched on the lawned area that ran along the far side of the house. It squeaked as it gently turned in the breeze. "Why don't you tell me what happened?" he said.

Nancy wriggled the hem of her dress down, embarrassed that she was still wearing last night's clothing. The fresh cut stung and although the world was no longer swaying around her, her head still felt heavy. She blinked, a little clarity of thought filtering through. "What are you doing here?" she asked.

Jackman watched Davies rip open a cotton wool pad and pass it to her. "We're investigating a fire that took place in the barn in the next field last night," he said. He pointed towards the hedge. "A body has been found there. Place that over the cut and press gently."

Nancy pressed the pad to her forehead and winced. "Near the blackberry bushes?"

"That's the one. Do you know it?"

Nancy nodded. "It's called Lowlands Barn, belongs to the farm. They rent it out, I think. Evan would be able to tell you more."

"Where can I find him?"

Nancy shook her head. "I don't know. He wasn't here when I woke up this morning. I've tried to ring his mobile, but he's not picking up." She turned and gazed through the windscreen at the gravelled driveway surrounding them. "He can't be far away, his truck is still here."

Jackman followed her eyeline to the Land Rover parked at the end of the house. "Does he have another vehicle?"

"No. He sold his car when the owners went away. No point in keeping it. He uses the truck for everything."

"When did you last see him?"

Nancy hesitated a moment, desperately trying to pull on the scant memories that were hiding in the shadows of her mind. She explained how they had eaten at The Fish pub at Wixford last night, a hazy memory of them sharing a couple of glasses of wine.

"You said you didn't live here with Evan?"

25

"No, but I must have come back here, stayed last night." The wellingtons she still wore squeaked as she shifted uncomfortably in her seat. "I do sometimes." A sharp thought clutched her. She turned her head, met the detective's gaze. "You don't think it's Evan, do you, in the barn?"

"We don't have any reason to think that," Jackman replied. "The body hasn't been identified yet. But we would like to locate Evan."

Nancy placed a hand to her chest.

"Is there anyone he might be with?"

She shook her head blankly.

"Why don't you tell me a bit about him," the detective said gently. "How was his mood last night?"

Nancy pressed harder. Willing the cogs to turn. "Okay... I think."

"You didn't argue?"

She thought back to the house, waking up on the floor, the broken glass in the back door. "Not that I remember."

"How long have you been seeing each other?"

"Almost three months yesterday. Last night was a sort of anniversary." Nancy explained how she had woken on the floor that morning and searched for Evan. And even as she spoke the words, she realised how sketchy and unsure they sounded. But as hard as she tried, she couldn't tap into her memory of last night. A wave of fear pressed down on her. "You don't think somebody broke in, do you? And took Evan?"

"We've no reason to think that at the moment. But the glass in the back door is broken. Can you think of anybody that might want to hurt either of you?"

Nancy shook her head slowly.

"Okay, I'll need a description of him. And a recent photograph if you have one. Do you have his mobile number?"

Nancy opened her mouth to speak, but her words were drowned out by excited barks, shortly followed by the sound of a slow engine approaching. She reached into her pocket, pulled out her phone, clicked some buttons and handed it over.

Gravel crunched beneath the wheels of the ambulance as it pulled up beside them.

Nancy watched a paramedic jump out. "What's going on?" she asked.

"We need to get you checked over," Jackman said. "And that cut on your forehead needs attention."

# Chapter **Four**

Davies spread the stills of Evan Baker they'd taken off Nancy's phone across the desk in front of them. Most of them were vague, distant shots where his head was turned away from the camera. A photo of them standing side by side indicated he was of average height, several inches taller than Nancy, with long legs and a short body. Wispy fair hair edged a bronzed complexion and the makings of a cheeky smile. She emptied the contents of a brown envelope – photos of the victim taken at the barn from a variety of different angles – sorting through them until she found the face frontals and placed them next to Nancy's photos.

Their eyes worked from one photo to another. A few strands of hair remained on the victim's head, but it was difficult to see what the original colour had been. Although the victim's eyes were closed, Jackman thought he could see a vague resemblance in the contour of his nose and the shape of his jawline.

Davies picked one up, peered in closer. "Look at that." She was pointing at one of Nancy's pictures. A brown speck sat beside Evan's left eye. It was to the side, at the corner of his temple and out of shot on many of the photos, almost as if he'd grown accustomed to tilting his head a certain way to avoid it showing. They both looked closely at the victim shots.

"Look." Davies' hand shot forward.

Jackman followed her finger and could just about make

out an enlarged mole on the edge of the photograph. He put the two photos side by side and compared them. "Could be our guy. The height matches, but we'll need a formal ID to be sure."

His phone buzzed on the desk beside him. *Janus* flashed up on the screen.

Davies glanced at the phone, gathered up the photos and made a hasty retreat.

Jackman answered on the fifth ring, just before the voicemail kicked in. "Morning, ma'am."

Superintendent Alison Janus didn't waste time on pleasantries. "I hear you've got another body?"

Her impersonal approach to homicide never ceased to amaze Jackman. "A man's body was found in a burnt-out barn this morning," he said. He went on to update her on the investigation so far. "Our first priority is to get a formal ID on the body. We've already started looking into the background of Evan Baker who is at present missing. We'll take a close look at his girlfriend too."

"Initial thoughts?"

"Difficult to say. The girlfriend is at Warwick Hospital, suffering from concussion. The house was seemingly broken into, no vehicles apparently taken. The gun cupboard looks like it's been raided, but with the owners away, we'd need to check with firearms licensing and establish whether there were still guns stored there. It's possible they disturbed a burglar. I'm waiting on forensics and hoping that delving into their backgrounds will uncover something."

"Okay, Will. Go ahead with a media statement appealing for witnesses in and around the pub last night. If they had a row amongst themselves or with someone else, somebody'll have seen something. DCI Reilly is still sunning himself in the Seychelles, and Peverell is on a review team at the Met. You're going to have to carry this one for the moment." She paused. "It'll be good evidence for your promotion board next week. That's assuming you wrap it up quickly, of course."

"I've based myself at Rother Street station for now, just getting everything set up." Jackman held his breath. The current trend was to use the readily available 'homicide suites' at force headquarters in Leamington, something that management like Janus championed. But Jackman hated centralised incident rooms. He preferred to be close to the enquiry, so they could peruse the ground, speak to local people, show a close presence in the vicinity.

To his surprise, he was greeted with a heavy sigh. "Okay. How's Alice?" The mention of his wife, out of the blue like that, knocked him sideways. "We haven't spoken about her in a while. How's she doing?"

Jackman inclined his head back. The image of his wife's head, wedged between the dashboard and the crushed roof of their Ford Focus flashed up in front of him. A little over twelve months had passed and the accident was still as fresh in his mind as if it had happened yesterday. "The same," he said.

"Right. Let me know if there's any more help you need there. I'll be guided by you."

The 'help' she was referring to was a series of mandatory counselling sessions he attended as part of the force's agreement to him returning to work, six months earlier. During the accident his wife had suffered damage to her basilar artery, leaving her in a severe state of locked-in syndrome. Her body had shut down, yet there was every chance her brain remained as active as ever.

Every now and then his mind would torture him with cruel flashbacks of the real Alice – trudging over the fields with their Labrador, Erik; watching her beloved American soaps, baking in the kitchen. No amount of counselling was ever going to make that more palatable.

He thanked Janus, was just about to ring off when she spoke again. "There is something else I need to talk to you about, or rather someone," she said.

"Who?"

"Carmela Hanson."

"Should I know who that is?"

"DCI Hanson. Former head of training and development."

"Never met her."

A tut filled the phone line. "Well, you need to get to know her. She's coming across to Stratford for a course starting today and I've given her your mobile number. Thought she might be able to help you with preparation for your interview board next week. She's worked for Thames Valley, knows the area, will be able to help with all the key words and phrases you need to mention."

Jackman massaged his eyes with his free hand. Right now, this was the last thing he needed. "I'm not sure I'll have time—"

"Make time. You'll find it useful."

The line went dead. Jackman glanced up into the incident room. Phones were already starting to ring, indicating that word was getting out about the fire. He reached for his policy log and started outlining his initial strategy for the investigation.

When he finally pulled himself from his notes and checked the time it was 9.30am. He opened the drawer, retrieved a navy tie, stood and wound it around, twisting it into a knot, then combed his fingers through his hair. Within a few minutes the tie started to clutch at his neck and he was tugging it down, loosening his collar as Davies stuck her head around the doorframe. "Oh, very smart, sir. How did you get on with the Super?"

Jackman pulled a face. "We've got a week to clear the case before the DCI gets back."

"That'll give everyone the incentive to pull out all the stops."

Jackman smiled. Paul Reilly had joined them last year as a newly promoted DCI. A self-confessed career policeman, he was more focused on impressing his superiors and giving flash press statements, than actually getting his hands dirty. A fact that had done nothing to endear himself to the team. "At least you're not the one who married him."

"Christ," Davies said, "I'd have to murder him first." She chuckled. "Do you have time to do the briefing before you give the press statement?"

"Sure. Give me a couple of minutes." Jackman waited for her to retreat, then began gathering together the notes on his desk. It wasn't Reilly that bothered him right now. He hadn't told Davies about the upcoming interview board and it was starting to feel like a stone in his shoe. If he was successful it would mean an imminent move to the neighbouring force of Thames Valley. He wasn't sure why he hadn't mentioned it. At first it seemed like a good idea, he hadn't expected to get this far through the process, especially after all the time he had taken off after Alice's accident. No point in building it up. The morning he received the letter, two weeks earlier, he'd pocketed it, fully intending to share the good news. But she was off that day, her baby was sick. He'd meant to tell her when she returned, almost had several times, but the moment had never felt quite right.

Jackman smiled inwardly. Davies and her husband, John, had been great friends to him and Alice. They'd shared BBQs together, evenings out. She was probably the best and most reliable Detective Sergeant he'd ever worked with, her ability to inject humour into the darkest of situations was refreshing. He watched her now through the glass window that separated his office from the incident room. She was laughing, nudging a colleague. She caught his eye, winked. Jackman had been holding out for a board in the Warwickshire force at Christmas, although with no announcements forthcoming it was looking more and more unlikely. This opportunity meant he would manage his own homicide team, without the likes of Reilly poking his nose in, playing the political game. It was too good to pass over but as the interview date drew nearer, he was starting to realise just how much he'd miss everyone if he got through.

Jackman stared at the board littered with photos of the burnt barn taken at various angles. His eyes rested on the victim. He leant forward and planted photos of Nancy and Evan beside them, drawing a line to join them together, then turned to face the handful of detectives and support staff scattered in a rough semi-circle around him. "So far we know that the barn is owned by Upton Grange Farm, and the owners, Ronnie and Janine Lawton, are away in Australia. From photos we have obtained, we suspect the victim may be Evan Baker, one of the farm workers who has been house-sitting in their absence and is currently missing. His girlfriend, Nancy Faraday, was at the farmhouse when we arrived this morning and we found signs of a possible break-in: the glass in the back door was broken and she had a visible injury to her head. She is now at Warwick General with a suspected head injury and concussion. DC Russell is with her, so hopefully we'll get something more from her soon.

"Nancy wasn't able to tell us much this morning," Jackman continued. "Apparently they went out to The Fish pub at Wixford for a meal last night. She vaguely remembers leaving the pub with Evan in his Land Rover, then waking up on the kitchen floor of the farmhouse this morning, alone. Nothing in between."

"Could they have had an argument? Thrown something and broken the glass by accident?"

Jackman followed the words to DC Andrew Keane who was leant up against the sidewall of their makeshift incident room. His mustard shirt stretched across his paunch.

"It's possible." Jackman considered the kitchen entrance. "Although most of the glass in the back door spilled into the kitchen, indicating it was broken from the outside. And Nancy claims she woke up on the kitchen floor. There are bloodstains there. We'll get that checked to make sure it matches hers."

"A break-in, then. Somebody knocked her out, abducted him?"

"I think that's probably more likely. The gun cabinet was empty. Looks like someone had prised it open with a crowbar or something similar. We're trying to reach the owners, but in the meantime could you check with firearms licensing to see if they have any guns licensed to them?"

"Anything else missing?" Davies asked.

"There's plenty of farm machinery still parked up in the yard," Jackman said. "Land Rover hasn't been touched, in spite of all the keys hanging in the kitchen. The rest of the house looks relatively undisturbed."

"Maybe they interrupted a burglar when they arrived home? Whoever it was stole the guns, took the barn keys," Keane said. "Unless the girlfriend staged the break-in?"

"She'd have a job to give herself a blow to the head like that," Jackman replied. "Unless she had help, of course. We can't rule anything out at the moment, but we need to establish motive and means. CSI are still examining the barn and the surrounding area; another team are at the farmhouse. Let's see what they dig up." He looked across at Davies. "Anything from intel?"

"Nothing on Evan. He's not known to us. There's a little intelligence on Nancy. Her mother, Cheryl Faraday, has been convicted of shoplifting and some minor thefts over the years. Nothing major and she's never done a stretch. She's a known alcoholic, so I guess it was to fund her dependency. Nancy was raised by her maternal grandmother. Cheryl moved in with her daughter after her grandmother died."

"I remember Cheryl," Keane said scratching the corner of his temple. "We had to scrape her off the kerb a few times when I did overtime on uniformed response the other year."

"Probably the sight of that shirt," Davies said.

Keane pulled a face in mock surprise as everyone laughed. "Nancy was listed as her contact," Keane continued. "Nice kid. Always felt a bit sorry for her actually."

Jackman nodded his thanks. "Okay, we've established the barn is owned by the Lawton family so Evan and possibly Nancy too would have had ready access. Let's do some background checks on Nancy Faraday and Evan Baker. Work history, friends, family. Pull both their phone records and check the police cameras for any sightings of their vehicles over the past couple of weeks. We'll also need to get the helicopter up to take some aerial photographs to highlight any access points across the fields to the barn."

A phone rang in the distance. Jackman cast it an annoyed glance and turned to Davies, "We need to interview the other residents of Cherwell Hamlet to see if they saw or heard anything, and everyone who was at the pub last night to establish who their friends and close associates were, and see if anyone remembers them there."

His watch read 10am. "I'm off to do a media appeal for witnesses. Be prepared for the deluge of phone calls in about an hour."

The eyes of the room turned to Keane who was having an animated conversation with someone on the telephone. He replaced the receiver and looked up. "CSI have found a passport and a bunch of wage slips belonging to Evan Baker at the farmhouse, along with his phone."

"Excellent," Jackman said. "Check his phone records for any sign of life since yesterday, and get onto the Department of Work and Pensions. See if they can trace any family through his national insurance records. We'll need someone to give us a formal identification of the body, especially if Nancy is still in hospital. And speak to the morgue too, make sure they only do prelims. We don't want them cutting him up until we have him identified.

# Chapter **Five**

Nancy sat up in bed and stared blankly out of the window. A pair of blackbirds fluttered about on the rooftops, against the backdrop of an inky-blue sky. Stray leaves danced about betraying a breeze that was picking up, gathering momentum, although she felt none of it. The small hospital room, with just enough space for a bed and a plastic chair at either side, was airless.

She stretched out her back. The seams of the hospital issue gown scratched at her sides. The morning's events had felt surreal, almost as if she'd been watching herself from afar. The ambulance's arrival at Upton Grange had been closely followed by a petite detective with ginger hair who'd introduced herself as DC 'Call me Kathryn' Russell and accompanied her to the hospital. When they arrived, she'd pulled off a long piece of hospital roll, laid it on the floor and requested that Nancy stand on it and remove her clothes, even before she was examined by a doctor. Nancy watched her wrap the clothes in the hospital roll, place them in brown paper bags and label them. 'Just a precaution,' the detective had said.

The chair leg squeaked on the polished floor as her mother fidgeted in her seat beside the bed. The thick stench of nicotine that surrounded her like a bubble was oppressive in the tiny space.

After a day of being pulled and poked, lights shone in her eyes, her brain was still embroiled in a misty fog. Nothing made sense. The mention of the body found in the barn that morning swung in and out of her mind like a pendulum. It wasn't Evan. It couldn't be. But as much as she tried to erase the idea, it pushed itself back in. *Where was he?*

Her mind rewound to their first meeting. She'd been in the shop on her own that Monday afternoon when he'd walked in and asked for directions to the library. She could see straight away that he was older than her, more mature. He'd flashed her a smile and immediately her breath had caught. They got talking about books and before she knew it they were relating lines from *Catch-22*, sharing their favourite authors – he liked Michael Connelly, she Jeffery Deaver. His manner was engaging, he carried himself with ease. By the time she went out back to find him a map, she felt like she'd known him for months rather than hours. It wasn't until after he'd left the shop that she'd found the telephone number he'd scribbled onto the pad beside the till.

She'd waited until the evening before she'd called him, half expecting it to be a dud number, and was surprised when he picked up on the second ring. It had been the first time she'd felt a sense of excitement since breaking up with her boyfriend earlier in the year and it felt good. Although when Evan suggested they meet at The Fish at Wixford for their first date she'd been disappointed. Living close to the centre of Stratford, she'd only been to a few of the rural pubs. Her main haunts were usually the bars and clubs of Stratford town, with cheap drinks and easy music to dance to. Wixford was almost a twenty-mile round trip and cost more in petrol than it was worth. Right up to the last minute she'd almost changed her mind. But he sent a string of texts that were charming and sweet and she wasn't doing anything else that Wednesday evening.

As soon as she walked into the bar she recognised him, seated on a stool near the end in a white open-necked shirt that showed off his golden skin.

He'd given her a slightly lopsided smile that lit up his face

37

and immediately her stomach bounced. She hadn't expected him to be so tender, so interested in her life, so caring. It was chilly when they left. She'd shivered, goosebumps appearing on her bare arms. He'd removed his fleece, wrapped it around her shoulders and kissed her gently on the cheek, said she would have to see him again to return it. And she'd driven home immersed in his freshly showered smell, a warm feeling swirling her insides.

During the weeks and months that followed, they'd texted and talked most days and met up a few times a week. It was intense. She'd have liked to have got together more, but he had a lot of work to do on the farm that seemed to keep him out all hours and she respected that. He wasn't a big talker, but he was thoughtful, bought her presents, made her feel special.

A pang shot through her chest.

The fire. The detectives kept asking her about the barn, what it was used for. She'd been out on the farm with Evan in the Land Rover many times, done the rounds and fed the cattle during the first few weeks of their relationship. In the beginning it was exciting to bump down the country lanes in the sunshine. But the novelty soon wore off, especially when rain smeared the windows and the ground was muddy. She'd never visited the barn though.

Kathryn, the detective, had questioned her, the same questions she'd been asked at the farmhouse earlier, and compiled them into a statement. 'Statement.' The very word induced a wave of unwarranted guilt. She thought back to the kitchen that morning, the broken glass in the door. She hadn't done anything wrong. It was she who had woken up bleeding on the floor. Although jabs of fear kept poking her in the side. *What happened last night?* If only she could remember.

The sound of a phone ringing pulled Nancy from her thoughts. She blinked, sat forward just as the detective said, "Excuse me," rose and left the room.

There must be some news. As she stared at the door,

willing the detective to return, a bony hand curled around her forearm.

"You all right, love?"

Nancy turned to face her mother, "I'm fine." But she wasn't fine. Her head was thick and fuzzy, her stomach was churning inside.

She laid back into the pillows, thought hard. Maybe the fire had nothing to do with Evan. Maybe he'd been caught up somewhere, and later he would turn up at her door in his truck, plaster that wicked grin on his face and say, "Fancy a night out?" Her life would be complete once more. They would enjoy more nights out, picnics on the lawn, walk the dogs together.

The door loosened on the latch, clicked open. Nancy craned her neck, listening hard for traces of the detective's voice. But any sound was drowned out by a commotion in the corridor: a patient screaming, soothing voices trying to placate. She tried to decipher the sounds but they merged into a distant din.

Her mother's incessant picking at the skin around her fingernails was starting to grate. "Cheryl, why don't you go and have a smoke?" she said. "I know you want one."

Her mother didn't flinch at being called by her first name. 'Mum' conjured up images of a woman holding their child's hand as they took them to school, standing at the gates to meet them at the end of the day, cooking them tea, reading them a story at bedtime. And Cheryl would be the first to admit, she'd never done any of those things.

She cleared her throat and scratched the gap in her parting. "Shall I wait for the detective to come back? Just in case?"

Just in case. Just in case Evan was dead. Her mother had never known the meaning of diplomacy. Nancy took a deep breath and fought to keep her voice even, "No, really. I'll be fine. You'll only be a few minutes." She patted Cheryl's hand in the most affectionate gesture she could muster.

Cheryl grabbed her black leather bag at the side of her

chair and removed a packet of Dunhills and a green plastic lighter. "Well, okay then." She held them up as she dashed out of the room. "I'll just have a quickie."

Nancy rested her head back on the pillow as the door slammed behind her. Cheryl was hopeless without her cigarettes. This was difficult for someone like her, to be removed from her home, sit here with Nancy in this room and be denied the comforts she relied upon so heavily.

A flashback: standing in a line in the primary school playground, next to the hopscotch markings and the coloured climbing frame, waiting to be collected at the end of the day. The other childrens' mothers were young and fresh faced with broad smiles and colourful clothes, some with ponytails bouncing as they approached. Nancy's grandmother sported the same smile that lit up her face and made her beautiful. But her attempt at smart clothes were worn and dated, and she walked with an arthritic limp. Nancy wasn't the only one collected by someone other than her mother. Another boy in her class had a mother who worked in London and a childminder collected him. Although his mum was still able to come to parents' evenings and school concerts. Nancy had struggled to understand her mother's gaping absence when she was young and by the time she reached her teenage years she bitterly resented Cheryl's occasional visits, when empty bottles lined the chairs at home, ashtrays overflowed and the thick stench of alcohol filled the air.

Oddly, Evan viewed things differently. He had more of a sympathetic approach to her mother's condition, emphasised to Nancy that this was an addiction. She needed help, treatment, like any other patient in this hospital and over the last couple of months, Nancy had tried to be more tolerant, allowing the early seeds of a relationship to develop. Evan was perceptive like that. He knew things about people. Tried to help them.

The sound of the door opening pulled her back to the present. She looked up to see Kathryn.

The detective's mouth turned up very slightly as she approached the bedside.

"Have you found him?" Nancy held her breath.

"Not yet."

"What about the body?" she asked, trepidation prickling her voice. "Do you know what happened… in the barn?"

"We're looking into it, working on an identification. Please try to stay calm and rest. I'll tell you more as soon as I can."

A crack of thunder sounded in the distance. It sent the birds flapping off the rooftops in panic. Nancy watched them disappear into the sky. She closed her eyes, tried as hard as she could to pull on her memories from the night before. But instead of order, a mixture of confused thoughts raced around her mind, dissipating into a cloud of nothingness.

# Chapter **Six**

Jackman was leaning down, plugging in his mobile phone charger behind his desk when a knock at the door caught his attention. Keane's face appeared, his mouth stretched into a wide smile that exposed a wide gap between his two front teeth. "Just to let you know, we've traced Evan Baker's sister, sir. Hampshire police have been out to see her. She's living in Southampton, coming up in the morning to do a formal identification."

"Good. Was she able to tell us any more about him?"

Keane shook his head.

"Probably in shock," Jackman said. "Might get a bit more out of her tomorrow."

"Doubt it. The detective I spoke to said she claims she hasn't seen him in six years. We've gone through his phone and he's made no calls since yesterday. Last text was sent to Nancy's phone at 5pm."

After Keane had left the room, Jackman swivelled his chair and stared out of the window into the car park below. The lack of phone activity strengthened the notion that Evan Baker could be their body. But what struck him was the dearth of information about him. He appeared to keep himself clean: no police record and no intelligence on file. They'd done the normal checks and so far been unable to trace anyone who knew him well, apart from a distant sister. Was he really such a private person, or did he have something to hide?

He turned back and idly stared through the slats in the

open blind. As his eyes focused, he could see the incident room was a hive of activity, buzzing with the wealth of calls the press appeal had prompted. Jackman loved the excitement of working a new case, uncovering clues, piecing together events. It reminded him of his earliest days in homicide in the Met. With over one hundred murders a year the unit had been busy, fast moving. Warwickshire saw fewer murder cases, but when they did they were accompanied by the same fizz of excitement as everyone pulled together, worked extra hours and put in the inevitable legwork to solve the case.

His phone interrupted his thoughts. A text message from DC Russell.

*Nancy is being kept in hospital overnight due to the head injury.*

He chewed the side of his mouth. Nancy was close to Evan. Even if she couldn't remember what happened on Sunday night, perhaps she was now feeling well enough to furnish them with background details on his friends and local associations so that they could build up a pattern of his life.

He clicked the button, called back. "Hi Kathryn, thanks for your message. What's happening there?"

"They're keeping her in overnight for observations due to the head injury."

"Do you think she's up to doing an ID on the victim?"

A short silence followed. "I'm not sure. She's still very confused."

"Any more insight into what happened last night?"

"Nothing. I've been trying to gain a little of her background, but she's very vague. Doesn't seem to know anything about his family either."

As Jackman ended the call, his phone rang again. It was Mackenzie Oliver, the pathologist. He didn't waste time with introductions. "Any news on an ID?"

"We've traced a sister. She's coming up in the morning. How did you get on with preliminaries?"

Jackman heard the rustle of paper in the background.

43

"We've done his hands and fingernails. They're too badly burnt for prints. There's a crack in the back of his skull. Possibly the cause of death."

"Could that have come from the rafters collapsing on top of him?"

"Doubtful. Looks more like a definite blow. Deep. Consistent with a blunt instrument. If it wasn't enough to kill him, it would more likely have knocked him out. The front of his body shows some bruising too."

"Do you think he put up a fight?"

Mac hesitated a moment. "Not sure. It doesn't look like the defensive bruising we'd usually find on a victim's arms. More concentrated on his torso. As if he'd been dropped. Possibly when he was placed in the barn or when something fell down onto him."

Jackman looked up to see Davies marching through the incident room in his direction. She was animated, shouting something across the room, her face flushed. "Thanks, Mac." He rang off, reached the door almost as she did and pulled it open. "What's up?"

"Obnoxious guy in the front office downstairs. Claims to be the owner of the cars in the barn. Will only speak to whoever is managing the investigation."

\*\*\*

Eamonn Benwell was a tall man of middle years with dark features and a protruding Adam's apple that wobbled as Jackman introduced himself. He strode into the interview room, clearly affronted by their surroundings. "What is this?"

"I'm sorry, this is the only spare room I could find," Jackman said.

"I'm not being taped, then?"

"Not unless you want to be."

A muscle flexed in his jawline. "When am I going to get my cars back?"

Jackman sat and invited Eamonn to sit on the spare chair opposite before he spoke. "This is a murder investigation, Mr Benwell. The cars at the scene where the body was found have to be forensically examined."

"How long does that take?"

"I can't say at the moment. Our priority is to ascertain what happened. Everything at the crime scene needs to be carefully examined."

Eamonn threw his head back. "You don't think they used my cars?"

Jackman shrugged a single shoulder. "I couldn't say at this stage."

"Can you at least tell me what state they are in? They said on the news there was a fire."

"I can confirm there was a fire at the barn. The body was located away from the vehicles, but there is some damage. That's all."

Eamonn sat forward, placed his head in his hands.

"What sort of cars are they?" Jackman asked.

"Classic. American."

"I'm sure they'll be covered on your insurance."

Eamonn raised his gaze, incredulous.

"They were insured, weren't they?" Jackman said.

"Of course. But insurers won't give me my cars back. The Corvette L88 is a special edition... took me years to find one." Beads of sweat were collecting on his forehead.

Jackman watched him a moment before he spoke. "How long have you known Evan Baker?"

"I first met him in The Fish pub earlier this year. I go in there a couple of times a week to unwind." He lowered his eyes. "Just recently I've had a few marital problems. My wife and I separated. I moved out and had nowhere to store the cars. When I told the landlord he suggested I approach Evan to see if there was anywhere they could be stored on the farm."

"Had you spoken to Evan Baker before that night?"

He shook his head. "I'd seen him, sitting at the end of the bar by himself, head in a book. He rarely spoke to anyone."

"What happened when you broached the idea?"

"He was reluctant at first. Said it wasn't his decision, he was only house-sitting. He brightened up when I said it was only for a short while and I'd pay him."

"How much did you pay?"

"Forty quid a month. Seemed to work well. Until yesterday."

"How did you pay him?" Jackman asked.

"I set up a direct debit from my business."

"Which is?"

"Steel fabrication. I have a factory on Timothy's Bridge Road."

"And where are you living now?"

"I'm renting a flat on St Peter's Way. It's close to work, but only temporary. Somewhere my kids can come and stay until we get the finances sorted. I'd planned to move the cars then too. Arrange for some proper storage."

"Do you go up to the barn at all?"

"Occasionally. Not as much as I'd like. The cars have been stored there since March and I've probably been up half a dozen times. We've been so busy at work I haven't had time to take them for a run in a while."

"How do you get access?"

"I have to contact Evan. He meets me there, unlocks the barn and makes sure he's back there when I return."

"He didn't give you a key?"

He shrugged a single shoulder. "Don't suppose it was his to give. I was just grateful for somewhere to store them."

"Did you ever see anyone else there?"

"No. The track's always empty. You wouldn't go up there if you weren't heading to the barn."

"What's the generator for?"

Eamonn shrugged. "Maybe he was thinking of heating it over the winter, stop the cars from seizing up. He's not much of a talker."

Jackman watched him a moment. Although tense, his body language was open. He looked like he was being honest, telling the truth. "How well do you know Evan?"

"Like I said, I saw him in the pub. At the barn occasionally. That's all."

"Did you ever go to the farmhouse? Or meet his girlfriend?"

"I never went to the farm. No need. I have seen his girlfriend, I think they call her Nancy. He brought her to the pub sometimes."

"How did they get along?"

"What do you mean?"

"Did they argue a lot, or seem happy?"

"Didn't see them arguing but I didn't really pay attention. They were just other people in the pub."

"What about friends, mutual acquaintances, family?"

"He seems a bit of a loner. I haven't seen him talk to anyone else, apart from his girlfriend."

Jackman pressed his lips together, leant forward. "Eamonn, where were you between the hours of 10pm and 3am on the night of Sunday the 9th of August?"

Eamonn looked indignant. "I worked Sunday and had an early night. Why?"

Jackman ignored the question. Silence hung between them.

"We have a big job on at the moment with a penalty clause," Eamonn continued. "I've pretty much spent the last few weeks at the factory, weekends too."

"You have witnesses?"

"None of my guys came in on Sunday. And I walked home. So, no. No witnesses." He enunciated every syllable. "You don't think the body in the barn is Evan, do you?"

"Do you?" Jackman replied.

"When it was reported in the press they just said a man."

"We are still waiting for a formal identification of the victim, but Evan is missing. Can you describe him for me, approximate height and weight?"

"God!" Eamonn looked physically taken aback. It took him a moment to recover himself. "Er, blond, average height. Slim-ish."

"I'll need specific details."

"Of what?"

"Makes and registration numbers of the cars. Dates when you spoke to Evan, visited the barn and took the cars out. Do you know of anyone who might want to hurt him?" Jackman asked.

Eamonn shook his head, any ounce of earlier belligerence now melted. "Like I said, I really didn't know him well at all."

\*\*\*

The detective stood and excused herself to go to the ladies. The emptiness of the room induced an overwhelming sense of loneliness. Anxiety clawed at Nancy's chest. What she really needed right now, more than anything, was Evan.

She pictured the barn in her mind. All she knew was that there'd been a fire. Somebody had died. Frustration ate away at her.

The door clicked open. She raised her eyes hopefully and gave a relieved smile as a familiar face entered.

"Nancy, what happened?" The young woman rushed to her bedside and embraced her in a tender hug. She pulled back slowly and saw the wound on Nancy's forehead. "Ouch, that looks sore."

It was such a comfort to have her best friend here. She'd known Becca since they started secondary school together, nine years earlier.

Nancy could feel tramlines gathering on her forehead as she stared back at her friend. "Have you heard anything… from Evan?"

Becca shook her head slowly. "How are you?"

"I don't know. Tired. My head feels heavy. Did you call him?"

"I did and left a message. Try not to worry. Have they done any tests?"

"They do nothing but tests and 'observations'."

"At least they're looking after you. What a horrible thing to happen."

"I'm worried it's him, Becca. The body in the barn. They won't tell me anything, but Evan's missing. I'm sure they think it's him."

Becca patted her arm. "Come on. You mustn't think like that."

Becca's dark hair was arranged into a long French plait swung over her left shoulder. Nancy watched her wind the end of it around the fingers of her free hand as she spoke. Becca had always faffed with her hair. Although their buses came from opposite ends of town, the girls met at the school gates every morning and invariably, Becca would be fixing or refixing her hair as she waited for her friend. Nancy wondered whether Becca would have followed her into floristry if it hadn't been so easy with them both working in Becca's mother's shop and later sharing the flat above together. She would have been far more suited to hairdressing.

Becca grabbed the plastic chair in the corner. It scraped across the floor as she dragged it over and sat down. "Has Cheryl been in? I rang her as soon as I heard."

"She was here earlier."

Becca raised a thick, drawn eyebrow. "Well, what happened?"

The birds were back on the roof, fluttering about on the felt in the corner of her vision as Nancy relayed the events, as far as she could remember them.

"What a nightmare. How long do you think you'll be in here?"

"I don't know. It's driving me crazy."

"Well, listen, don't worry about work. Take as much time as you need. We can cover things until you're ready to come back."

49

"Thanks. Did you manage to get me a phone? I can't believe the police still want my phone. What on earth could be on it that they'd be interested in?"

Becca reached into her bag. "Working next door to a mobile phone shop does have some benefits." She pulled out a white Samsung. "I put it on the business. Be useful to have a spare. I've put in mine and Mum's numbers, and Cheryl's. You can do the rest. It's only pay as you go, but it'll sort you out until you get yours back."

"Thanks. You're a star. How was the shop today?"

"Pretty quiet really, thank goodness. But listen, Mum says don't worry about a thing. It's more important you get well."

"Have you heard anything, on the news I mean?"

Becca frowned, lowered her voice. "It was on the radio in the shop. Mum turned it up. They said there'd been a fire, a body had been found."

"And?"

"The fire inspectors are still investigating. They suspect arson."

# Chapter **Seven**

Jackman meandered up the winding driveway to Broom Hills Nursing Home and parked up. The sun had passed over, leaving the red-brick Georgian frontage cast in shade. He passed through the entrance, paused briefly to make small talk with the receptionist and sign the visitor's book, and continued on into the day room.

"Here he is now, Alice." A warm smile accompanied Christine's soft Irish accent as he approached. She patted the forearm of the patient beside her and hauled herself up.

Jackman returned Christine's smile and bent down to envelope the woman beside her in a hug. He planted a kiss on her forehead before he stood back. "How was your day?" he asked.

His wife's glassy eyes stared into space.

"It's been just fine, hasn't it," Christine said. "Watched *Gone Girl* this afternoon, didn't you?"

Alice's cardigan hung off her shoulders, a testament to the amount of weight she'd lost in recent months. He stood back while Christine busied herself with checking the straps that harnessed her to the chair, tucked a light blanket around her legs. "Lovely evening for your walk too," she said as she finished up. "You must check out the rose garden. It's beautiful at the moment."

Jackman thanked her, took the handles of the wheelchair and pushed his wife through the doorway, across the foyer and down the ramp into the gardens where he pulled the blanket to the side, exposing his wife's bare calves, and let her hair loose, allowing the fragile breeze to lift strands of it as they crossed the car park.

Erik, their four-year-old chocolate Lab, was jumping around on the back seat causing the car to rock slightly as they drew nearer. Jackman paused to make sure no one was around and let the dog loose. He leapt out of the car and circled the wheelchair twice, each time licking Alice's fingers.

"Calm down, mate," Jackman said and patted his back. Erik raced ahead as he pushed the wheelchair around the back of the main house and across the lawn. The rear of the property offered breathtaking views across the surrounding rolling Warwickshire countryside. He pushed Alice into the gardens. They were divided into a herb and vegetable garden, a rose garden and a long lawned area, each separated by low, manicured privet hedging.

Erik trotted on ahead while Jackman wheeled Alice around each of the gardens in turn, pointing out the new flowers in bloom. Jackman was no gardener himself, but this area had been carefully planted to offer something different throughout the summer months and he'd learnt to appreciate the changes as they took place. It was important to him that Alice saw these changes too, that she was aware of what was going on around her. They paused next to the honeysuckle for a while, taking in the fresh aroma, before entering the rose garden.

The soft rattling of the wheels and the pants of Erik's breath were the only sounds to be heard. He talked Alice through the case, the body at the barn, the frustrations with early enquiries and felt the tension of the day filtering out. He'd grown accustomed to Alice's silence over the past year, filling the gaps in the conversation himself, although it still left him hollow. He missed her chirpy voice, singing as she moved around the house; the quiet spells when she'd lay on the floor in her study and listen to Bach. If he closed his eyes he could still see her before the accident, chatting to his daughter in the kitchen, filling every corner, every crevice of their home with her presence.

Part of him clung on to the tiny thread of hope that one day there would be an eye movement, the edge of a smile, some little spark of recovery. But the more time that passed, the less likely a recovery was. And the idea that his effervescent wife might end her days in this sorry state made her tragic demise all the more difficult to bear.

Jackman's mobile buzzed. He pulled it out of his pocket, swiped the screen and brought up the text message.

*Hi Will, this is Carmela Hanson. Alison Janus gave me your number regarding your interview board. I'm in Stratford all week. Give me a call when you are free.*

Jackman groaned inwardly and pocketed his phone before moving on.

He parked up beside a bench in the rose garden and sat down next to his wife. Erik appeared from behind a bush and laid down next to them, his tongue hanging to the side. The air was cooler here. Jackman pulled the blanket back over Alice's legs, tucking in the sides. They were seated next to an old English rose, the edges of the huge flower head were brown and tinged, just over their best. Jackman leant forward and breathed in, allowing the sweet smell to linger in his nose. It was fresh, all encompassing. Absently he picked the flower and held it up to his wife's nose a moment.

The smell in the barn filtered into his mind. It was pungent, familiar. Even through the smoke it felt distinct. As they sat in silence he thought about the generator out back, probably used to keep the cars warm in winter as Eamonn had suggested. His mind wandered around the barn and the charred remains of the cars when a thought struck him. He hadn't seen any radiators. The generator couldn't warm the cars over the winter without a heating system.

He sat forward and worked it through in his mind. It didn't make sense.

# Chapter **Eight**

Jackman grabbed the coffee and climbed out of the car. The sun was rising, slowly uncovering the fields. Apart from a couple of birds flapping in a nearby tree, rising early from their roost, and the low hoot of an owl in the distance, all was quiet.

The uniformed officer standing beside the barn entrance looked surprised as she watched him climb over the blue-and-white police tape. Jackman recognised her as one of the youngsters from the response team at Stratford station and smiled as he approached. "Hi, Shelley. I brought you a coffee," he said, handing over the cardboard cup.

Her eyes shone as she took it and peeled off the lid. "Thanks, sir. What brings you here at this early hour?"

Jackman stared out over the fields of rapeseed stretching out in front of him. He thought fleetingly of Sheila Buckton and her allergies. The crime scene had niggled away at him all night, forcing sleep aside. He'd churned it over again and again in his mind, but there was one question that picked away at the side of his brain: *Why go to the expense of installing a generator to a barn stuck in the middle of nowhere?* "Thought I'd take another look around," he said. "What time did the CSIs finish?"

The officer's fringe fluttered as she blew across the top of the coffee. "They left about 8.30pm. It was getting dark by then and they'd photographed and filmed everything."

"How long are you here for?"

She glanced at her watch. "Relief comes at seven. Can't wait."

Jackman gave her a knowing smile. Memories of guarding a manufacturing plant in East London during the coldest December in years filled his mind. He'd joined the Metropolitan Police less than six months earlier and, even for an ex-Marine who'd been stationed in the Arctic during his training, he was freezing and by the end of the shift could barely feel his own feet.

He left Shelley and walked around the outside of the barn, pausing at intervals to eye the surrounding fields, looking out for alternative routes the killer might have used. The aerial photographs hadn't shown up any bridle ways, designated pathways or breaks in fencing or hedging nearby. From where he was standing, he couldn't even see a badger route. He halted beside the generator. It was silent. He could see Cherwell Hamlet from here, the only place it seemed, where any kind of view of the barn could be found.

The light was brightening as he returned to the main entrance, opened the doors wide and wandered inside. The interior looked larger this morning. He walked around the edge of the cars. An earthy dampness mingled with the scent of burnt metal. Jackman tried to pick through the smells. He was just starting to wonder if he'd imagined it earlier when he caught it again – a musky sweet smell.

He made his way over to the remains of the shed in the corner. There was barely anything left there apart from some metal racking which had melted and bowed in places, but was miraculously still fixed to the wall. Something puzzled him as he stood and looked at it. Earlier he'd assumed that this area had been enclosed before the fire and used as some kind of office, but it lacked any electrical equipment or the remains of a desk.

Jackman walked around the perimeter. He wasn't sure what he was looking for. He knew it had been checked and rechecked by his team earlier, but something didn't feel quite right. The pathologist was pretty sure that the victim was placed here after he'd died. But Jackman couldn't understand why his body would have been left in the barn he was looking after.

He stood beside the entrance awhile, looking out towards the track. The officer was sitting on an upturned crate, coffee cup cradled in her hands, staring out into the murky countryside. Even though the barn had doors that opened both ends, this was the only entrance route by car. The track was long and winding, almost a quarter of a mile back from the road and situated several hundred yards from the farmhouse. The road at the bottom was rarely used, other than as a through route to the village nearby. It must have taken the killer a while to find this isolated spot. But why go to so much trouble? It's not like they sought to hide his body. The presence of the fire drew immediate attention to it.

Jackman tried to put himself in the killer's shoes. Nancy said the last thing she remembered was them leaving the pub. Perhaps they disturbed somebody when they got back. Or somebody crept up on them and broke the glass in the back door to gain entry. Surely it would be difficult for one person to break in and incapacitate them both? Unless of course there was more than one offender.

Evan Baker's bank statements had come in last thing yesterday evening. Coupled with his phone records, they could find no sign of activity since Sunday evening, strengthening the notion that the victim was Evan. Jackman ran a hand down the side of the entrance door. Blisters of rust tugged and pulled at his rubber glove. The doors opened almost the width and height of the barn at both ends. The killer could have opened them, reversed a vehicle up and placed the body down before starting the fire. Evan wasn't of muscular build, but it would have been an effort to haul him into the boot of a vehicle, even with help. Maybe that was why his body was laid out on its front, so close to the entrance.

He viewed the floor where the body had laid and looked back up at the entrance. The more he thought about it the more he thought it the most likely explanation. Evan's body was around fifteen metres from the cars. Jackman walked over to them and around the edge of the first car. He continued along. He was just heading down past the last one, back towards the entrance when something caught the toe of his shoe. He stepped back, looked down. A tiny lip of concrete sat proud. He wiped his foot across the floor, clearing away some of the soot. It wasn't a lip. It was a line of concrete, the edge of something.

Jackman pulled his torch from his pocket and lit up the area, scraping his foot across the floor, moving away the debris, his actions quickening. He called out to the uniformed officer.

Shelley came rushing in. "What is it?" She immediately looked down, following his eyeline. "What's that?"

"It looks like some kind of door," Jackman said. He bent down, pushed some more of the soot and debris away from the join. The door was recessed slightly. A flat handle sat at one end. He hooked his fingers around the handle and tried to prise the metal back. It was distorted and melted in places. Sweat coursed down his back, but as much as he tried to heave and pull, it refused to budge even an inch.

"What do you think is down there?" Shelley asked.

"No idea. But we need to get inside. Now."

\*\*\*

Jackman stood outside and glanced at his watch. It was almost 6.30am. Thankfully the weather had been warm since the weekend. Thunder had threatened a few times, but the rain hadn't broken through and the mud track was packed hard. But, after a bright start, the sky was now blanketed with patches of grey cloud, bringing with them the fresh threat of rain.

He caught the low drone of a motor, louder as it approached and turned in time to see a fire engine rumble up the track. Shelley, who had been doing her rounds, walking the edge of the barn, came back to join him. Jackman waited for them to park up and exchanged pleasantries with the firefighters that jumped out, who introduced themselves as Rob and Carl, relieved to find that they'd already been briefed on his phone call.

"Do you want us to wait for your CSI team before we start?" Rob asked.

Jackman cast a fleeting glance down the track. He'd asked Shelley to record the area with her body worn video camera. And he couldn't afford to waste any time right now. "No, we need to be quick in case somebody is trapped down there. Do you have your cutters?"

Rob nodded his head, waited while his colleague retrieved the disk cutter from the truck and followed Jackman into the barn. "It's a metal door, warped by the fire," he said. "I've covered the handle area with some exhibit bags I had in the car, in case of fingerprints."

Rob nodded. "We'll cut around the door, see if we can pull it out. That will limit the damage to whatever there is below."

"Thanks."

The roar of the disk cutter filled the barn. Within moments it penetrated the metal. It took less than twenty seconds to cut around the door and pull it back.

That familiar smell immediately filled the air around them, more pungent now. The fire fighters grimaced, stood back. Jackman covered his nose, bent down and shone his torch inside the space below.

# Chapter **Nine**

A sea of faces turned as Davies rushed into the room later that morning. Janus paused mid-speech, raised her eyes for long enough to frown, and turned back to the room as she continued speaking. "We've made a discovery that takes the investigation in a new direction." Her eyes slid to Jackman. "Perhaps you could fill us in."

Jackman shared the events of earlier that morning. "There's a hidden room beneath the barn, around twelve metres long by five metres wide. It looks like it's being used to grow cannabis. We need to let the forensics team examine it quickly before the search team can go in with cutting equipment and open it up properly. That'll give us a good idea what state the cultivation is in."

"That would explain the disgruntled CSIs in the canteen this morning," Keane said, sniggering. "They don't like anyone messing up their scene."

Jackman rolled his eyes. "We had no choice, there could just as easily have been another person down there. Get the DNA test fast-tracked, will you?" he said to Davies. "We need to know who the victim was. Some of those plants are just about to crop. It's likely they aren't the first crop, but he must have known something about them. Any news from the other residents of Cherwell Hamlet?"

"Nobody has noticed anything unusual, either on Sunday or recently. They don't seem an observant lot," Keane said.

Jackman pictured the informant's inquisitive face. "Send

someone out to have another word with Sheila Buckton, will you? She seemed interested in the general comings and goings, might remember something of significance in the weeks running up to the fire."

He turned back to the room. "Any news from the press appeal?"

"Nothing yet," Russell said. "Usual time wasters. Early feedback from interviews at The Fish suggest that they were a happy couple, quite lovey-dovey on Sunday night. No one has mentioned an argument."

"What about the victim's habits?" Jackman asked.

"We've gone through his bank records," Keane said. "There's a few regular payments into his bank each month, one of which looks like his salary; a direct debit for his phone, and he withdraws at intervals, seems to work mainly in cash. Nothing of interest. We're going through the numbers listed on his phone, the entries on his billing. CSIs also found a couple of grand in used bank notes stuffed in a box at the bottom of his wardrobe."

Davies gave a low whistle. "Sounds like drugs money."

"Any luck on tracing the farm owners?"

She shook her head. "They're still driving around the perimeter of Australia in a camper van. We've spoken to the daughter. The last contact she had was a phone call from Adelaide on Sunday."

"No mobile phones, iPads?"

"Apparently they've gone *au naturel*. Reliving their youth. There were no mobile phones twenty years ago. They're using Internet cafés to keep in touch with relatives in the main towns and cities. We've emailed them, asked them to get in touch urgently."

"Let's make an application to examine their bank accounts, both personal and business," Jackman said. "See if there are any large injections of cash, anything to indicate they might be involved." He turned back to the main room. "I want Davies and Keane at the crime scene this morning to supervise the excavation. CSIs will be removing the cars before the search team move in. We want minimal damage."

"I'm meeting Russell at the hospital. We've got the victim's sister coming for the ID, so we'll join you there later."

Janus stood. "Right. Let's keep this one tight. Everyone at the barn, make sure you wear coveralls. That's all."

Jackman watched Janus rush off to her next meeting in her usual perfunctory manner and made his way back to his office. He was just gathering some papers together on his desk when Davies popped in with two coffees. She still seemed flustered. She reached out, passed him a mug.

"Everything okay?"

"Sorry, one of those mornings. Typical when all this has happened."

"John stay away?"

"Yes. His course finishes this evening. He should be back late tonight, thank God. My mum's away in Cyprus. We arranged for my mother-in-law to help out with the little one, but that woman's got no sense of urgency."

"I take it you've still not found a nursery, then?"

Davies plonked herself down in the chair opposite and blew a long sigh out of the corners of her mouth. "We've looked at a few." She looked past Jackman out of the window beyond. "Oh, I don't know. He seems so little." She hesitated, as if the question was too difficult. "What about you. When's Celia off to Sweden?"

Jackman smiled. When Celia, his daughter, had been selected as one of twelve students for a six-week field trip in Sweden, a special project as part of her course, he'd been so proud. "This weekend. She's back on Thursday to get packed up."

"Nice to have a couple of days together before she's off."

"I'm not sure about that. She's bringing the boyfriend home with her."

"Now that should be interesting."

61

Jackman sidestepped a family clogging the entrance to the lifts and made his way up the stairs to the neurology department. As soon as he stepped out into the corridor, he spotted the back of DC Kathryn Russell's ginger hair, tied into a bun that was bobbing up and down as she nodded, a mobile phone glued to her ear. She ended the call, turned and smiled as he approached.

"Morning, Kathryn. How's our patient this morning?"

"Tired. Confused. She had a CAT scan first thing, which I understand showed up nothing significant. But there's something not quite right."

"What do you mean?"

"She's not eating."

"Possibly the shock."

"Probably. But it seems like something else. Something I can't put my finger on. She keeps asking about Evan, understandably, then looks lost."

Nancy was sitting on the edge of the bed, fully dressed in jeans and a red T-shirt. She looked up as Jackman followed Russell into the room. Her hair was tied back from a face which still looked pallid and drawn. He introduced himself.

"You came to the farmhouse yesterday," Nancy said.

Jackman nodded. "How are you feeling this morning?"

"Okay." She hesitated. "Do you have an identification on the body yet?"

"Somebody's coming this morning. We should know more after that."

"Have you found Evan?" she asked, her voice brittle.

"Not yet. Do you feel up to answering some questions?"

She stared at him blankly as he asked her again about the night of Evan's disappearance. He watched carefully as she repeated that she didn't know anything, couldn't remember. At one point she closed her eyes, as if willing her brain into action. He changed tack, asked about the barn and she repeated that she'd never been there.

"Take your time," Jackman said.

But despite all the breaks, nothing new was forthcoming. A nurse pushed open the door, carrying a tray of beans on toast which she passed across to Nancy. "For the hungry patient," she said.

Russell smiled as she watched Nancy stare at the plate of food on her lap. "You'll feel better if you eat something."

Nancy surveyed the fork for a moment before lifting it awkwardly and placing it down again. She looked as though she wanted to cry. "I'm not hungry," she said, pushing the tray of food away.

Realising how intimidating it might feel to have people crowding her, Jackman rose and indicated for Russell to join him. "We'll leave you to eat," he said. "If you remember anything, anything at all, no matter how insignificant it might seem, please give us a shout. You have our number."

He caught sight of a familiar face in the corridor and left the room swiftly to catch her up. "Lucy!"

The woman turned and briefly frowned over the top of her glasses, before her mouth broke into a toothy grin. "Will. Good to see you." She crossed the corridor and hugged him affectionately. "It's been a while."

Jackman introduced Russell and the two women nodded at each other. "I thought you were at Coventry," he said.

"Been reorganised. I cover neurology for the two hospitals now. Bit of travelling," she wrinkled her nose, "but I don't mind it so much. How's Erik?"

"As bouncy as ever. What about yours?"

"Still a nightmare. Keep thinking I should take her back to training classes, but I don't think it'll make any difference. What brings you here?"

"On a job." Jackman tilted his head towards Nancy's room.

Recognition spread across Lucy's face.

"Actually, you might be able to help."

"Well, I can't discuss individual cases as you know. But if it's general?"

"Sure."

They all moved across and sat on the chairs opposite as Jackman ran through Nancy's version of the events of Sunday night. "Obviously, it would help us tremendously if she remembered anything leading up to her boyfriend's disappearance."

"I presume they've run toxicology to check for alcohol levels, presence of drugs?"

Russell nodded. "I was with her when they gave her the results. No trace of any drugs. She admitted she'd been drinking on Sunday night, but they didn't find excessive traces of alcohol in her system."

"I saw her on the Monday morning before she was admitted," Jackman said. "She seemed pretty sober then."

"But she is vacant and very vague at times," Russell said. "As if she doesn't really know what's going on."

The doctor took a deep breath. "If she's had a CAT scan and there is no obvious damage to her brain, then it sounds like she's suffering from temporary amnesia brought on by concussion. In such cases some patients may regain the lost memory, others may not. It depends on the extent of the damage and where the bruising is. Only time will tell, I'm afraid."

Jackman rolled his shoulders. "The injury to her head is at the front if that helps."

"There could be bruising to the frontal lobes," she said. "In those cases it is common for some patients to experience memory loss. Sometimes their cognitive abilities are affected too."

"How do you mean?"

"Their ability to complete routine tasks. In extreme circumstances it can be basic hygiene – washing themselves, cleaning their teeth, getting dressed. With milder injuries it's more likely to be intermittent, things like tying shoelaces, changing bedclothes or making a cup of tea. Often they speak perfectly coherently, then forget key processes in tasks or get them mixed up."

Jackman recalled Nancy's bewildered face staring at the fork in front of her when she'd been served her food. "What happens in those circumstances?"

"The specialist brain injury team are called in. They carry out a number of tests to assess the level of cognitive understanding and help them to relearn the methodology of tasks. Recovery depends on the extent of the damage."

"That sounds time consuming."

"Nothing in neurology is a quick fix I'm afraid. I thought you might understand that more than most." Lucy touched his forearm briefly. "I need to get on. Give my love to Alice." She stood and glanced across at Russell. "Good to meet you."

He watched her walk off down the corridor, grateful for the efficiency of her concern. No dramas, no awkward questions. Just a brief mention of his wife, a passing of thoughts.

Russell's phone rang. She moved away to take the call. Jackman sat back and ran through Nancy's scant account of Sunday in his mind. The single bang to her head suggested whoever broke in wasn't really interested in Nancy. She didn't live there, so perhaps they weren't expecting to see her. Although he couldn't rule out the possibility that she was working with somebody to get Evan out of the way. But there was something about her, behind the eyes, that made him uneasy. It was difficult to tell whether she was telling the truth about her memory loss. Whether it was the result of a head injury, or she was using it as a ruse to mask what really happened.

A woman of her petite frame would never be able to lift his body into the barn. Not without help. And why would she, unless she'd discovered the drugs or was involved in some way?

Russell's footsteps along the corridor brought him back to the present. She was holding her phone out at an angle. "That was Keane. He's confirmed there are three shotguns still registered to the farm."

"Might explain a break-in," Jackman said. "But why take

Evan up to the barn? They could just as easily have killed him at the farmhouse." He paused for a moment. "Get onto the station and have the source handlers out in the field to check with their intelligence contacts, will you? We need to find those weapons before anyone has a chance to use them."

# Chapter **Ten**

Karen, Becca's mother, cast a look into the back of the car through the wing mirror. "You all right in the back?"

Becca immediately turned from her seat next to her mother, craned her neck and pressed her hand on Nancy's. "We'll be home soon."

Nancy offered a weak smile. It was all she was capable of right now.

The car pulled up at a red light. The engine sounded louder, piercing the silence as they sat stationary. Nancy turned, looked out of the window. A man in a suit rushed past, a file tucked under his arm. Two women stepped out of a café, laughing together in the sunshine. A cyclist in fluorescents slowed to a stop next to them. The people of Stratford town were going about their business, blissfully unaware that the fabric of her world was being torn apart at the seams.

She stared at the cyclist. A satchel hung loosely from her left shoulder. Wisps of dark hair poked out from beneath her helmet as she pulled a mobile from her pocket, dialled and chatted animatedly to someone at the other end. The normality of the situation caught Nancy. At that moment she felt a longing to be the cyclist – chatting to her partner, arranging to meet a friend later, on her way to work. Not travelling back from the hospital, confused and tired, waiting to hear if her boyfriend had been killed.

After Becca had mentioned arson yesterday, a million thoughts had reverberated around her head. *Did the body in the barn die from some kind of accident, or were they killed?*

She glared out of the window, a rage building in her chest. She couldn't understand how they could all carry on as if nothing had happened. She wanted to wind down the window and shout, "A man has died. Maybe murdered." The thought made her recoil.

For the last twenty-four hours, from the moment the police had told her about the body, she'd been stuck in a vortex; aware of voices going on around her, but her senses seemed to have numbed.

The detectives had said they were waiting on an identification.

Identification… She held onto that word. That meant they couldn't be sure. And they hadn't asked her to be involved which had to be a good sign.

*Don't let it be Evan.*

She thought back to when she had lost her grandmother, three years earlier. Nothing prepared her for the hollow sense of loneliness that scoured her insides, leaving her raw for days and weeks afterwards. And the world continued around her, oblivious to her distress.

She remembered the anger and resentment at her being taken. But this was different. Evan was in the prime of his life, soon to be making plans to settle down and have a family of his own. The very idea that someone, somewhere might have taken this away from him, from both of them, was incomprehensible.

*It can't be Evan.*

The cyclist pocketed her phone. The lights changed. Sharp tears pricked Nancy's eyes, blurring her vision as the car moved forward.

\*\*\*

Evan Baker's sister, Sharon, was a small horsey woman with sharpened cheekbones and a sheet of dirty-blonde hair that hung down her back. She was accompanied by her husband, a softly spoken man who introduced himself as Simon and must have been well over six foot five. It'd been a long time since Jackman had looked up to speak to somebody.

Jackman led them into the morgue waiting room. "Thanks for making the journey," he said. "Can I offer you a tea or coffee?"

They both shook their heads. "We were early, stopped at the services on our way up," Simon answered.

Jackman indicated for them to sit. "I realise this is a difficult time for you, but I do need to ask you some questions before we go in." He paused as Simon pressed his hand on his wife's arm. "Can you describe your brother to us?"

Sharon looked confused. "I thought you were pretty sure it's him?"

"We found a wage slip at his address. But we need to be definite. Does he have any distinguishing features around the face?"

Sharon flicked her gaze to her husband fleetingly. "I don't know... Like I told the detective yesterday, I haven't seen him for some years."

Jackman softened his tone. "The victim has been in a fire." Sharon gasped, placed her hand over her mouth. He gave her a moment to compose herself. "Some of his body has been burnt, but his facial features remain intact. I'm going to take you into a room where you will see him and ask you to confirm whether or not he is your brother. Please only say yes if you are absolutely sure."

He guided them out of the room, along the corridor and through a door that led to a half-room, separated by a Perspex screen in the middle. Beyond the screen was a trolley covered in a white sheet that was crumpled around the edges of what was clearly a human shape. The room smelled clinically clean.

Sharon turned to Jackman. "Where do we go in?"

"We can't, I'm afraid. The body still needs to be subjected

to a full forensic examination. We have to view him through the screen to avoid any cross contamination. I'm sorry."

He watched her step forward. The trolley was almost within touching distance. Russell entered the outside room, dressed in white coveralls. A hood was pulled over her head, booties covered her shoes. She moved towards the trolley, glanced towards them before she lifted back the sheet to reveal the side of a green body bag, the edges of a zip undone. A white sheet was wound around the victim's head, covering the burnt hairline, the blistered ears.

Evan's sister leant in closer. Her husband rested a hand on her shoulder.

"Could you confirm—"

She whisked around, stopping him mid-flow. "No."

"I'm sorry?"

"I mean no, that's not my brother."

Her face hardened as Jackman registered her words. "Are you absolutely sure?"

"Definitely. Evan's got a scar that runs the length of his forehead. He pulled a glass table down on himself as a kid when he was seven. I'll never forget it because we spent the whole afternoon in A&E on Christmas Day."

"Could he have had surgery?"

"It doesn't even look like him," she said. "Evan's head is squarish, I used to tease him about it when we were young. And he's taller."

Jackman indicated to Russell they were finished and led the couple back to the waiting area.

Now seated, Sharon reached into her bag, pulled out a bottle of water and took a huge gulp, wiping the back of her hand across her mouth as she passed it to her husband. Her face had visibly paled. "What I want to know, Inspector, is what made you think that was my brother? You must have been pretty sure to have dragged me all the way here."

"We believe the victim was using his national insurance number. Evan's passport was also found at his address."

"How did you manage to trace me?"

"Through the national insurance number we traced the date of birth. He was the only Evan Baker born on that day – so we went through births, deaths and marriages to trace the next surviving adult. It's routine police work."

She chewed the side of her lip, mulling this over.

"When was the last time you saw your brother?" Jackman asked.

She glanced across at Russell who had removed her notebook from her bag and opened it. "About six years ago. We're not close."

"Can you remember the circumstances?"

She averted her gaze. When she spoke, her voice was distant. "It was my parents' thirtieth wedding anniversary. They had a party at their home in Southampton. He turned up late, got drunk and spewed in the lounge. It was embarrassing, but only to be expected." She raised her eyes. "My brother was the only boy in our family, Inspector. My parents gave him everything: designer sports kits, school trips abroad, a car. It was never enough." She smiled to herself. "My sister and I used to joke that when he had steak for tea, we'd be given burgers."

"Your sister?"

Sharon was silent a moment. "Clara. She was two years younger than me. She died with my parents in a coach crash just over three years ago."

"I'm sorry," Russell said.

Sharon looked from one detective to another. "It was a long time ago."

Jackman waited a few moments before he spoke again. "Did your parents keep in contact with Evan before they died?"

"I'm not sure. I don't think so. After their accident I tried to trace him, to give him the news myself that we were the only ones left. That's when I discovered he was living in Thailand. He'd flown out with a friend who'd long since returned and had left him in a hostel in Chang Mai in the northern region. I spent ages going through addresses, hostels nearby, trying to find him. We even went out there. I found hostels where he'd stayed, but nobody knew where he'd moved on to or what happened to him. You don't give a forwarding address when you're travelling." She took a deep breath. "It became a bit of an obsession. I had a job, a life back here. Had to give up the search and come home in the end. But I always wondered whether he would walk through the door one day. And whether he ever knew."

Jackman watched the knuckles of her husband's hand whiten as he squeezed her hand.

"Anyway, he didn't bother with them when they were alive, so why would he bother with them after they were dead?" They sat in silence a moment until she spoke again. "What bothers me is, if that man was claiming to be Evan, using his national insurance number, his date of birth, what does that mean about my real brother?"

"Did you ever report him missing to the police?" Russell asked.

"No. As I said, we weren't close. He could have been anywhere. And I had no reason to think he'd come to harm. Until now."

Jackman made his excuses and left the room. Walking back down the corridor, one question pounded inside his brain: *If the man in the morgue wasn't Evan Baker, who was he?*

# Chapter **Eleven**

Jackman waited for the lights to change and continued on his journey, leaving the town of Stratford behind him. The frustrations of the morning ate away at him. Just when he thought they were making progress with an identification, it had fallen through. Now they had new, additional enquiries as to where the real Evan Baker was. And why the victim was using his identity. There was also the added complication of finding out who the deceased was. He'd requested an urgent DNA test, but with current backlogs goodness knows how long that would take.

He hiked up the volume to the Bach CD and drove across the rolling Warwickshire countryside to Upton Grange. The combination of the scenic route and rich classical music would have ordinarily calmed him, but today his mind was so occupied by the morning's events that he barely heard anything.

His mobile rang. He pressed to answer. Instantly the music stopped, interrupted by Davies' Geordie accent. "Hello. How did the ID go?"

"Not good," Jackman said. "She's adamant the victim isn't her brother – or certainly not the Evan Baker whose national insurance number he was using. We're getting dental records checked from a surgery her brother used some years back, close to where they lived in Southampton, just to be sure."

"Where does that leave us?"

"With somebody using an assumed identity, for whatever

reason. All we know so far is that the guy in those photos, the victim in the barn with the mole beside his eye, is not the Evan Baker whose passport and national insurance number he was using." Jackman paused as he reached a junction and pulled across the main road. "How's it going there?"

"The CSI team have been a nightmare. Wouldn't let anyone from the search team near the scene until they'd photographed everything and brought in cranes to remove the cars for examination. The POLSA search team have only just gone in." Her tone was infused with excitement. "It's like a gold mine down there—" Davies cut off.

Jackman could hear raised voices in the background, the edge of what sounded like an argument. "What's going on?" he asked.

It was a while before Davies came back on the line and when she did, she was out of breath. "Sorry, can't talk. A bloody journo has got through the cordon. Must have come across the fields. I think you need to get down here."

***

Jackman drove up the track and parked up behind the profusion of cars, vans and trucks next to the police cordon. Just as he exited his car, he spotted Davies, coming down to meet him. "Drama over. DC Keane has escorted her off the premises," she said.

"Who was it?"

"Elise Stenson from the *Stratford Mail*. Claimed she didn't see the tape. Some of it was ripped, pulled back at the bottom of the field behind the barn. Bloody liar. Not sure what she picked up though."

"Pull the cordon out wider and make sure it's guarded. We don't want any more unwanted visitors."

Davies nodded, pulled out her phone and made the call as they strode up the track.

The same musky smell wafted out of the barn, although

it had dissipated somewhat from first thing that morning, the open doors at each end providing welcome ventilation. Jackman crouched down beside the gap in the floor. He could see further into the room now that it had been opened up further, his vision assisted by a temporary police lamp illuminating the area with a strobe of light. Reflective silver hung off the walls. Rows of plants lined the floor, in various stages of growth. Lights and cables were scattered around. A fan stood in the corner.

Dave Mason, the search team sergeant, joined them as Jackman stood. "It's an old shipping container," he said. "Looks like two welded together actually." He raised a hand, scratched at his beard. "Insulation, a generator to provide heat and light. The perfect place for a cannabis farm."

"Must have taken a lot of work to get that down there," Davies said.

"Not really. The doors are big enough to get proper diggers in. Just a couple of days work to make the hole, slot it in and skim over with concrete."

"But if they welded it—"

Mason shook his head. "I'm pretty sure they'll have bought it like that. Fairly easy to get hold of, there will be loads on the Internet. People use shipping containers for all sorts of reasons. I've seen them used for storage, converted to workshops, even went to one with a toilet in it last year. Never seen one sunken in the ground before, although it's an ingenious plan." He looked around him. "Stuck out here, even the installation wouldn't attract any interest."

"Especially with the ruse of the cars stored on top. You wouldn't think to look any further," Jackman said.

"Quite right, although I'm not sure this barn would attract much interest." Mason turned around. "The entrance to the container was covered by some old wooden boards. They got burnt and singed in the fire, but were largely saved by the cars. The heat buckled the handle of the door, that's how you noticed it, but the room beneath was relatively undisturbed."

"Seems like a lot of trouble to go to for a crop of cannabis," Davies said.

Jackman looked down at the plants. He recalled a raid he'd attended early in his career in East London. The three-storey terraced house had been completely given over to the crop on all floors – even the cellar was used to dry out the harvested crop. The market in cannabis was huge and ever-expanding, drugs gangs were always searching for new and unusual locations to cultivate the plant.

"It's usually the electricity board that sound the alarm due to overuse of electrics, or the strange smell that gives these places away," Mason continued. "But stuck out here with a generator there'd be none of that. I doubt even the heat sensors on our helicopter would pick it up beneath the floor."

Jackman recalled Sheila Buckton's comment about them working late. Lots of farmers operated the machinery by night. It wouldn't have raised alarm. But it was the perfect mask to set up this kind of operation. Someone had given this considerable thought and invested a substantial amount of money. "Do we know how long it's been here?" he asked.

"Not sure at the moment," Mason said. "The generator out the back doesn't look particularly old though."

Jackman turned to Davies. "Have we heard from the farm owners?"

"Not yet."

"This kind of operation must have taken some organising," Jackman said. "Get on to the local building firms, see if anybody has been approached to install a container here. Find out how easily it is to source one of these containers and how it's transported, and see if you can source the generator too."

Davies had just raised her phone to her ear when Jackman had another thought. "Try skip companies in the area as well. There must have been a huge amount of soil and wastage to dispose of afterwards."

Jackman thanked Mason, moved away and took another look around the barn. The cars had been parked at the far end, on boards obscuring the entrance to the room below. The body was found in the opposite corner, beside the entrance and some makeshift shelving which he now realised was used to dry out the cannabis before it went to market. This whole operation was probably why Eamonn Benwell wasn't given a key. So that Evan could keep an eye on him.

Davies was winding up her call when he joined her outside. "Do you want me to get someone out to see Nancy? Deliver the news about the identification?"

Jackman's mind turned over the CSI photos of the victim. He couldn't deny that the resemblance between the victim and the stills they had taken off Nancy's phone was uncanny. "I'll call in there on my way back. I want to see what she's got to say."

"Want me to come with you?"

"No, I'll take Russell. She's been doing the liaison with Nancy. Be useful to have her input. Get Keane to pick up Eamonn Benwell, would you? I'd like to have another word with him."

# Chapter **Twelve**

A knock at the door pulled Nancy from her slumber. She blinked, laid there a moment, desperately trying to gather her thoughts and work out where she was. The white wardrobe and chest of drawers backed onto a pale pink wall. A picture of Evan and her sat on the bedside table – they were seated in the Land Rover, eyes hidden behind sunglasses. He was wearing the old Tilley hat he wore when he was doing the rounds on the farm. Muffled voices filtered through from the hallway. She couldn't make out what they were saying. Footsteps. The sound of a door handle. The voices faded. More footsteps, closely followed by the sound of knocking on the bedroom door.

"Nancy. You awake?"

Her head was heavy. She mustered enough energy to lift it from the pillow. "Who is it?" Her voice was full of sleep.

"The police are here to see you…" Becca's voice tailed off as she moved away.

Nancy laid her head back on the pillow. Becca hadn't left her side since they'd arrived home from the hospital that morning. For a while Karen had stayed too, both of them fussing over her until Karen had finally relented and gone downstairs to take over their florist shop beneath the flat that Nancy and Becca shared. She knew that even after she'd retreated to her bedroom to rest, Becca had been back and forth checking on her.

Nancy slowly eased herself around, dropping her legs off the edge of the bed, catching her reflection in the corner mirror as she did so. Her usually manicured hair hung lank onto her shoulders. She combed her fingers through it, tucked her T-shirt into her jeans. But when she turned to the door something stopped her.

Police officers. That meant news. Part of her didn't want to open the door. She didn't want to hear what they had to say in case it was bad. A sense of foreboding wrapped around her. If the news was bad, there was no going back.

Nancy took a deep breath and forced herself forward, concentrating on putting one foot in front of the other. In the hallway she could hear low voices. They quietened as she pushed open the door to the sitting room.

"Hey." Becca plastered her kindest smile on her face. "This is…"

Nancy looked past her. "I know who they are," she said, eyeing Russell.

Russell angled her head. "How are you feeling?"

"Like I've been tossed around in a tumble dryer." Her words were pithy, she knew that, but she couldn't bear to soften them. Curtness was a part of the armour she needed to shield herself from the news that was about to break her world in two.

The male detective sat forward. "Why don't you sit down?" Her eyes were drawn to him. His voice was soft, gentle, releasing the plug and letting every ounce of fight trickle from her.

"Nancy, how long have you known Evan?" he said.

Nancy frowned. "About three months. I told you."

He hesitated a moment. "Have you ever known him go by any other name?"

"No." Bubbles of irritation gathered in her chest. "What is this?"

"The body in the barn wasn't Evan Baker."

Nancy inhaled, a sharp intake of breath. But the tenseness in the room told her something wasn't right. She switched from one detective to another. "That's good, isn't it?"

Russell leant forward. "Evan's sister was able to confirm it wasn't him, not least because Evan doesn't have a mole beside his left eye."

The bell of the shop door trilled beneath them. Once again life was going on around her, pretending that nothing had happened. The irony was not lost on Nancy. "I don't understand."

"Her brother has different features. He also has a deep scar across his forehead from a childhood accident," Jackman said.

"Maybe it was a different Evan Baker."

"We think he was using the passport and the national insurance number of her brother."

"What are you saying?"

"We are going to need you to come along with us to ascertain whether the body in the barn is that of the man you knew as Evan Baker."

\*\*\*

The door clicked closed behind Jackman. He sat down opposite Eamonn Benwell, placing the file tucked underneath his arm on the table between them.

Eamonn looked at the file and back up at Jackman. "What's going on?"

Jackman waited for Keane to switch on the tapes and make the relevant introductions before he spoke. "Eamonn Benwell, can you please explain what you were doing between the hours of 10pm and 3am on the night of Sunday the 9th of August."

Eamonn glared back at him. Keane said he'd been surprised when they'd arrived at his factory and asked him to come back to the station. But he'd come along amiably, waived his right to legal representation. "I've already told you…"

"For the purposes of the tape, please."

"Is it Evan?" Eamonn said, ignoring the question.

"Pardon?"

"The body in the barn. Is it Evan? I can't get it out of my mind."

Jackman surveyed him. They hadn't released any details about the identity of the body to the press and he wasn't about to share anything with Eamonn Benwell now. "We're still waiting for the body to be identified."

Eamonn took a deep breath, slowly releasing the air through pursed lips.

"Could you answer the question please?"

Jackman ignored the anger creeping into Eamonn's voice as he gave an account of his movements on Sunday and Monday. He went on to ask him how he'd met Evan and formed the arrangement with the cars. The tapes continued to turn as Eamonn repeated his answers.

"Did you ever see anyone else at the barn?" Jackman asked.

"No, I told you. I only went there to use the cars."

"Does anyone else use your vehicles?"

"No."

"I believe one of the cars is a Buick. Can you tell me when you last drove this vehicle?"

"I don't know. A few weeks ago, maybe."

Jackman removed a photograph from the file and placed it on the table between them. It was the front of a car, blurred slightly. The driver wasn't visible, but the number plate was clear. "I am showing Mr Benwell Exhibit DAL3. Mr Benwell, can you confirm this is your Buick?"

Eamonn stared at the photo for some time. "Yes."

"This image was recorded by routine police cameras on the A46 approaching Stratford centre at 4.56pm on Sunday."

"I don't understand."

"Are you telling me you didn't drive your car last Sunday?"

"Somebody else must have used it."

"Does anyone else have keys to your vehicles?"

"Not that I'm aware of, but…"

"And you have no witnesses to confirm where you were on Sunday?"

Eamonn looked away. "No."

Jackman opened the file again and removed a single piece of paper. "I am now showing Mr Benwell Exhibit DAL4. This spreadsheet details your bank accounts and business records over the past twelve months. Can you explain to me how a man whose business appears to be failing, whose bank account is in the red and who has accumulated huge debts is able to pay for the upkeep of those vintage cars?"

Eamonn's face clouded. "You went through my stuff."

"This is a murder investigation. We're obliged to make all necessary checks into any persons connected with the victim."

"I'm going through a divorce."

"So you said." Jackman angled his head, waiting for Eamonn to continue.

He drew a deep breath, spoke through his exhalation. "We've been working on a big job, building a new conveyor for one of the supermarket chains. It's the biggest contract we've had, but they pushed us to the wire on pricing and wouldn't agree to a deposit. The material costs have drained us, but if we pull it off in time, we'll beat the penalty clause and move back into the black. It's a temporary blip."

"I guess the insurance from those cars might have given you a nice little injection of cash."

"I love those cars. Took me years to collect them."

"Do you have any other sources of income?"

Eamonn's brow furrowed. "I don't know what you mean."

"We are pulling the barn to pieces. If there is anything else stored there we will find it."

"Look," Eamonn said through gritted teeth. "I don't know what Evan Baker does with the barn, who else he rents space to, how he manages the farm. All I know is my cars were there. And now they're ruined."

"So, to your knowledge, there wasn't anything else stored there?"

"No. Why should there be?"

"Did you and Evan ever argue?"

Eamonn shook his head in disbelief. "We had crossed words a couple of times, yes."

"Why?"

"He wasn't always available when I wanted to use my cars, refused to give me a key."

Jackman narrowed his eyes. "What were the racks in the corner of the barn used for?"

"I don't know."

"You never saw anything there? What about on Sunday?"

Eamonn stared back at him blankly.

"You do realise we can enhance the image to show exactly who was driving the car?"

"I was at work."

"May I remind you we are investigating an arson and a murder? If something comes to light at a later date that you failed to mention…"

Eamonn stood. "That's it. I want a solicitor."

# Chapter **Thirteen**

Nancy watched the officer peel back the sheet. She held her breath, pressed her palms to the glass.

"Is this the man you knew as Evan Baker?"

Nancy swallowed hard, suppressing the tiny wail fighting to rise within her. The longer she kept it inside the longer she could refuse to believe. But the more she stared at the strong cheekbones, the familiar jawline, the eyes gently shut, the more the tears pushed through. Her fingers curled in despair. With the white sheet wrapped around him, Evan looked like he was sleeping.

Voices in the background merged together. She was stuck in a trance, almost like a dream. She needed to break through the screen, to get to him, to save him.

A banging in the distance. Somebody was creating a furore, wailing, giving voice to her distress. She blocked it out, her mind focused. Pain shot through her body. The tug of a heavy weight, a bracing hold. She could hardly breathe.

As she was pulled back, Nancy blinked back to the present. Her knuckles were red raw and burning. She looked down at them and suddenly became aware that it had been her own fists banging at the screen, her own screams filling the room. Strong arms guided her across to a chair in the corner.

The hard plastic was cold through her jeans. She stuck her head between her knees and obeyed the detective's words, encouraging her to take deep breaths in and out. When the dizziness subsided, she lifted her head. But the dead figure of her boyfriend through the screen did nothing to curb her rattled nerves.

The room started to spin again. Bile rose in her throat. She looked at the officer talking to Becca, back at the corpse, jumped up and fled from the room.

Nancy raced down the corridor, only just reaching the toilet in time for the contents of her stomach to meet the empty pan. She laid back on the cold tiles. She was aware of the door flapping open, heard her name being called, but couldn't answer.

Finally, when she felt strong enough, she moved forward and rinsed her hands and mouth in the cubicle sink. She looked up and stared at her reflection in the small mirror. Her face was white, her mind torn into two pieces – one side of her consumed with the loss of her boyfriend, the other side befuddled at how little she knew of him.

\*\*\*

"What do you think?" Davies asked. They were back in the incident room, Jackman relaying the relevant points of his interview with Eamonn Benwell to his team.

"That he has good reason to lie. His debts give him a motive for starting the fire. They, alongside his divorce and child support, also give reason for him to find another source of income."

"Like cannabis."

"Maybe he thinks it was destroyed in the fire. Or maybe he thinks we won't find it. Either way, he's not going to admit to being party to a cannabis cultivation. The trouble is we have nothing, apart from his car on camera to put him nearby. We need something else." Jackman placed his hands behind his neck, stretched his shoulders back. "What about Nancy?"

Russell explained what had happened at the morgue. "I took her home afterwards. Poor kid was distraught. We won't get any more out of her today."

"That leaves us with an unknown victim using the identity of Evan Baker. So where is the real Evan Baker? His sister last saw him six years ago, says he left for Thailand some time afterwards. What happened to him and how has the victim come to use Evan's identity?" Jackman looked across at Keane who was sat at a desk making notes while shoving the end of a bread roll into his mouth. "Andrew, can you get onto the Passport Agency? See if you can find out if an Evan Baker has ever reported a passport lost, when he last left the country, and if he ever returned. Anything more from the pub, his associations on the farm?" Jackman asked.

Keane wiped the crumbs from his mouth; they fell softly onto his yellow tie. "I have spoken to the other farm workers, but they weren't able to give me much at all. It seems that nobody goes to the barn and nobody really knows Evan very well."

"What about Sheila Buckton?"

"Hopeless cause." Keane rolled his eyes. "She's more interested in how the investigation is going than helping us with any more sightings of the victim in the past few weeks. Kept me there for almost an hour too."

"Okay, let's give Nancy some time to work it through. Keep an eye on her, Kathryn, and see if you can get her in for more questioning tomorrow. At the moment she's the closest person to our victim. Interview her as a key and significant witness, rather than a suspect, in one of the less formal rooms. Might encourage her to be a little more open."

Jackman rubbed his chin. "The car puts Benwell at the barn on Sunday, which he initially denied. Should give us enough to get a warrant to search his flat. Mac is pretty sure that whoever put the body into that barn had struck him over the head with some kind of blunt instrument beforehand. We could do with finding that weapon. The barn keys are still missing too. Any news on the missing firearms?"

Heads shook around the room.

"Let's get that warrant and search Benwell's flat and business premises. We need those guns out of circulation."

"Davies glanced at her watch. We'd have to be quick. It's after three."

"Shouldn't take too long. There are some benefits to sharing a building with the magistrate's court."

***

Eamonn Benwell's flat was on the first floor of a block of modern fixtures on St Peter's Way, close to Stratford town centre. Jackman stepped over the post that littered the black-and-white mock-tiled flooring in the hallway, past an array of jackets and coats hung over the top of one another, and moved into a long room at the back of the flat. The combination of minimal furniture – television, sofa and small corner coffee table – with the patio doors gave it a light and airy feel. Jackman could almost see Eamonn Benwell languishing on the sofa after a heavy day at work, working through the channels, remote in hand.

He wondered how Davies was getting on. The warrant had given them permission to search both Eamonn's business and home address. They'd organised two separate teams, taken one each, to avoid any chance of cross-contamination. For some reason, Jackman felt Davies was more likely to find whatever they were looking for at the business unit.

He moved to the end of the sofa, knelt down and looked through the plethora of magazines scattered at the side, which appeared to be vintage car magazines of varying ages. He stood, pulled back the net curtain and peered through the double glazed doors. House roofs peeked in the distance; a towel hung over the balustrade outside. *It must have cost a fortune to keep this two-bedroomed flat so close to Stratford centre*, Jackman thought, *especially on top of maintaining his family*. He could hear the search team pulling open drawers in the bedrooms, banging them closed as he wandered around. The kitchen was an assault on the senses. Although the slim window at the end allowed limited lighting, the cupboards and fittings were all finished in chrome, with sparkling white splashback tiling that made it dazzlingly bright. Jackman opened a few cupboards. Most were empty, apart from one containing a white dinner service that looked like it had never been used and another with a few tins of baked beans, half a loaf of bread and an onion sprouting shoots. It seemed that Eamonn Benwell didn't eat at home a lot.

"Sir!" The sound of Keane's voice turned his attention to the bedroom at the front. The room smelled musty, as if it needed a good airing, although the bed was made and there was a folded pile of navy overalls on the chair beside the wardrobe. Keane was kneeling down in the far corner.

"What is it?" Jackman asked.

"Looks like the carpet here has been disturbed recently," he said.

Jackman watched him a moment. He picked at the edge, tugged at the fibres. The carpet loosened from its gripper rod beneath.

Jackman was itching to get in closer, take a look for himself, but Keane's paunch filled the area between the bedside table and the window wall. "What's there?" he asked.

Keane shuffled back a little. "Doesn't look like anything." He ran a gloved hand over the chipboard beneath, moved back further and tugged on the carpet until the whole corner was exposed. "Well, well, well," he said.

Jackman peered over Keane's shoulder. There was a cut in the floorboard that looked like it had been done with an electric saw, almost a perfect circle. Keane curled a nail around the edge, pulled back. It lifted slightly and dropped. He snapped his hand back and sucked his finger, a pained expression on his face. "We need a screwdriver, or something to catch the edge," he said, heaving himself up.

As he left the room, Jackman picked up the photo on the

bedside table. It was a girl and boy sitting on a beach next to a sandcastle. She was smiling through a squint, but his face was taut as if he had been told to pose for the camera and didn't feel like it. Neither of them looked more than ten years old. He was just replacing it when Keane returned with a palate knife. He held it up and grinned. "Only the best in our toolbox."

Jackman watched as he worked the knife around the edge of the circle, loosening the wood. It lifted as he dragged it back, just enough for him to slide a finger underneath and pull it away. They both moved forward. Loose wires ran along the cavity beneath the floor, but apart from that it was empty. Keane shot Jackman a puzzled look, retrieved his torch and shone it in the gap, leaning down and looking in from different angles.

"I don't get it," he said. "Why go to so much trouble?"

He dug his gloved hand in further, beneath the boards, scrabbled around a moment, and pulled out an orange carrier bag. He opened it up to reveal two large bundles of cash and a mobile phone.

"Get the CSIs in to run a check over the area, will you?" Jackman said to Keane. "See if they can pick anything up." He moved out of the bedroom, pulled his phone out of his pocket and dialled Davies. He didn't bother with pleasantries. "How's it going there?"

"Slow." Davies gave a heavy sigh. "It's a working factory and he's not the tidiest of people."

Jackman relayed their findings.

"What do you think that means?"

"Not sure yet. We need to get the phone examined. In the meantime, make sure you check every nook and cranny for any more compartments. And get the drugs/firearms dog out to run over the premises. He obviously has something to hide."

# Chapter **Fourteen**

Jackman became aware of Superintendent Janus' knee juddering next to him. Most people suffered nerves at press conferences. The media weren't just looking to report to the public, they were looking for some nugget of information to sensationalise, make it entertaining; the police only released what was essential to drive an investigation forward. It was like an unhappy marriage, they both needed each other for different reasons. But it never ceased to amaze him how it rattled the usually calm and collected Superintendent.

A light flashed in the distance. Jackman blinked as he stared out to the audience in front of him. "May I reiterate that we are looking to speak to anyone who was in the vicinity of Upton Grange Farm and anyone who visited The Fish pub that night? You might not think you've seen anything, or have anything to add, but please come forward, even if it's just to enable us to eliminate you from our enquiries."

A voice came from the back of the room. "Can the Superintendent tell us why the excavators were at the site of the barn this morning?"

The room fell silent. Anyone that had been fiddling with phones and making notes before looked up. A glimmer of fresh interest shone in the eyes that faced them. Janus folded and unfolded her hands on the table in front of them. When it was obvious she wasn't about to respond, Jackman leant forward and gave the journalist his full attention. "Elise Stenson, isn't it? From the *Stratford Mail*?"

She gave him a sly smile. "Indeed, Detective. Now are you going to answer the question?"

Jackman gave a cool smile back and paused before he spoke. The room was silent, as if there were only the two of them present. "This is a murder investigation. Our priority here is to the victim and their bereaved family and to the people of Stratford. We need to find out what happened and track down the killer. Time is of the essence. And we are asking for the help of the people of Stratford to be able to do that. The work carried out at the barn is routine police work to help with this investigation."

"But—"

"I repeat, our priority is to catch the killer. And it would be helpful if the press would respect our cordons in future. We don't want any cross-contamination of potential evidence."

"Do you even know the identity of the body yet, Inspector?"

Jackman watched her curl her top lip. "We are waiting for a full identification."

"So you have a lead?"

Jackman sighed inwardly. "I can confirm that there is a man helping us with our enquiries." He ignored her scowl as he stood. "Thank you, everyone." More cameras flashed as he exited the room, closely followed by Janus.

They moved down the corridor in awkward silence. Jackman's step quickened. He was keen to get back to the incident room to see if anything had come back from the drugs squad, informants, or the public appeals.

"Thank you, Will," Janus said as they climbed the stairs.

"For what?"

"Bloody Elise Stenson. She's the one who broke through the cordon this morning, isn't she? I'll bet she's seen something. She knows damn well that targeting drug-related crime is a current priority. We'd better keep a close eye on what is reported. She'll do anything to sex up the situation, score some points."

Jackman didn't answer. The discovery of the cannabis farm hadn't been released to the public and he wanted to keep it that way for as long as possible, to focus the public on looking for sightings of the victim. He wasn't about to get bogged down with the wider politics of policing right now.

At the top of the stairs she paused and caught his arm. "Did you speak to Carmela yesterday?"

Jackman looked at the ceiling and back at her. "Haven't had a chance yet."

"Really? Look, Will, you're a good detective. But if you want to get through this promotion board you're going to need to play the game. I didn't support your application to watch you fail." She glanced at her watch and marched off down the corridor in the opposite direction to the incident room calling, "Come on," over her shoulder.

Jackman gave a heavy sigh as he followed. "I really don't think—"

"She should be finishing up for the day now," Janus interrupted. "If we hurry we'll just catch her."

She paused outside an open door. The room was laid out like a training room, an array of chairs arranged in an arc in front of a wide screen. A slim woman in a dark trouser suit was gathering papers in the corner. She looked up as they entered, immediately placed the papers down and grinned a welcome. "Alison, it's good to see you." She rushed forward, touched Janus' shoulder who smiled back.

"Carmela, this is Will Jackman," Janus said, moving aside. "The DI I was telling you about."

Jackman extended his hand and was surprised when the shake was accompanied with a smile that lit up her whole face.

"So you want to join Thames Valley?" Carmela asked. "Good move."

He caught Janus throw her a look. "If you can spare a moment to help him prepare for his board next week, give that extra polish to his answers, he'd really appreciate it."

"Sure." She glanced around the room. "We could have a quick coffee now, if you want?"

"I've got a briefing—"

"I'm sure you can delegate," Janus said. "You'll need to do lots more of that if you get your promotion." She turned her back on him. "That sounds great, thank you, Carmela."

Carmela looked from one to another, sensing the tension. "Um... okay. Well, just give me a few minutes to finish up here and I'll be with you."

Janus looked pleased with herself as they moved out into the corridor. "Make time for this, Will," she said. "If anyone can help with interview preparation, Carmela can." She adjusted the strap of her bag on her shoulder. "Right, what's next on the case?"

Jackman stared at her in disbelief before he answered. "We're searching the premises of Eamonn Benwell and working through his business records. We're also waiting for the DNA on the victim, working through the results of the public appeal and hopefully preliminary forensics should come through any time. And, of course, waiting on any intelligence from the source handlers and the drugs squad. Somebody is going to miss that crop."

"Right. Make sure you check and double-check every connection with the drugs community. I don't want any review team coming in at a later date and discovering we've missed something, especially with Elise Stenson on our back. God only knows how far the press are going to push this one. And check on any intelligence for those guns, surely somebody'll know something."

She stuck her head back in the room. "Bye, Carmela!"

He heard Carmela shout back, "Oh, bye. We must catch up before I head back on Friday. It's been too long."

"Definitely. Give me a call."

Jackman watched Janus fly down the corridor, any ounce of her earlier nerves now rescinded, and cursed under his breath. He imagined her driving back to Leamington, working out in her mind how this was going to affect her crime figures, the relations with the press, the public.

He pulled his phone out of his pocket, was just about to call Davies when he heard a voice behind him. "Okay, ready?" Carmela had now arrived at the door, flashing that same smile.

"Sure." He followed her down the corridor with some reluctance. This coffee had better be quick.

\*\*\*

For the past half hour the rain had beat the window, little needles cascading in a torrent of anger. Apart from the occasional trill of the entrance bell in the shop downstairs and the bang as the door closed, it was the only sound that filled the room.

Nancy lay on the sofa, unfocused eyes fixed upwards. *Evan was dead. Gone.* She repeated it over and over in her mind, yet her subconscious blocked the words, preventing them from sinking beneath the surface. *He couldn't be dead.*

She could still see him in the Land Rover, trundling down the country lanes to feed the cattle, his blond hair flopping over his forehead and bright blue eyes staring back at her.

The image disappeared, washed away by a wave of sadness. She hadn't been out in the Land Rover in recent weeks, making excuses because of the wet weather, teasing him about the stench of damp cattle that his clothes carried back. Right now she'd do anything for another chance to take one of those trips. Even in the rain. She wouldn't worry about her hair getting wet or her mascara running.

A raindrop plunked off the window sill. Followed by another. The blocked guttering had finally given way, as it always did during heavy downpours, causing a steady staccato of blobs to bounce down.

Her mother hadn't called. She knew she ought to phone

her, to tell her she was home, but she couldn't face speaking to Cheryl right now.

She allowed her eyes to wander freely around the cream walls of Becca's lounge, floating over the gothic fringed curtains, the black rug and matching leather sofa Becca's mother had given to her when they'd moved in here. A mock-oil painting of Becca's childhood pet German shepherd hung above the fireplace. Coloured candles were scattered on the mantle beneath in various melted states. The lump in her throat hardened.

Her eyes rested on a photograph on the mantelpiece. It was a holiday snap of Becca and her, the colours faded slightly, taken when they were in Corfu together last year, a trip paid for them both by Becca's mother as her daughter's eighteenth birthday present. In fact, when she thought about it, Becca's mother had paid for almost everything in this room and the rest of the flat for that matter.

Becca would often say that they were as good as family. Nancy was the sister she never had. Karen and Becca had been good to her. They'd given her a job and the opportunity to work with her beloved flowers, somewhere to live when she had nowhere to go. She was grateful for everything, but they'd never truly felt like family. In some ways she'd grown accustomed to living on the edge of other people's lives.

It wasn't meant to be like this. She'd wanted to grow up, become a successful florist, have her own shop one day, get married, have children. Whatever happened she always knew she wouldn't be like Cheryl – she'd be a good mother, take care of her children, keep them safe. Tears trickled down her cheeks. Evan had wanted the same things as her.

If only her grandmother was still alive. More tears swelled in her aching eyes. Hazy images of life before school filled her mind: sitting at her grandmother's Formica table in the kitchen eating her tea, cuddled up on the sofa watching the television together. Gran read her stories at bedtime, smiling at her pleas of 'just one more page'. Abridged versions of the classics were replaced by Enid Blyton and Harry Potter as the years folded past. Her mother popped in, from time to time, but never stayed long.

Gran blamed her daughter's behaviour on the fact that her father had died when Cheryl was five – an industrial accident in a warehouse nearby. They'd fought a case against the company and lost, leaving them with debts which meant they'd struggled to pay the bills. In her early teens, Cheryl got in with the wrong crowd and starting drinking. Nobody even knew who Nancy's father was, or if they did they never told her. When she questioned her gran, she'd simply said that Nancy didn't need a dad. They had each other and that was enough.

Her gran loved books – encouraging Nancy to read the Brontë Sisters, Charles Dickens. But her greatest love was gardening. They might have only had a small garden in the terrace they shared but from a young age, Nancy remembered the anticipation and excitement of watching the first snowdrops and bluebells in spring that kicked off months of flowering plants.

Nancy's mind fast-forwarded to 16 January 2012. She was sixteen. She'd woken to the sound of the birds singing in the garden out front, checked her phone like she always did. Her grandmother hadn't woken her. It was 8.30am. She was late for school.

She'd jumped out of bed, dressed in a flurry. She could remember now, running into her grandmother's bedroom. The curtains were open, her bedclothes folded back, the same way they always were. Nancy had called out, shouting down the stairs, her voice disappearing into the stillness that filled the house. It wasn't until she reached the kitchen that she discovered her grandmother's crumpled body on the floor. Nancy remembered the fear, the anguish she'd suffered in the days that followed. If only she'd got up earlier. If only she'd used her own alarm. Maybe her grandmother would still be alive.

Nancy's heart sank. Evan was the only person outside Becca's family and since her gran that had made her feel loved and special in her own right. And now he was gone.

# Chapter **Fifteen**

Jackman locked the front door, wound the lead around his forearm and started into a jog. The rush hour was over and, apart from parked cars dotted along the curbside, Shipston Road was sleepily clear of traffic. Erik trotted along at his side, his tongue hanging loose. They passed the aperture beneath the bridge that led to the recreational ground, jogged past the numerous bed and breakfasts, and headed up the pathway into town.

The rain had long since passed, leaving a low sun to wipe the pavements clean and light up the evening, in spite of the late hour.

The case wormed its way into Jackman's head. He needed to work out why the victim had taken someone else's identity. And whether or not that had something to do with why he was killed. Evan was secretive about the barn. He must have had some connections somewhere in order to operate such a sophisticated cannabis cultivation, but so far, the drugs squad hadn't come back with any leads.

His mind wandered to the press conference, the meeting afterwards. He'd expected a quick cup of coffee, accompanied by tedious management talk. Instead he'd been surprised by their impromptu meeting – Carmela's manner was open, friendly. She'd been impressed with his knowledge of policing policy (as had he, considering he avoided reading the emailed news bulletins wherever possible). One cup of coffee turned into two and before he knew it he'd invited her around to the house the following evening to run through some mock interview questions.

He passed the garage at the end of Shipston Road, crossed the main road and quickened to a sprint over the bridge. It was a balmy Tuesday evening, the air calm and still. He slowed to cross the road as he passed the statue of Shakespeare and halted beside the Canal Basin, glancing into the water as he caught his breath. A pair of swans glided through the water, side by side, a line of cygnets at their tail. Jackman leant on the bridge and took a swig from his water bottle. Erik flopped down at his feet, clearly relieved at the break. A busker was singing a cover of 'Brown Eyed Girl' on nearby Bancroft Gardens, a small audience huddled around him. Groups of people dotted the surrounding grassy areas.

A man and woman strolled beside the water, hand in hand. He watched them a moment. It wasn't long ago that he and Alice had walked into town for a meal, or a drink. This was one of the things that Jackman loved most about living in Stratford. It was a sleepy town, compared to North London where they'd lived before, yet still offered the cultural highlights of the theatre, restaurants, the river. Alice used to say their home was perfectly positioned, close to the rolling hills of the Warwickshire countryside, yet within walking distance of the town. A beautiful place to raise their daughter.

Jackman secured his water bottle in his pocket, jogged down the side of the Basin and across the bridge towards home. At the last minute he veered off into the recreational ground, retrieved a ball from his pocket. The sight of the ball wound the dog into a frenzy and he stood there for some time throwing the ball, watching Erik retrieve it.

Eamonn Benwell's dark features flashed up in his mind. He had lied about being at the barn on Sunday. The search at the unit hadn't yielded any results, but the phone and cash at the flat had given him enough to keep Eamonn in custody overnight while they applied for billing on the phone. Although the look of sheer terror on Eamonn's face at the prospect of a night in a police cell sat uncomfortably. Somehow, somewhere in the deep corners of Jackman's mind, the thought of Eamonn being the murderer just didn't ring true.

*** 

Becca had just passed Nancy a fresh cup of tea when the doorbell rang. It was late, dark outside. Nancy heard the front door click open. Becca returned almost immediately, "Ryan's here to see you."

Nancy was just about to say she didn't want to see him when Ryan's freshly shaven face appeared in the doorway. He was wearing the Fat Face T-shirt she'd bought him last Christmas.

"What do you want?" Nancy could feel her shoulders tense.

Ryan put his hands in his pockets. "I heard the news, came to see how you are."

"Yeah, sure." Nancy looked away. "You made it quite obvious you didn't like Evan."

"I came to see you, to check if you were all right."

"Well, I'm not. So now you've seen me you can go." Nancy clenched her teeth in an effort to stop herself from crying.

Ryan was hovering in the doorway, his shoulder leant against the frame. He wasn't handsome in the traditional sense. His parents owned a garage on the Birmingham Road. He'd gone to work with his dad on an apprenticeship as soon as he left school and his lanky body was nearly always smeared with oil stains of some sort. A number two haircut complete with cowlick framed a skinny face. But there was something infectious in the way he carried himself that had drawn her to him, and his easy manner coupled with his sense of humour had made the pain of parting earlier that year all the more difficult to bear.

They'd been through so much together – he'd been there, many a time, when she'd had to help her mother into bed after a sleepless night worrying where she was. Nancy had stayed at his house on numerous occasions when things were bad at home after her gran died. It was Ryan who finally persuaded her to move out.

He was the first man she'd had sex with. The first man she'd truly loved.

"I still care about you, Nance. Six years is a long time. You can't switch off feelings like that."

"You didn't care when you decided you wanted your life back. When you said you were too young to be tied down."

"We *were* young."

"We're still young. I never asked anything of you. No commitment. You just wanted to go off and shag half of Stratford, then come back and pick up where you left off."

"That's not fair."

"Not fair?" Nancy was on her feet now. She could feel the anger pulsing through her veins.

Ryan shifted uncomfortably. "Come on, Nance. We're still friends."

"You hated that I'd found a new boyfriend, didn't you?"

"That's got nothing to do with it. I just—"

"You just what? Thought you'd come and gloat? I should think you're pretty glad he's gone."

"I didn't wish him dead."

Nancy could feel the burst of energy draining away at the mention of the word 'dead'. The finality of it, spoken aloud, made it so terrifying real. She swallowed back the fresh tears threatening to fall. She couldn't cry in front of Ryan. She wouldn't.

"Don't be like this Nance, I just wanted to see if I could do anything. You know, to help."

"I don't need your help."

He hesitated. "Okay. You've got my number. Call me if

you need anything, anything at all." He hovered for another few seconds before leaving.

As soon as the front door clicked shut, Becca emerged from her bedroom. Just in time to see Nancy collapse back down onto the sofa, throw her head in her hands and sob. Becca rushed to her side, cradling Nancy in her arms. The tears dripped through her fingers as she cried hard and fast, harder than she had done so in days.

Slowly, her breathing started to ease. Becca pulled back, passed her a box of tissues. "It will get easier you know. In time. I promise you it will."

Nancy looked up at her. "You didn't like Evan either, did you?"

"Oh, Nance. Don't say that. I didn't really get a chance to get to know him."

Nancy held her head in her hands. "Why me? Isn't it enough that I don't have a family to care about me? Why take him too?"

Becca hugged her close. "You do have family. You have us."

"I have you, but no one else."

"You have Mum, too." They sat in silence for a moment. "Ryan was only trying to help, you know?" Becca said eventually as she moved back and sat on the floor beside the chair. "I didn't call him. He heard about the fire on the news, came here because he wanted to."

Nancy sniffed, wiped her nose. That sounded just like something her gran would say. But right now the wounds were too raw. And the last person that she felt like talking about Evan to was Ryan.

# Chapter **Sixteen**

Layers of paper money juddered about inside the exhibit bag as Jackman held it up. "Mr Benwell. Why do you feel the need to keep cash under your floorboards?"

Dark rings hung beneath the eyes that stared back at Jackman. Eamonn scratched the layer of stubble coating his chin before he answered. "My wife does the company books. I have to keep something back, she's taking everything."

"Does she have keys to your flat?"

"No."

"Then why hide it?"

Eamonn let out a long sigh. "My kids stay over sometimes. I found my youngest searching through my bedside drawer a month ago. When I asked him why, he clammed up. An hour or so later he burst into tears, saying his mum told him to look for money." He placed a hand over his eyes. "She's bleeding me dry."

His solicitor looked up from her notes, switched her eyes from one to another. "Do you have something else, Inspector?"

Jackman ignored her. "Your raw products – the steel sheeting, tubing. Your business records suggest you buy a lot from China and the Far East. Why not source them in this country, or from Europe?"

"It's cheaper."

"How are they transported?"

"By sea."

"In shipping containers?"

"It's not a crime to save money."

Eamonn's solicitor leant back. "Do you have anything relevant to the crime to ask my client?"

Jackman narrowed his eyes. Pulled an exhibit bag out of the folder on his desk. A mobile phone sat in the bottom. "Would you like to tell us why you keep this under your floorboards?"

Eamonn cast a sidelong glance at his solicitor. "It's for personal calls."

"We know that. We're examining the call records right now. Why?"

He smacked his lips together. "I can't say."

"Can't or won't?"

Eamonn buried his eyes in the table.

"We will continue our investigation into your income and if we find that it is funded by illicit means, you will be charged and your assets seized. Are you sure there's nothing else you'd like to tell us?"

Eamonn shook his head wearily.

His solicitor made a play of checking her watch. "Right, Inspector. As far as I see it you have no direct evidence to link my client to the murder, which I believe is what he was brought here for in the first place?" She widened her eyes, started gathering her papers. "I think it's time you let him go."

"We'll take a break," Jackman said. They turned off the tapes and Jackman left the room with Davies on his heels.

"What do you think?" she asked as the interview room door closed behind them.

"He's living beyond his means, no doubt about that. It's possible he's been sourcing his materials in the Far East so that he could bring other stuff in. If he is involved in the cannabis chain, he might be into other drugs too. We could pass that onto the drugs squad. But his brief is right, we haven't got enough evidence to link him to the murder."

"What was on the phone?" Davies asked as they made their way down the corridor and climbed the back stairs.

"Looks like he only uses it to contact one number. The techies are having a problem tracing the source."

"Anything back from the labs?" Jackman called out as they entered the incident room.

A plethora of heads looked up from desks and shook in unison.

"What about the farm owners?"

"Not yet." Keane slammed a drawer shut as he spoke. "We've been in touch with their daughter. She thinks they're currently between Adelaide and Perth. It's a long stretch to drive."

Jackman was starting to feel itches of irritation beneath his skin. "Could we send them another email please? With a cannabis cultivation on their property, they are potentially involved in criminal activity. If we don't hear anything back from them soon, we'll have to get onto the Australian police to see if they can track them down. What about local skip companies or builders? Somebody must have arranged for that room to be put beneath the floor in the barn."

"We're working our way through local companies, but it's a mammoth task," Davies said.

"Nothing from the drugs squad?"

More head shakes.

"As it stands at the moment we'll have to let Eamonn Benwell go," Jackman said with a heavy sigh. "We've got Nancy coming in today, so hopefully that'll give us something. We've checked missing persons. Chase those DNA results again, will you? I'm sure once we know who the victim is, it will open up some more leads."

\*\*\*

The letterbox woke Nancy the following morning. After a night of broken sleep, she'd drifted off as the early morning light streamed into her bedroom. She could hear intermittent shuffles downstairs and muffled voices in conversation in the shop below. She lay there for a while, trying to clear a space in the tenacious mist that dogged her mind.

She grabbed her mobile phone from the bedside table. It was Wednesday, 10.30am. The last few days merged together. Two text messages lit up her screen. She opened the first from Becca.

*Gone to work. Text me if you need anything.*

Good. She was grateful to Becca for taking yesterday off to look after her, but it was a relief to have some peace today to work things through. She needed time to think. The second message was an unknown number.

*Thinking of you. Give me a call when you are feeling better. Rx*

Ryan again. Becca must have given him her new number. She tried to suppress the new wave of anger rising inside her.

What she really needed was a coffee, an injection of caffeine to kick-start her brain into action. Nancy hauled herself out of bed, plodded through to the kitchen and flicked the switch on the kettle. As the steam rose and swirled into the air, she moved around gathering her mug, making the coffee.

It wasn't until she walked back through to the hallway that she saw the white envelope on the mat. She placed the mug on the side, picked it up and turned it over in her hands. It was addressed to *NANCY* in wide typed letters. She pulled it apart, tearing the letter inside in her clumsy haste. It took a while to retrieve it and place it together before she could read.

*Debts pass to next of kin.*

Nancy turned the paper over, looked back at the envelope and reread the words. Her knees weakened. She moved through into the lounge and lowered herself onto the sofa. The only next of kin she had was Cheryl. She stared at it, barely able to comprehend.

Nancy stood, pulled the new mobile from her pocket and dialled her mother's number, clutching her elbow with her free hand, shuffling from one foot to the other as it rang out several times before the voicemail kicked in. She went back through to the kitchen, leant up against the side and looked at the note again. This could only mean one thing. But Cheryl had promised. Sat beside Nancy's hospital bed, she had said she hadn't touched a drop of alcohol in almost two months. The news was intended to cheer Nancy's spirits and it certainly had the desired effect.

Just like the last time.

Nancy recoiled as the memories came flooding back. After Gran's funeral Cheryl vowed to seek treatment, spending two weeks in a clinic to clean herself up. Nancy was wary when she was discharged and moved in with her, yet Cheryl worked hard to gain her trust. She went to the supermarket, cooked fresh meals, none of that ready-made stuff her gran disapproved of. She spent her days cleaning the house, listening to Nancy share the gossip at the florists over dinner in the evening, even got up and made her breakfast before she started work, although she didn't need to.

It lasted almost two months. Until Cheryl disappeared.

Nancy had been frantic. She'd phoned around friends, mutual acquaintances, walked the streets looking for her. Becca and her mother joined the search. They alerted the police. Even now Nancy could remember the raw feeling of fear that at any moment officers might arrive at the door, explain that something terrible had happened, some cruel twist of fate had taken her mother away, just when she'd got her back.

Four days passed before Cheryl returned, slotting her key into the front door one evening as if nothing had happened. Nancy remembered how she'd rushed out to the hallway. And froze. Cheryl's clothes were filthy. She'd peered up at Nancy through a lank fringe, her eyes dark and sunken. Nancy had seen that look before. Now she understood why her gran had shouted at Cheryl so many times over the years, thrown her back to the streets to 'sort herself out' when she'd turned up at their door. She'd fallen back into the clutches of alcohol once again and it would take nothing but a minor miracle to bring her mother back.

Nancy had grown accustomed to the hollow reassurance, the false promises. From as young as eight, she'd sat on the stairs and peeped through the bannisters at her mother and gran arguing. Yet this time Cheryl had been so enthusiastic, seemed so convincing.

But the more she turned it over in her mind, the more Nancy was sure it could be the only possible explanation. It would also explain why Cheryl hadn't been in touch since she left hospital.

There was a time when a letter like this would have scared Nancy, left her mind spinning at what events might befall her if she didn't comply. Now she just felt numb.

She would have loved a normal mother. Those brief intervals in her life when her mother had been clean had represented some of their happiest moments and she cherished them like a baby's comfort blanket. But it wasn't meant to be.

During their short time together, Evan had cautioned Nancy to be gentle, comforting, try to help her mother, wean her off the drink. Against her better judgement, formed by years of disappointment, she'd been persuaded by his words. But this now... This was too much.

Only Cheryl could be selfish enough to create a drama like this amidst her own daughter's anguish. Nancy ripped the note in half, and half again, and several more times before she shoved it in the bin. This time she wouldn't be there to pick up the pieces.

A knock at the door startled her. She pulled her robe across her chest, tightened the straps as she made for the door. Instead of pulling it open, she stood back and called out, "Who is it?"

"It's Kathryn."

Nancy picked at the locks and opened the door, only to be met with a smile from the petite detective. "How are you feeling today?"

# Chapter **Seventeen**

"The basic equipment to set up this kind of operation costs around £2,000." The slick detective in the sharp black suit turned and looked at the photos plastered across the wall behind him of the inside of the container found at the barn. "Fans and ventilation, heat lamps, lights – looks like quite a sophisticated operation. Pretty easily available online, or if you know the right people. You'd expect a crop worth around £5,000 every ten weeks or so."

Janus' chair squeaked as she sat back. They were gathered in the incident room with Mike Clarke, head of Warwickshire Drugs Squad, who'd driven over from Leamington to discuss the discovery at the barn.

Jackman shot Keane a look. "Any sign of big withdrawals in the victim's bank records?"

Keane shook his head. "There's little cash in there, and not many payments either in terms of direct debits or standing orders. His salary's quite meagre, paid once a month. I'm guessing it includes his lodgings. The owners pay the farm bills and he uses their Land Rover as his vehicle so he doesn't need much. He withdraws cash a couple of times a week, but not in huge quantities. We've gone back over the last twelve months, before the Lawtons left, and can't find any significant payments. Although there is that stack of used notes, just over £2,000, that CSIs found at the farmhouse."

Jackman couldn't help but think of the cash they found

in Eamonn Benwell's flat. "On face value the victim didn't seem to lead the lifestyle one might expect of a drug dealer," he said. "They usually plough their cash into flash cars, property, anything to avoid placing large payments into the bank. Which suggests he's either stacking the cash up somewhere, or he had help."

"That's not unusual in this sort of operation," Mike said. "Towns are generally split into patches, controlled by organised crime groups. Most law-abiding sorts never see it, but if you delve deep enough you'll find them. Setting up an operation like this without help isn't likely to last long without the right people getting involved or backing it."

"You're suggesting the victim provided the space and someone else is reaping the rewards?"

"Not quite. He'll either set up a new supply chain, or he's contributing to one already established. If it's established, he'll be paid for the use of the barn with each crop he yields. And it would explain why you can't trace the building firm who installed the container, or the generator. They'd do it off the books, be paid for their discretion."

"What about the Lawtons' bank accounts?" Jackman said to Keane.

He shook his head. "Direct debits for farm bills, utilities – nothing of any significance. They have a personal bank account which has about £16,500 in it and pays what looks like their monthly credit card bill and travel expenses, and a savings account which shows a few chunky withdrawals, but no large injections of cash."

"Is it possible a rival gang discovered the cannabis farm?" Davies said. "Burnt it down, with Evan in there to send a message?"

"Possible. These guys are very protective. They don't like anyone else muscling in on their business."

"What can you do to help us?" Jackman asked.

Mike paused, looked at the photos again and turned back to his audience. "We've got our source handlers out there, talking to people in the field as we speak, to try to see who this operation belonged to or who supported it. If they were supplying locally, the discovery of this farm is going to leave someone short for a while – hopefully we can find out who and where."

"How long do you think that'll take?" Janus asked.

"Hard to say, but we'll keep in touch, feedback any information as soon as we have it."

"What about the missing firearms?"

"Nothing yet. We're still working on it."

Jackman ignored Janus' loud sigh. He briefly shared Eamonn Benwell's account, their findings at his flat. "Is Benwell known to you, at all?" Jackman asked.

Mike thought for a moment. "It's not a name I'm familiar with. But of course I'll share it with my team."

"Is there any way of knowing how long the cannabis farm has been there?" Jackman said.

"The equipment doesn't look particularly old. Part of the crop looks almost ready to harvest, although it might not be the first one. I've seen many cannabis farms," Mike continued. "Some were in factory units, others in backstreet houses where the whole ground floor was taken over by little pots of compost and heat lamps. Someone was paid to look after them, living in one room of the house on their own while managing and harvesting the crop. But it's a risky business in a residential area with people coming and going. Being stuck out there where police cars and helicopters rarely venture. It's ingenious."

Jackman turned to face the room. "We know the victim's been managing the farm since the Lawtons left in November. He must have access to their suppliers. I think generators like this one run on diesel. We need to find out who he is getting it from and whether there has been a spike in his diesel spend."

*\*\*\**

"Let's talk about Sunday, the day in general." Detective Russell sat back in her chair.

Nancy leant her arm on the corner of the sofa. Her heart had sank to new lows when she had opened the door to the detective that morning, and was asked to come down to the station and answer more questions. After passing through the stark entrance she'd expected to be led into a small room with a table in the middle, plastic chairs and a bare light bulb in the ceiling like on the TV crime dramas she'd seen. But this was more like somebody's front room with carpeted flooring, curtains at the windows and comfy cushions on the sofa.

"How was Evan's mood on Sunday?"

Nancy hesitated, struggling to see the relevance. "Same as normal."

"Did he talk to anyone at the pub, or on the way?"

"Not really. We were having a meal together."

"What about in the last few weeks? Have you noticed a change in him at all?"

Nancy fidgeted, glanced at the camera in the corner. It was odd being watched from afar, and strangely disconcerting. "No."

"Why don't you tell us how you first met Evan?"

"He came into the shop one day, left me his number. I've already told you this."

"We're just building up a picture of his life," Russell said with a kind smile. "It'll help us to fill in the gaps. When was your first meeting?"

She swallowed. "The 13th of May."

"Can you remember where you met?"

"At The Fish."

"The same place you visited the night he disappeared?"

She watched Russell pull her notebook out of her case and click her ballpoint pen before she answered. "We rarely went anywhere else."

"Was there a reason why he chose to go there? It certainly wasn't the closest pub to the farm."

"I think he liked their beer."

"But he had to drive there."

She shifted in her seat. "He liked the atmosphere. We used to play pool in the covered area outside. Sometimes we sat beside the river. Evan didn't like crowds."

"What can you tell us about his friends?"

"I never really met any of them." Nancy shuffled awkwardly. In truth, she'd asked him several times whether he'd like his friends to join them. But he always refused, said he preferred to have her to himself. She'd been flattered at the time. But now she thought of it, he never really mentioned friends. Yet he knew everything there was to know about her: when her gran died, her mother's situation, where she lived. He'd even met Becca, although he'd never stayed over at her flat. When she'd asked, he always said it was easier if she stayed at the farm.

"What did he think of your friends?"

"He only met them a couple of times. He was very busy at work."

"What about friends at the pub? You said he went there a lot. The landlord maybe?"

"He did talk to him. Sometimes. But I wouldn't say they were close."

"What about other workers on the farm?"

"There are two casual workers, Stephan and Luca. He tends to text them jobs, send them off. He was the only permanent one."

"So you never met any of his friends?"

Nancy could feel Russell's eyes boring into her. "We were a bit consumed with each other, I suppose. It was all very new. And I only saw him a few times a week, the summer is a busy time on the farm."

"What about family?"

"He talked about his mother."

"Where does she live?"

"Northampton, I think. He was planning to take me to meet her when things quietened down on the farm."

"No brothers, sisters?"

"He has a sister. Hasn't seen her in years, didn't like to talk about her."

"Did you ever hear him use a different name?"

"No. I thought Evan was his name. That's what people called him."

"People?"

Nancy rubbed the side of her head. The criss-cross questions were starting to make her feel disoriented. "The landlord at the pub. People like that."

"How long did he say he'd been at the farm?"

"About two years. He did some casual work and they offered him a full-time job. He did seem close to the owners, Janine and Ronnie. He said he'd introduce me to them when they came home."

"Did he ever talk about what he did before working at the farm?"

She shook her head. "He wasn't a big talker."

"What, never?"

Nancy was starting to feel uncomfortable. Evan was a very private person, she'd tried to respect that. When she'd asked questions he'd always said that what was important was the here and now; he didn't believe in dwelling on the past. She remembered him telling her about an old friend he'd lost to a heroin overdose, some years ago. They'd been close, the scars ran deep. She'd guessed that was why he was so good to her mum, he knew how to deal with addictions, was patient.

"What about where he used to live before, old workplaces, friends, family?"

A memory crept into Nancy's mind. Almost a month after they'd got together. She was sitting at the side of a field, watching him repair the fencing. The sunlight was warm on her skin as she sat splitting tiny green stems to make daisy chains. The conversation had been idle. Nancy talking about her grandmother, the long evenings they shared watching

115

films on television with chocolate and popcorn. Evan listened in silence, smiled when she said they'd watched *Sense and Sensibility* at least a dozen times.

Nancy had looked across at him, closing one eye to cut out the dazzling sunshine. "What about your mum?" she'd asked. Evan didn't respond, almost as if he hadn't heard her. He continued to work the fence. "Come on, I've told you all about my family. What about yours? I don't even know your mum's name, where she lives."

She lifted her hand to shade her eyes. The muscles in his back tightened. "What is it? Are you okay?"

Evan sucked on his forefinger a moment, his forehead creased in pain. "It's nothing," he said. "The hammer slipped. We're done here."

He'd collected his tools and made off towards the Land Rover, leaving Nancy to scurry after him. The change in his mood, the dent in his usual affable manner, only served to make her feel more determined. She'd pressed him on the way back about his mum, they'd bickered. He didn't want to talk about his family and she couldn't understand why. Suddenly, he'd stopped, braked hard in the middle of the country road. She'd flown forward, then back as he reversed.

"What are you doing?" She placed her hand on his thigh. He'd pushed it away, roughly.

He didn't answer. Drove back in the direction of Stratford.

For a day they hadn't been in touch, both too stubborn to break down the barriers. When he started texting, he didn't mention his mother and that only served to irritate her even more so she ignored him. Three days later he'd turned up on her doorstep.

She'd made them both tea. He sat in the lounge, apologised and told her that he wanted them to be together. To have no secrets. He hadn't had a relationship in a long time and she needed to bear with him. But he did tell her that his mother was called Audrey and she lived in Northampton. Their relationship was complicated but he promised to take Nancy to meet her when the farm settled down for the winter. Nancy could relate to complicated. Her upbringing certainly wasn't textbook.

At the time, that day had felt like a pivotal moment in their relationship. She remembered it clearly, it was the only time he ever stepped foot into her bedroom. They'd made love passionately, more deeply than before. It was as if they'd passed a new hurdle and their relationship had elevated to a new level. Although, when she thought of it now, he hadn't mentioned his mother again. And there never seemed the right moment for her to raise the issue.

Nancy swallowed as she stared back at the detective. "He was quite private."

"So you never asked him about his background, old relationships, that sort of thing?"

"I did ask. A few times. But it just seemed to make him sad. Evan was deep. I thought he'd tell me in his own time."

# Chapter Eighteen

Jackman clicked off the screen and swivelled his chair. Janus had returned to Stratford shortly after her meeting that morning, motivated by the assistant chief constable's keen interest in the case. The press were circling. It was only a matter of time before the discovery of the cannabis was made public.

"Do you think she's being deliberately mysterious?" Janus asked. She was perched on the edge of a desk, peering across at him over the top of her glasses. They'd been watching Nancy's interview, listening to her answers, focusing on her body language for any signs of latent guilt.

"It's possible. She speaks coherently, yet she still claims to have no knowledge of what happened on Sunday. Difficult to tell if she genuinely can't remember, or if she's covering something up. We've been through her phone records, bank statements. She has a few credit card debts, but nothing of any significance. The CSIs found some money in the farmhouse, presumably dirty drug money, so she hasn't done much digging."

"Maybe he had an affair and she found out?"

"We've nothing to suggest anything like that at the moment. Witnesses who have seen them over the past few weeks have said they looked close, happy. We are struggling to get much on him though. It seems he didn't like to form close associations, kept himself to himself."

"Which is pretty much what Nancy said. Understandable

if you are living under a false identity. You wouldn't seek to draw attention to yourself."

Jackman's laptop bleeped, indicating a new email. He leant across and clicked it open. "That's interesting," he said.

"What?"

"Mike Clarke has received some intelligence that might help us. Too long to share on email apparently, he's on his way over from Leamington."

"Thank God for that. Let's hope it's good. With the assistant chief constable breathing down my neck, I could really do with some news. And soon."

\*\*\*

Nancy closed the door behind her. It was good to be back in the privacy of her flat, away from the police station's cameras watching her every move. She checked her phone. Another message from Ryan and a missed call. She ignored them both.

She made her way into the lounge, switched on the television and slumped onto the sofa. The man on the screen was stood outside the front of a terraced house talking about rendering. Nancy loved home renovation programmes. She usually watched them on her days off, enjoying seeing how peoples' homes were transformed. But today she stared at the screen blankly. Time passed by. All of sudden she was watching the end credits and became aware that she hadn't actually seen any of the programme.

A key turned in the lock, footfalls on carpet. Becca's face appeared around the doorframe, "Hey."

Nancy managed a weak smile.

"How're you doing?"

"Did you give Ryan my number?"

Becca rolled her eyes. "Don't be angry. He's only trying to help. Anyway…" She held up the bag in her hand. "I've brought you McDonald's, chicken nuggets and chips. Your favourite!"

The sweet gesture brought fresh tears to Nancy's eyes. She blinked them back. "You don't like McDonald's."

"I'm having a chicken sandwich. Come on, we can share the milkshake."

Becca pulled out the coffee table and began arranging the food.

Nancy didn't feel like eating at all. She forced herself to look interested. "Thanks."

"What are you watching?"

"Nothing much." A presenter with a huge smile filled the screen, talking about people seeking a new home in the country.

"Oh, I love this." Becca sat down next to her, unwrapping her sandwich.

They ate in silence, eyes fixed on the screen. When she'd finished, Becca screwed up the paper, put it back in the bag and sucked on her milkshake. "How are you feeling?" she asked.

Nancy poked the last few chips in the bottom of the carton. "Awful. Angry. Numb. I can't stop thinking about him."

Becca pressed her lips together. "I'm sorry."

"I wish people would stop apologising."

"Sorry."

Nancy gave her a hard stare and they both smiled.

"Any post?" Becca asked, staring towards the door.

Nancy thought about the note this morning, opened her mouth to tell Becca, but at the last minute something told her not to. "No, nothing."

They sat in silence a moment. "I want to come back to work." Nancy said finally.

"I'm not sure, Nance. Mum says you need time."

"I'm going out of my mind here, rattling around the flat. Give me something to do. Please?"

Becca stared back at her a moment. "I'll speak to Mum. We have those two weddings coming up at the weekend. They're taking all our time. Maybe you could update the Facebook page or something."

"Thanks. I really appreciate it."

Becca took a deep breath and rested back into the sofa. "What do you want to do tonight?"

Nancy shrugged.

"I vote we watch a film. I'll pop out, grab some wine if you like?" She didn't wait for a reply, leaning forward to clear up the mess on the coffee table.

"Becca?"

"Yeah?"

"Thanks."

"For what?"

"You know."

"Oh, don't be silly. You can get rid of this lot. Make sure you put it out in the dustbins so Mum doesn't see it or she'll panic about my diet. Insist I'm incapable of looking after myself." She chuckled as she grabbed her bag. Wandering through to the hallway, she called back, "I'll leave the door unlocked for you."

After Becca left, Nancy pulled all the wrappers together, crossing to the kitchen and placing them in an old carrier bag before taking them outside. She climbed down the metal stairs that led to the entrance to the flat, which was situated at the rear of the property above the shop. There was a yard area at the bottom where they kept their bins and an open passage that ran down the side of the shop and out onto the street.

The air was clean and fresh, providing a welcome relief from the stuffiness of the flat. Nancy placed the rubbish in the bin and stood for a while, taking long deep breaths. The thought of immersing herself back in her work gave her a glimmer of hope, of being useful for the first time in days. At least it would dull down the chilling sense of loneliness that now surrounded her.

She wandered down the passage, out onto the street and stood beside the front entrance to the shop, absently taking in the activity on the road outside. A few cars filtered through but the rush of the day had long since passed. The sun had slipped below the buildings out front, leaving an amber glow in its wake. She turned and made her way back through the passage, halting at the bottom to take in one last gulp of air when she felt a presence behind her. Just as she was about to turn, she felt a hand grab her hair, pulling it tightly.

She made to scream, but only a high-pitched whimper came out.

"We are watching you, pretty lady. You can't hide for ever." The voice was a low growl. The aroma of old chewing gum, past its flavour, hung on his breath.

Nancy froze. Her heart pounded her chest. Then, as quickly as he arrived, she felt her hair released, her body pushed forward. He was gone.

Nancy scrabbled up the stairs, not leaving time to look back. It wasn't until she was in the flat, leaning against the locked door that she breathed out a shaky breath. She heard a noise. Her chest tightened. It came again. A tap. On the other side of the glass.

Nancy jumped forward, turned. The shadow of a man stood on the other side of the door.

She started to shake as she backed away from the door.

"Nance, it's me. Open up!"

It was a familiar voice. She rested her hands on her knees, tried to regulate her breathing.

The letterbox flicked open and she looked up to see Ryan's eyes appear through the hole. "What are you playing at? Open up."

Nancy's hands were trembling so much, it took her a moment to unlock the door. It juddered as she wrenched it open. She stuck out her arm, pulled Ryan inside, then locked it again.

"What's going—" His words were stifled as she hurled herself at him, burying her head in his chest.

"Hey!" His voice softened. He held her tight and stroked her hair as she started to sob.

Nancy wasn't sure how long they stood there. Time stood

still as she cried out the events of the past few days – Evan's disappearance, the head injury that continued to plague her, learning of his death, her mother's decline, the notes, the threats. A raw tirade of misery came pouring out of her. Slowly the tears stopped and she pulled away. "What are you doing here?" she asked.

He threw her a look. "You're not answering my messages. I came to see if you were all right." He peered down at her. "Which clearly isn't the case."

Nancy felt a twinge of guilt. "I thought you were him."

# Chapter **Nineteen**

"Nick Anderson. Forty-two years old, lives out on the Saturn Way estate."

With the conference room busy, the team were crammed into a meeting room, the only space Jackman had been able to find at short notice for their meeting with Mike Clarke. He angled his head past Davies' mop of black curls to get a better look at the screen. The man was standing beside a Range Rover mid-conversation with someone just off the edge of the photo. He was tall, unassumingly dressed in a pair of black chinos and white T-shirt. Dark sunglasses rested on his bald head.

"Married to Carly; two kids, Grace and Kyle." Mike clicked another button and the photo on the screen changed to reveal a family shot of them leaving a restaurant on the High Street. The children barely looked old enough for secondary school. He turned back to face them. "We've been gathering intelligence on Nick for a while. We believe he's not only involved in the supply chain, but is steering it. He's got his legitimate businesses of course. Carly owns a nail bar in town, he has a car repair garage and a snooker hall."

"Venues that work in cash. Perfect for passing dirty money through," Davies said.

"Exactly."

Janus cleared her throat. "How is this linked with our murder?"

Mike held up a flat hand. "We're getting there, ma'am."

He clicked again. Another photo, this time of a burnt-out industrial unit. "A month ago there was an arson attack on his garage on Timothy's Bridge Road. So far, police haven't traced the offenders. Our source handlers were told that there were rumours he'd upset somebody and it was a message. When we put it together with the other intelligence we had, we applied to put a covert GPS tracker on his car."

Jackman raised a brow. Covert intelligence was one of the most difficult to set up and required authorisation at the highest level to prove that police involvement was necessary, otherwise it was considered an infringement of human rights. "You must have some interesting stuff on him to secure that," he said.

"It was touch and go. I didn't think we'd get it for a while, everything we have is speculation, but when you put it all together... I think the current policing priority to crack down on drugs finally pushed it through. Anyway, we've been watching his movements for the past two weeks. And we can tell you that last Sunday his Range Rover was in the car park of The Fish pub at Wixford at 10.41pm. He didn't stay long, just a couple of minutes, then drove across to the Upton Grange farmhouse."

"What time was this?"

"He arrived at the farmhouse at 10.52pm, and stayed almost fifteen minutes, before he drove back home."

"Nothing at the barn?"

"Not on Sunday."

"And he didn't go back?"

Mike shook his head.

"So we know he was there when the victim and Nancy were in the pub. But not later when he disappeared?"

"Not personally. Or his car wasn't. Maybe he was checking up on something, or setting something up for later. In any case it shows a link between the victim and him."

"Maybe he was the one who broke in?" Janus suggested.

"He was there almost fifteen minutes," Jackman replied.

Seems a long time to hang around if the farmhouse was empty." The room fell silent. "Any connection with Eamonn Benwell?"

Mike shook his head. "I'm drawing a blank on that name."

"Can we use this?" Janus asked.

Mike shot her a look. "We've invested a lot of money on a tracker and surveillance team. The intelligence we're gathering has the potential to pull down the whole network, lead us to those in charge, those bringing in the stuff. That's what we're interested in. Unless you have something tangible, some unconnected evidence that Nick Anderson himself is involved, we have to ask you to tread cautiously."

"Where is Anderson now?" Jackman asked.

"Ah. That's the tricky part. We last tracked him to Birmingham Airport. We've checked with the airlines and he flew out to Prague on Monday morning, a stag break for one of his friends, it seems."

"Don't people usually go on stag weekends?" Davies said.

"Not this lot, the weekends are their busiest time."

"Great." Janus swiped a hand across her forehead. "Do we know when he's due back?"

"It was a one-way ticket. We're checking with the airlines, trying to find a return booking. I can't see him staying out there long. His family are still here."

"What about the group he's gone with?" Jackman asked.

Mike shook his head. "They're a secretive lot at the best of times." He cast a glance back at the screen. "It's difficult to pinpoint exactly when your man started supplying. We know cannabis plants like these, in forced conditions, can be ready in around eight weeks, then need another two weeks to dry out. They're looking for a continuous supply, hence the plants are in various stages of growth."

"What does that mean?"

"Not a huge amount on its own. But local sources in the field have reported drops in the price of cannabis around three months ago though. The price comes down when there is an abundance of supply, which might suggest he hasn't been operating it long, probably only four or five months since his first crop."

"And he's been operating locally, on Anderson's patch?"

"Seemingly."

Jackman was deep in thought. They knew that the Lawtons had left the country in November, around nine months earlier. It would have taken him a while to obtain the container, get builders in to dig up the floor and set it beneath.

The door clicked open and Keane appeared. He held his phone up like a trophy. "Found the diesel supplier."

"And?"

"We phoned around some trade suppliers. The farm use Aitons, a local firm. We've been in touch with them and they checked through the last 24 months. Traditionally there's an increase between March and September, the more active months on the farm for machinery usage, but from January the spend has practically doubled in comparison to last year."

The Lawtons flew out to Australia in November. It all suggested that the victim had everything planned and in place. As soon as the owners went away, he was setting everything up. "How is it paid for?"

"Direct debit from the Lawtons' business account."

"So, are we thinking Anderson was an investor or a competitor?" Jackman said.

"That's what we really need to find out."

Another knock at the door. "Come in!" Jackman called out.

He recognised Jan Leyton, one of the civilian case workers, appear in the doorway. "There's a phone call for you, sir."

"Who is it?"

"A woman. Won't give her name. Sounds pretty desperate. Asked for you specifically."

\*\*\*

Nancy took a sip of tea. Milky white with two sugars; baby tea her gran used to call it. Very few people knew how to make it just right, and Ryan was one of them. The incident outside her flat had dissolved her earlier anger towards him. Right now she was grateful to have him here.

He listened as she gave an account of what had happened and waited until she'd finished before he spoke, "What does that mean, 'You can't hide for ever'?"

"I have no idea."

"Is this something to do with what happened to Evan?"

"What do you mean?"

"They're calling it a suspicious death in the newspapers. Saying the fire was arson. You don't think he was involved in something, do you?"

Nancy could feel her defences returning. "Like what?"

"I don't know. But this is scary stuff, and just after…"

Nancy turned away. "No. I'd have known."

"It's a bit of a coincidence though, don't you think?"

She turned back to Ryan. "You just want to find something, anything to make him look bad."

"Well, hang on, that's not fair."

Ryan leant forward, moved to place his hand on her shoulder, but she shrugged it off. "I'm sorry, Nance. I'm only trying to help. Maybe if you told me what actually happened last Sunday?"

Nancy blew out a heavy sigh. Going over the events of Sunday evening only served to remind her how little she could remember. By the time she had gone through her experience at the morgue, the pain in her head had soared to new heights. She decided not to mention the different identities of Evan. She didn't want to give Ryan any more reason to think badly of him right now.

"I'm so sorry, Nance. I can't imagine what it's like to be going through all of this."

She gave a feeble attempt at a nod.

"But there's no reason anyone would be interested in you.

128

If they'd wanted to kill you, surely they'd have done so on Sunday. Did you get a look at him? The man outside."

She shook her head.

"Maybe it was kids messing about. It could have been just a prank."

"It didn't feel like a prank."

Ryan scratched his chin. His face was impassive, although she could see the concern he was so deftly hiding. "There's something else." Nancy placed her mug on the coffee table and wandered out into the kitchen. She could feel him beside her as she rummaged through the waste bin.

"What are you doing?"

Nancy ignored him. She pulled out a drinks carton, pushed aside a couple of crisp packets. When she couldn't see what she was looking for she delved deeper until her fingertips brushed the top of torn paper. Nancy grimaced, reached in further and dragged out the pieces of the note.

She could feel Ryan's eyes on her as she washed her hands, wiped them with a tea towel and tried to piece the torn paper together.

"'Debts pass to next of kin'," he read out loud. He glanced at her. "What does that mean?"

"Next of kin," she repeated. "There's only one thing it could mean."

# Chapter **Twenty**

Jackman felt the heat of a pair of eyes trailing him as he turned off the Birmingham Road and crawled down the side of the Premier Inn. He parked around the back of the hotel beside the canal. A woman in a black jumper sat beside the window in the corner of the Thyme Café, cradling a mug of coffee, watching him as he approached. She didn't look away when he met her gaze. By the time he had pushed open the door and crossed the threshold she had placed her mug down and was standing to welcome him.

"Mr Jackman?"

He nodded. "Amanda Grayson," she said. "Thank you for coming to meet me here."

He'd deliberated over sending one of his team when he'd taken her call in the incident room. She said she'd seen him doing the press appeal earlier in the week, insisted on speaking to him personally. Public appeals always attracted a number of time wasters and attention seekers and it was difficult, at times, to separate truth from reality. But there was something in the way this woman crafted her words that piqued his interest. She spoke clearly, enunciating every syllable. And when she mentioned Eamonn Benwell's name, he'd felt compelled to come along and meet her himself.

Grey-blue eyes set in a clear complexion stared back at him as he shook her extended hand. Her hair was pulled into a loose French plait.

Jackman ordered a coffee and sat himself down. "How can I help you?"

She rubbed her lips together before she spoke. "It's rather awkward. I've come to talk to you about Eamonn Benwell."

"So you said." Jackman kept his face expressionless and let the silence linger in the air.

"I know you've been questioning him about his movements last Sunday evening, the day the man was killed in the barn. I've come to say that he wasn't involved. He couldn't have been." She sucked in a deep breath. "Because he was with me."

"Mr Benwell said he was at work."

She looked down into her coffee. "He was. Until early evening. He met me at a lay-by on the A46. We went for a ride in his Buick."

"Why?"

"Pardon?"

"Why was he with you? How do you know Eamonn Benwell?"

"We've been…" she paused, turning her eyes to the right, "seeing each other for the past eight months." She winced slightly as she spoke the words. "Since his marriage ended. But nobody knows, not his wife and certainly not my husband. Eamonn would never tell. He wouldn't break my confidence. I've got children, two of them, at primary school. It would rip my family apart, and it wouldn't do his any good." She stared out of the window for several moments. "But I can't see him being arrested and questioned for something he didn't do." She looked up. "It's not fair."

The waitress arrived with a mug, placed it in front of Jackman and retreated.

Jackman stared at the coffee and looked back at Amanda. "How long have you known Eamonn?"

She moved her hand to her neck, wound the gold chain that hung there around manicured fingers before she answered. "Almost a year. Our daughters were in the same class at primary school, they played at each other's houses. It was invariably Eamonn that would be there when I collected my Lily, or dropped her off. Sue, his wife, worked full-time. He runs his own business and seemed to be able to drop out of work to look after his kids and ferry them around. We exchanged numbers, mainly to arrange play dates for the children. It was nothing much at first. The odd look, a smile here and there. He sent a few texts. Just flattering stuff really. I thought he was being friendly. Then just before Christmas last year I was out shopping on my own, picking up the last few stocking fillers. The children were with my mother. And we happened to be in the same store. The shops were heaving, so we went for a coffee. And... I'm not proud of myself, Inspector. I love my husband. I never intended for anything like this to happen. It just sort of started."

"How often do you meet?"

"Whenever we can. Sometimes once a week. Sometimes less often."

"Where?"

She cleared her throat. "Sometimes we go to a hotel in Leamington."

He felt her recoil as he opened his notebook, took down the details.

"If we didn't have much time, which was often the case, we'd go for a drive. Take one of his cars if Evan was around to open the barn."

"Did you go to the barn?"

She shook her head. "No. Never. Eamonn would pick the car up first. Meet me along one of the country roads. I'd leave my car in a lay-by and we'd go out in his. We had to keep to the country roads in his American cars, in case they drew attention. I used to wear sunglasses." She placed a hand across her face. "God, you must think I'm awful."

"My job isn't to make judgements. It's to establish the truth." The silence lingered awhile before Jackman continued. "Did you ever meet Evan?"

"No." Her voice was barely a whisper.

"When was the last time you saw Eamonn?"

"Today. Only for a few minutes because the children were at a club. That's when he told me about the police interviews. I couldn't believe it. He's a good man, Inspector. He's just had a difficult year."

"When did you last see him before today?"

"On Sunday. He texted me in the morning. My children go to a swim class early evening. Michael, my husband, was golfing. I met with Eamonn, he was in his Buick. We drove down to Warwick Road Lands.

"What time was this?"

"From around 5pm for an hour. I collected the children at 6.15."

"Is there any way that I can confirm this?" he asked.

She hesitated briefly, swallowed and fumbled in her bag, moving across her purse, a packet of tissues, unzipping a side pocket inside. The phone she pulled out was switched off, the blank screen bare. "This is the phone I use to contact Eamonn. It has details of all our calls and texts. He has one similar. I don't use my own phone, for obvious reasons, and his wife checks the billing on his mobile."

Jackman picked up the phone, switched it on and scribbled down the details he needed along with her contact details. When he passed it back to her he could see tears in her eyes. She didn't look like the kind of woman that would be paid to manufacture a fictional alibi, but then criminals didn't look like the comic book monsters he was raised with as a kid.

"What happens now?" she said.

"We check out your story."

"How?"

"It's routine police work."

"Is there any way of keeping this confidential?" There was desperation in her voice. "I know it's a minor issue for you. A man has been killed." She placed a hand on her chest, clearly fighting to keep her composure. "But I don't want my husband to find out about the affair."

"I can't make any guarantees."

"I realise that, but I have children. Please?"

Jackman surveyed her a moment. "It's not unusual to treat a report like this as confidential intelligence. People would never come to us if they thought their every word, every detail they gave would be made public. I will need to keep your contact details on file, just in case, but if your account is proven, and you are not suspected to be involved in any way, it's possible the details may not need to come out."

"Thank you." Her words were laced with relief, but her face still looked anxious. She stood, indicating an end to their conversation.

Jackman watched her go, pulled some money out of his pocket and left it on the table. He was walking across the car park as she drove out in a green Volvo. She flashed him a brief grateful look, and was gone.

He sat in his car for several minutes, letting their conversation percolate in his mind. He would have his team cell site her phone and check the police cameras to correspond her movements on Sunday, although he was pretty certain she wouldn't have given the account if there wasn't an element of truth in it. But one thought coloured all others. By her own admission she was keeping her affair from her family, her loved ones. Eamonn Benwell was keeping things from his family too – the affair, the money in his flat. Both of their accounts, however true, were laid on a foundation of deception.

He leant his head back, pushed it into the headrest. Her statement explained the reason why Eamonn Benwell was at the barn on Sunday, but it didn't give him an alibi. He still had to return his car to the barn, which gave him plenty of chance later to carry out the murder. But if he was the killer, Jackman still didn't have a motive for him. And he couldn't see what Eamonn would stand to gain from burning the barn down.

# Chapter **Twenty-One**

On his way back into the station, Jackman felt his phone vibrate in his pocket. He paused in the corridor to check it. A missed call from Celia, his daughter, followed by a text.

*Sorry I missed you. Call you later x*

He was just pocketing his phone when he heard a door slam. Almost immediately he felt a presence behind him. "What are you doing lurking out here in the corridor?"

He turned to face Davies who was smirking up at him. "On my way back to the incident room." He made a play of sniffing the air around them. "Back on the fags, then?"

"Only at work. Keeps me sane." She chuckled. "Any news?"

"I just popped out to meet a friend of Eamonn Benwell's. Claims they've been having an affair for the past eight months. Apparently she can prove he was with her on Sunday. He met her in his car, they went for a drive." Jackman explained about their journey to Warwick Road Lands.

"Doesn't mean he wasn't involved."

"No, but it makes it less likely."

"So where does that leave us? Surely we're not beholden to Mr Drugs Squad?"

Jackman couldn't resist a grin. Mike Clarke was certainly the kind of detective that took his job overly seriously. "Let's look into the farm owners' backgrounds," he said. "Everything points to them not being involved, but with all the investment in this operation, I can't see that the victim would have planned to shut it down when they returned. Also, see if Keane can chase the international liaison angle. What happened to the real Evan Baker and why did the victim steal his identity? And chase that DNA. Again. Finding the true identity of the victim is a priority, pay extra if you need to – I'm sure Janus will have something to say but we'll deal with that later. I guess we've exhausted missing persons?"

A familiar voice came from behind him. "Will, fancy bumping into you." He turned to see Carmela's wide smile and found himself grinning back. "Still okay for later?"

"Sure."

An awkward silence followed. Davies shot Jackman a look, stepped forward and introduced herself.

"Nice to meet you," Carmela said and shook her hand. She gazed up at Jackman. "Well, I'll see you later, then." She pulled that smile again and moved along the corridor.

"Mixing with the high flyers now, I see?" Davies said, just as Carmela was out of earshot.

"It's not like that."

"Didn't know you two knew each other well enough for a 'later'," Davies said.

"We don't." Jackman paused, scratched the back of his neck awkwardly. "She's just helping me with something."

Davies widened her eyes. "I bet."

Jackman turned and watched Carmela push open the door at the end of the corridor. As soon as she disappeared he decided it was time to share his secret promotion board with Davies. But as he turned back to face her she'd gone. He spun, just in time to see her push through the door at the other end of the corridor on her way back to the incident room. Jackman rested his back against the wall. Another chance gone.

*\*\**

The first thing Nancy noticed when they drove down Lodge Road and pulled up was that the front curtains were drawn.

The clock on the dash read 3.30pm. She bit her lip and glanced around. Apart from a few parked cars, the street was empty. She turned to face the house she'd been raised in. It had changed so much in the few years since her grandmother died. Clumps of grass and weeds hung out of the stone tubs out front that had once housed fuchsias, petunias and begonias in a kaleidoscope of colours at this time of year. Her eyes slid to the neighbouring house next door whose pretty window basket was overflowing with red geraniums. Mrs Gibson lived there. When she was growing up, Mrs Gibson's granddaughter, Isabel, used to come and stay with her in the holidays. Isabel was the same age as Nancy and the two girls played out together; she remembered them roller-skating up and down the pavement one summer until their legs ached. On the other side an elderly man called Roger lived alone, his wife long since passed away. These people had been friends of her grandmother, smiled and exchanged pleasantries when they saw her out in the street, took parcels in for her at Christmas; attended her funeral to pay their respects.

After Cheryl had moved in, they became distant. Nancy suspected it was the regularity of police vehicles outside and the company her mother kept that pushed them away. If she saw them in the street, she would smile at them sympathetically. But sympathy soon turned to embarrassment. She cringed when they started to ignore her. They could clearly see what was going on in their quiet street and disapproved of the comings and goings next door. It was sad to think what her grandmother would have made of it all.

The boarded lounge window was an indelible reminder of what happened last time her mother hadn't paid her debts: the window had been smashed when a brick had been tossed through it. Nancy thought back to her visit that day. The neighbours had alerted the police, who eventually called her. She'd been at the farm with Evan and, despite only knowing her a few short weeks, he insisted on coming over to help.

The front door had been swaying in the breeze when they'd

arrived. She remembered the huge sense of trepidation as she'd walked through the hallway and stared into the lounge. A female police officer sitting on the sofa immediately stood. "She's upstairs. The paramedics have given her the okay. We'll be back to take a statement when she's sober." And with that she'd left.

A couple of empty bottles had sat on a coffee table, which was strewn with plastic lighters and an overflowing ashtray. The kitchen was filthy, dishes and glasses stacked up in the sink.

Evan had followed her up the stairs where they found her mother laid across the bed, a line of spit hanging out of the side of her mouth. Nancy recalled shouting, snapping Cheryl out of her sleep. They'd bickered, words flying across the room, until Evan had stood between them. He was amazing that day. He'd placated Nancy and sent her out, while he spoke to Cheryl alone. She wasn't sure but he was so insistent that finally she relented and stood out on the landing, desperately trying to make sense of the muffled words spoken through the wooden door. Finally, she gave up. She was sitting on the top of the stairs when Evan emerged, closing the door behind him.

Evan refused to tell her what they discussed and moved past Nancy and downstairs. When she found him in the kitchen he was tackling the huge pile of washing-up in the sink. The moment felt surreal, they didn't talk as she started to empty the ashtray and clean up the house, just like she had many times before. Evan went to the builder's yard down the road, returning with a sheet of chipboard and proceeded to board up the window before they left.

But what was more remarkable over the weeks that followed was how Cheryl sought help in an effort to wean herself off the alcohol. It hadn't been easy, she'd been interned in a clinic that Evan had arranged for several days, came out and had counselling. She was withdrawn, but she'd been free from alcohol for two months and she seemed to be more responsive, to be eating, cleaning the house, coping.

Evan even offered to replace the window in the weeks that followed, but Cheryl refused his offer. She wanted to save and pay for its repair herself. It was a remarkable turn of events and Nancy remembered how grateful she'd been to Evan for his efforts.

Nancy snapped back to the present. But as she walked down the short pathway today, she felt the same uncertainty. The curtains shouldn't be drawn in the daytime. It was a bad sign, and only served to confirm her fears that her mother was back on the drink.

"You okay?" Ryan asked, as they reached the front door.

Nancy searched in her bag for her key. "Think so." She could hear the babble of conversation in the background as she crossed the threshold. The sound confused her. Maybe her mother had company. As they approached the door to the lounge she suddenly felt relieved to have Ryan with her.

Nancy halted at the bottom of the stairs and called out. "I don't think she's home," she said to Ryan when there was no answer. She pushed open the lounge door and peered inside. It had been a while since her last visit. She noticed the dining room table and chairs had disappeared from the sitting room, no doubt sold to fund her mother's habit. The sticky smell of nicotine pervaded the room.

Ryan followed Nancy up the narrow staircase. Although dull, the conversation was stronger up here and more animated. The door to the back bedroom, where Cheryl slept, hung open and was empty. Voices emerged from a radio in the corner.

"She must have gone out," Ryan said. "Left the radio on."

Nancy ignored him. She crossed the room and started opening the drawers to her mother's dresser, searching through the piles of clothes.

"What are you doing?" Ryan asked.

"Searching for bottles. She always used to keep a spare in her underwear drawer." But although she ruffled up the tops, bras and pants, nothing came to light.

Ryan looked uncomfortable. "Maybe we should come back?"

Nancy fished her mobile out of her pocket, selected Cheryl's number and pressed dial. The voicemail immediately filled her ear. "She's not picking up. Where is she?"

Nancy bent forward, switched off the radio. The encounter beside her flat flashed into her mind. "We'll wait," she said.

Ryan peered over his shoulder. "I'm not sure, Nance."

Nancy sat on the edge of the bed, sweeping back her arm. She felt her sleeve catch something. Turned quickly. Too quickly. Her cuff caught the edge of a glass on the bedside table, sending it crashing to the floor.

Ryan leapt forward. It bounced on the deep rug once, twice before he caught it. He placed it back on the side and gave Nancy a guarded look.

The sound of a door snapping open was followed by a croaky voice. "Who's there?"

"It's me," Nancy said.

Cheryl's head appeared around the doorframe. She was dressed in a long nightie, her mousy hair sticking out at odd angles. She frowned at them. "What are you doing in here?"

Aware that she'd left the top drawer of the dresser open, Nancy felt sheepish. "We were looking for you."

"I was asleep. You never said you were coming." Her mother's eyes slid to the top drawer of the dresser hanging open, the second drawer with edges of clothes peeking out. "What are you doing?"

Nancy could feel the heat rising in her cheeks. "Just checking."

"For what?" Her eyes spanned the room. She glared at Nancy. "How dare you?"

"You can't blame me. You haven't been in touch."

"I phoned the flat. You were sleeping. Becca said you were okay."

"When?"

"Yesterday."

They stood in silence. "You didn't get my message so you thought I must be drinking again? What gives you the right to come over here and snoop around?"

"You weren't in your room."

"I sleep in the front when I have a migraine, away from the barking dogs over the back. I can't believe you thought I was back on the bottle, just like that."

For a split second Nancy felt guilty. Then she remembered all the other broken promises made with the same convincing face. "Well, it wouldn't be the first time, would it?"

"That's not fair, Nancy."

"Where's gran's old dining room suite, then?" She spat the words out, feeling the heat of the venom beneath them.

"I lent it to a friend from AA. She just got a flat and she's got nothing to sit on. It's only until she sorts herself out."

"Likely story."

"How dare you? You know how hard I'm trying."

"How dare I? After all you've put me through. I've just lost my boyfriend and it's all about you. It's always been about you."

"Nancy, please…"

"Please? What about the people following me, demanding money. I'm sick of paying your debts."

Cheryl started. "I don't know what you mean. I don't owe any money."

"Well, you obviously owe somebody. And, as usual, it's me that gets the hassle."

"Nancy, you have to believe me. I'm clean, I have been since you and Evan—"

The mention of Evan drove a spear of anger into Nancy's chest. "Don't you dare mention his name." She turned back to Ryan who had stood there mute, watching them both. "We're going."

Nancy couldn't wait to get out of the house and back to the car. It wasn't until they'd pulled out of the road and were on their way back to the centre of Stratford that she tried to make some sense of the conversation. Her mother had been insistent that she hadn't borrowed any more money. 'Next of kin', the note had said. She was an only child. She'd never met her father. Her mother was an only one and her grandmother before her. They had no other family, apart from some very distant relatives that she'd never seen. The note had to be related to her mother. Didn't it?

# Chapter **Twenty-Two**

Erik's low gruff brought Jackman in from the garden where he was stretching after his run. Jackman yanked the door open, surprised to find Carmela standing on the doorstep. She almost dropped the bottle of wine in her hand when Erik hurled himself at her, wagging his tail so hard that his whole body moved in unison.

Jackman reached forward and grabbed the dog by the collar. "Sorry, I'd never have let him out if I'd known it was you." Erik made another friendly lunge, but Jackman held firm and pulled him away. "Please come in."

He gestured for Carmela to go into the lounge and put Erik behind the stairgate in the kitchen. By the time he arrived back, she smiled up at him, her usual serene self. "You didn't put him away, did you? I'm dog-friendly, you know."

Jackman grinned. "Good job. I only let him through because I thought it was somebody selling something. Erik is able to put the most ardent sales person off." She chuckled. "I thought you were coming over at eight?"

"I had time to kill, so I left early to pick up a bottle of something." She passed over the wine. "Then I was really early, so it was either stop for a coffee, go back to the hotel, or come now and find out what you get up to when you're not working."

An awkward silence followed. "I'll get you a drink."

"Just a small one, I'm driving," she called after him.

Jackman opened the stair gate and busied himself with

uncorking the wine and finding a glass. He could hear Carmela chatting to Erik through the open door. By the time he wandered through with a glass of wine, Erik was sat on the sofa beside her. "Ah, sorry about that. We've got him into bad habits," he said, handing the wine over.

"It's no problem, really. He's adorable." She took a sip of wine and rubbed Erik's head with her free hand.

"Well, he isn't going to move now," Jackman said. "Look, I was just about to get a shower..." He pointed his thumb towards the stairs.

She raised a hand. "Don't let me stop you."

Jackman rushed upstairs, quickly undressed and climbed into the shower. It had been a long time since he'd entertained at home, certainly not since Alice's accident. But strangely he'd been looking forward to this evening. Carmela was such easy company, at least it made discussing the tedious subject of management policies slightly more bearable.

By the time he had dried off, dressed and was back downstairs, Carmela had finished her glass of wine. A whiff of her perfume caught him as he grabbed the empty glass. "Another?" Before she had time to answer he'd picked up the glass and made his way to the kitchen. He returned with a fresh refill and passed it over, placing his own glass of water down on the coffee table beside him and squeezed in beside Erik.

Carmela looked at the water, "You don't like wine?"

"I don't drink."

She nodded but said nothing, leaning down to retrieve some papers from her briefcase. "Okay, where would you like to start?"

They sat there for a while, Carmela firing questions at Jackman. She smiled at him when he gave the wrong answer, corrected his language. The time passed easily. Before Jackman realised, the light had faded. He rose, flicked the switch on the lamp, brought in the bottle and passed it across to Carmela. "I shouldn't," she said. "I have to drive back."

"I'll take you."

"You're too kind." She poured another glass, took a sip, then placed it on the floor beside her and stretched her arms above her head. The movement exposed the sleek curvature of her breast. "You interview well," she said. "Just remember the key terms. It's all about getting those in. And the current policing priorities. If you do that, I can't see you going far wrong."

"Well, it's not my first time."

She averted her gaze. "I did hear."

A raised voice in the road outside cut through their conversation. Erik lifted his head, growled. The voice grew louder, accompanied by intermittent bangs. Jackman crossed to the window. A man was shouting outside the house opposite, punctuating his yells with kicks at the front door.

"Excuse me." Jackman left the house and crossed the road. "Hey!"

The man didn't turn. The door bowed as he booted it again. "Bitch!" he yelled.

The house looked empty, bathed in darkness. "What's going on?" Jackman said. He'd reached the man now and was immediately assaulted by the pungent smell of alcohol.

"Nothing to do with you." Another kick. The door juddered.

Jackman moved forward. "That's enough." He made to grab the man's arm, but was forcibly pushed back. A sharp pain emitted from Jackman's temple as he collided with the brick edging around the doorway. He swung forward and struck the man on the shoulder. The man wavered, just long enough for Jackman to move forward and wrestle his arm up his back into a tactical hold.

The man cried out in pain. Then leant forward and cast the insides of his stomach over the doorstep.

\*\*\*

Jackman flinched as Carmela pressed the damp cotton wool to his forehead. "Well, I can't say the evening wasn't eventful," she said.

In all the furore, Carmela had called the incident in. Uniformed officers arrived just in time for the offender to throw up again, this time in the back of their patrol car.

"Who was he anyway?" Carmela asked.

"No idea. Sounded like a spurned ex-partner from the slurred account he gave to uniform," Jackman replied. "A woman lives there alone. She's waved a few times whenever I've seen her, but we've never spoken. She's only lived there a few months. He obviously didn't realise she lived near a cop."

"Always on duty, eh?"

"Isn't that what we're taught?"

Carmela replaced the cotton wool pad with a clean one. "At least the cut's in your hairline. Are you feeling okay. No dizziness, blurred vision?"

Jackman gave a mock smile and shook his head.

"Are you going to make your statement tonight?"

"No, I'll do it in the morning. He'll only be in a cell, sleeping it off."

"Well, your neighbour'll have a shock when she comes home and sees the state of her door."

Jackman moved his head away. "I think it's stopped bleeding now."

Carmela put the cotton wool in the bin, washed her hands and tidied the medical box. "Wow. You've got a mobile ambulance here by the looks of things."

"Alice was very organised."

"Your wife?"

He nodded.

"How is she doing?" she asked. Jackman reached across to his glass and took a gulp of his water. "I'm sorry. Should I not ask?"

"No, it's fine. The answer is we don't know. The doctors aren't sure how much she knows or feels because she can't communicate."

"That must be hard."

Jackman looked away. This wasn't the usual tea and

146

sympathy he'd grown accustomed to. Nobody, apart from his damn counsellor had ever referred to how Alice's condition affected him. "What about you?"

"Divorced." She sniffed. "Long story."

Jackman snorted. "Shall we talk about something else?"

"We could talk about your mean right hook. Although that's one skill I wouldn't recommend sharing with the interview panel." They both laughed.

Carmela finished the last drop of wine. Her glass wobbled as it touched the side. "What happened at the last promotion board?" she asked.

"Alice's accident." The night of the collision slid into his mind. It was a friend's retirement party. He'd drank. Too much. Couldn't drive. Alice had been irritated about coming out to get him and arrived late. They'd had crossed words on the way back. The car appeared from nowhere. A pair of headlights rounded the corner on the wrong side of the road. Jackman blinked, pushed the vision away.

Carmela was still putting the contents back into the medical box when a pile of plasters glided to the floor. She crouched to pick them up. He bent down to help, inadvertently brushing her shoulder with his.

"Sorry," Jackman smiled. They rose together. Clumsily.

Carmela moved closer to him, staring into his face sincerely. The soft aroma of her perfume filled his senses.

The ring of his mobile made them both start. Jackman excused himself and moved into the lounge, picking it up without checking the screen.

Celia's chirpy voice filled the line. "Hey, Dad! Looking forward to seeing you tomorrow." Jackman hesitated momentarily. The sound of his daughter's voice induced a deep feeling of guilt, although he had no idea why. "You've forgotten."

"No, I haven't. You're coming back with Adrian. Staying until the weekend."

"Are you okay? You sound odd."

"It's been a long day. Got a case on."

"Okay, well, we should be there around seven-ish. Don't worry if you're not home, we can sort ourselves out."

"Sure."

"And, Dad?"

"Yes."

"Be nice to Adrian, please? He's really looking forward to meeting you."

*** 

An hour later, Jackman heeled the door closed behind him. It had been an eventful evening, but he'd enjoyed it nevertheless. In fact, he couldn't remember when he'd laughed so much. He moved into the kitchen, tucked the medical box away in a cupboard. As he poured the rest of his water down the sink, Alice's face entered into his mind, sobering his thoughts. He knew he wasn't responsible for his wife's condition, but the problem was, she would never have been on the road that night if it wasn't for him. And he'd never forgive himself for that.

He was just drying his hands when Erik sauntered over. Jackman ruffled his fur. Erik enjoyed the moment for a split second, then jumped back, skipping about in mock combat. "Celia's coming to see you tomorrow," Jackman said. A smirk grew on Jackman's face as he remembered Celia's final words, 'Be nice to Adrian.' Of course he'd be nice. What else did she think he was going to be? Just as long as Adrian was good enough for his daughter.

# Chapter **Twenty-Three**

The sound of his phone ringing woke Jackman. He blinked, staring at the illuminated digits of the bedside clock a moment, desperately trying to focus. It was 6am.

Jackman grabbed his phone and swiped the screen, just before the voicemail kicked in.

"Morning." Davies' jaunty tone made him flinch. "Sounds like you've had a busy night."

Jackman rolled his eyes. Davies had obviously already seen the incident log that morning. "Tell me that's not why you called?"

"Not the only reason. The DNA results are in."

Jackman sat up. "When?"

"The labs are working through the night at the moment, trying to clear their backlog. The email came through half an hour ago."

"And?"

"His name is Richard Garrett."

Jackman detected a hint of excitement in her voice. "I take it he's known to us?"

"Oh, very much so. How quickly can you get down here?"

Jackman glanced back at the clock. "Give me half an hour."

\*\*\*

Twenty minutes later a freshly showered Jackman raced up the back stairs of the station, two at a time. The incident room was empty apart from Davies who was sitting at a computer screen with her back to him. She appeared to be searching through a plethora of photos. She turned her head as he drew near, her mouth curling into a teasing smile. "You took your time."

He ignored her quip, perched himself on the edge of her desk. "So, who is Richard Garrett?"

Davies pulled a typed A4 sheet from the side of her desk and thrust it at him before turning back to the screen. "Richard Garrett. Born 16.3.81, to Bryan and Audrey. Father deceased. But the interesting part is…" She scanned down the screen. "Here it is. He was arrested for rape, five years ago. Charged too. The case went to trial and he was acquitted."

"Anything else?"

"A reel of intelligence reports. Antisocial behaviour when he was young, connections with drugs and firearms, but no charges. Until the rape allegation."

"What about the victim?"

"Not good. Her name was Alicia Wainwright. She committed suicide eighteen months after the trial."

"What about her family?"

"The Wainwright family still live in Harlestone, a village in Northamptonshire." She leafed through the pile of printouts on her desk. "I've been trying to track down Garrett's last movements, see when he changed his name. He was still Garrett four years ago when he applied for a new passport. Nancy said Evan, whom we know now to be Richard, had been at the farm two years. So we just need to fill in the gaps."

"What about his family?"

"Father deceased. He was living with his mother in Northampton when he was first released. Sister moved to Canada about four years ago."

"How did he get acquitted? They must have had some pretty strong evidence to keep him in custody."

"I've been reading through the file online. He was seeing

her for several months before the incident. She didn't come forward for a couple of days afterwards, so there wasn't much to go on. Came down to consent in the end. I guess she couldn't convince the jury."

"When does our intelligence go quiet?"

"September 2011. Not long after he applied for the new passport. Nothing since then."

"I'd like to have a word with an officer on the case. See what was going on. And we need to check the Wainwright family too. It's a long shot after all this time, but if they'd discovered Richard Garrett's new identity and where he was living, the old case would give them a motive."

***

Becca withdrew her head from the fridge. "We'll need some more milk for later."

Nancy stared into her cornflakes. She could feel Becca's eyes on her.

"Why don't you pop out and get some?" Becca said. "The fresh air will do you good."

Fear prickled Nancy's scalp. The last thing she wanted to do was to leave the confines of the flat, on her own, after yesterday's experience. "I'm not sure."

"Come on. It'll only take a few minutes." She smiled until Nancy met her eyes. "Are you sure you're okay? I could ask for today off, if you want?"

The thought of having Becca here with her was tempting. The company would provide a welcome distraction. But she couldn't let Becca know there was anything wrong. She had to deal with this problem herself. "No, I'm fine. Really. I'll sort it."

"Okay. Well, I'm going to go downstairs before Mum wonders where I am. I'll be there if you have any problems."

Left alone, Nancy remained seated at the kitchen table. She dragged in a deep breath. It was a quarter to nine. Town would be busy, rush hour in full swing. Lots of people around. Yesterday, he'd come down the alley, out of view from the road. Which meant he didn't want a public display. It was easier to get lost in a crowd.

She went to the bathroom, brushed a little mascara over her lashes and pulled her hair back into a messy bun. In the hallway, she grabbed Becca's red jacket and placed it over her shoulders.

Her heart pounded as she opened the door, closed it behind her and descended slowly down the stairs, eyes darting about, keys grasped in one hand, phone in the other. She moved through the alley at the side of the shop quickly.

A car sped past as she reached the street out front. She looked each way. There were plenty of people around, striding in different directions. But no sign of anyone lurking. She tried to remain calm and turned onto the main street, joining the throng of bodies filling the pavement on this Thursday morning.

Nancy weaved in and out of the people as she made her way down the road, past the uneven Tudor shop frontages that Stratford was famous for. The sun was injecting a welcome heat into the day and by the time she reached the supermarket, she could feel sweat tickling her neckline.

The store air-conditioning provided a welcome respite. She picked up the milk and wandered over to the ready meal section to choose a pizza. Bacon and mushroom was Becca's favourite. She'd get one for them to share for dinner, maybe a bottle of wine too, as a thank you for looking after her these past few days, especially since she knew that Becca hadn't always approved of Evan. She'd hated the way that Nancy pushed everything aside and changed her plans at the last minute to meet up with him, how he never came out with her friends. Only last week he'd called her up to see her after she'd already arranged to go to the cinema with Becca. He was angry and short with her on the phone. Eventually she'd cancelled Becca. But he was busy on the farm, he worked hard and when there was a little free time he wanted to spend it with her. She understood that. They saw so little of each other as it was.

But the impression Becca had of him was all wrong. Evan was shy, which made him appear withdrawn, aloof even at times. But he was also generous and kind. So many people seemed to form judgements, without really getting to know him. She worked her way through the pizzas, placing one in her basket. Her fingers lingered on the garlic bread a moment. She was just wondering whether to go for freshly sliced or a loaf, when she sensed a presence close by.

Warm breath on her neck. That familiar smell of old chewing gum. It was him.

Nancy made to turn, but he was too quick, pushing his body against hers. She just caught sight of the cuff of a black sweatshirt, inked letters on the side of his forefinger before he jammed her against the fridge. "Still watching," he said. She jumped as he nudged her basket with his knee.

She spun around. Searching urgently for any sign of who it might be. The supermarket was busy but she caught a glimpse – the rear view of a man in denims. A black hoody pulled up over his head. She dropped the basket, rushed towards him, zigzagging through the other shoppers. He'd reached the door, turned out into the street. She followed. But as hard as she looked, she couldn't see him. She stood very still, raised her arms, swung them around the back of her head.

Her hands trembled as she lowered them. A wave of nausea hit her. The realisation of what had just happened. She glanced back at the store, desperate to be back in her flat. Behind the locked door, safe. But if she didn't pick up the milk, Becca would ask questions.

Nancy raced back into the supermarket, grabbed her basket and pushed through the bodies towards the checkout, fidgeting from one foot to another in the queue. The checkout girl eyed her warily.

Bodies filled Bridge Street as she left the store. Shoulders nudged her this way and that. Her eyes searched in all directions. When she was absolutely sure there was no sign of the black hoody she moved on, her speed kicking up. By the time she reached the corner, she'd broken into a jog. The back stairs leading to the flat resonated with every step. The key pressed into the lock. The door swung open. Nancy rushed in and slammed it behind her, pausing to check the lock before dropping her bags and sliding to the floor.

She could see his hand, stretching round to grab her. Grubby fingernails. Inked letters down the inside of his forefinger. CC… something.

She sat there for a while, listening to her breaths, short and sharp. Waiting for her heart to stop thumping.

# Chapter **Twenty-Four**

Jackman had just pulled onto the M6 en route to Northampton when he heard a phone ringing. Davies leant down, picked through her bag and pulled it out. "It's Keane," she said to Jackman. "Hi, you're on speaker," she answered. "Any news?"

"How's the head, sir?" Keane said. "We've been discussing whether we should rent you out to night patrol."

Jackman heard a chorus of laughter in the background and couldn't resist a chuckle. He'd met a similar response when he'd submitted his statement about last night's incident. Cops loved the opportunity for a laugh and it would take a while for this one to die down. "Have you got something for us, or did you just phone to take the piss?" he said.

"The forensics report has just come through from the farmhouse. We know about the cash, just under two grand, in a shoe box in the bottom of his wardrobe. No distinguishing fingerprints, plenty from Nancy and the victim but no one else. Keys and guns still missing."

Jackman exhaled. "Is that it?"

"Pretty much."

"Any news on Anderson?"

"The drugs squad have been in touch. There's talk of him flying back home tomorrow. We've checked the airlines. No bookings yet but maybe he's going for a last-minute ticket."

"What about the real Evan Baker?"

"I'm drawing a blank there, sir. His passport says he flew

out to Thailand on the 16th of August 2011 and returned on the 12th of June 2013. Richard Garrett flew out to Thailand on the 2nd of October 2011. We think Richard used Evan's passport to fly back, as there is no record of a Richard Garrett returning to the UK. So sometime between August 2011 and June 2013, the real Evan Baker seems to have disappeared. His passport was never reported lost or stolen. We've obtained an old email address from his sister, but it was only used a couple of times in August 2011. Nothing since."

"Do Garrett and Baker look alike?"

"Evan Baker's sister emailed us some photos. Garrett is shorter than Baker, and slimmer. But they both had blond hair, blue eyes and were the same age. It's possible they could be mistaken from a distance if you weren't looking too closely." Keane cleared his throat. "I've gone through International Liaison and the Thai authorities have been really helpful, but they've left us under no illusions. Evan's sister said she last had contact with him in Chang Mai, which is in the northern province of Thailand, just below the border to Laos. Most travellers go up there, stay a couple of nights in a hostel, go off trekking in the hills, then return to Bangkok. There's a plethora of hostels for the police to try and none of them keep general records of guests. It's cheap. Most of them are cash only operations. And given that it's four years ago, there's not much chance anyone's memory will stretch that far back."

Jackman thought back to his conversations with Evan's sister, how she'd been out there herself, painstakingly searched for her brother. "Okay. Leave the Thai police to search, but also get in touch with the Met. They have an office for British citizens that have disappeared abroad. See if they can give us any advice on how to take this forward."

The phone cut. Davies dropped it into her bag. "It's odd, isn't it, that we can't find anyone that can give us some firm background on either Evan Baker or Richard Garrett? It's like they are both one and the same. Do you think Richard was out there looking for somebody's identity to steal, saw Evan and engineered his death? But then there would have to have been a body, a suspicious disappearance."

"I'm not sure," Jackman said. "Alice and I travelled a little around Thailand. I've been to Chang Mai briefly. It's very much a transient area. People are coming and going all the time. It's doubtful anyone would question a disappearance. And there's lots of open space up there. Wouldn't be difficult to hide a body if you were minded to. There's always a chance that the real Evan Baker decided to stay in a remote area of Thailand, off the record, and sold his passport."

"So we'll never know what happened to him?"

"I don't know. We just have to keep trying."

\*\*\*

Jackman gave up on the doorbell, rapped his knuckles hard against the wooden door and waited. Soft rain was starting to fall, spotting the shoulders of his navy shirt. He felt Davies give an imperceptible shiver beside him and stepped back, looking up at the white pebble-dashed house. The curtains were open, the windows smeared with rain that was now gathering momentum.

"Can't see any movement," Davies said, peering through the front window.

Jackman turned and was just considering whether or not to rap the door again, or try one of the neighbours, when he saw an elderly figure in the distance hobbling up the road. Her face was set hard against the weather, the collar of her raincoat turned up against the wind. Bulging carrier bags filled both hands. He waited for her to approach before he could speak, but she beat him to it. "Can I help you?" she asked in a low raspy voice.

"We're looking for Audrey Garrett," Davies said.

The woman turned into the driveway, paused to look them both up and down. "What's it about?"

Now that she was closer Jackman could see that she was younger than she looked at first glance, although her face still bore the deep grooves of a difficult life. "We really need to speak to Mrs Garrett," Jackman said. He introduced them both and they held up their identification cards. "Do you know her?"

"You're speaking to her." She pushed past them and dropped a plastic carrier bag on the ground. The tins inside rattled against each other as they hit the paving. She fished a key out of her pocket and placed it in the lock.

"We need to talk to you about your son, Mrs Garrett," Davies said. "May we come in?"

A brief tensing of shoulders was followed by a sharp turn of the head. "If you must."

As she reached down for her bag, Jackman leant forward. "Let me help…" But she elbowed him back, grabbing the bags, heaving them into the hallway and straight down into the room at the back that Jackman guessed was the kitchen. By the time Davies had clicked the door shut behind them, he could hear the sound of a fridge door open and close, tins tapping cupboard shelving as they were put away. They exchanged a glance and waited several moments for her to return.

When Audrey did reappear the coat had been removed, revealing a pair of navy trousers and a white T-shirt that pulled against the roll of fat straddling her waistline. Cream slippers clad her feet. "You'd better come through," she said.

They followed her into a lounge room that overlooked the road. Off-white woodchip covered the walls. A grey velour sofa and armchair, scattered with floral cushions, was arranged around the television. A teak table and chairs were visible through glass doors at the other end. A blue Persian cat looked up from its position on the armchair and glared at them.

Jackman's eyes worked through the photos that littered the mantle: two different babies, taken separately; a school photo of a boy and a girl next to each other, both in red jumpers; a larger one of a whole family draped across each other in a 'professional portrait'-style pose. Beneath them a display of dried flowers filled the hearth.

"Please, sit down," Jackman said.

A mild tick flickered beneath Audrey Garrett's left eye, although she said nothing and crossed to the single armchair beneath the window, lifting the cat onto her lap as she sat. He purred loudly, nuzzling into her hands.

"May we?" Jackman indicated to the sofa.

She gave a single nod. "What is all this about?"

"I'm afraid we have some bad news," Jackman said. "Your son, Richard Garrett, was found dead on Sunday evening." Once the words were out, he watched, waiting for the inevitable reaction: the shock, the tears, disbelief or anger, poised to deal with it. But there was nothing. Audrey's face was expressionless, her eyes averted, staring blankly into space as if she were recalling a distant memory. Jackman looked across at Davies and sat forward. "Are you okay, Mrs Garrett?"

Audrey fixed her gaze on him. "Is that it?"

"Do you understand what I've told you? Your son—"

"I heard you."

A brief silence followed, broken by the sound of Davies shuffling off the sofa beside him. "Let me get you a drink," she said to Audrey.

Audrey didn't look up as she left the room. The cat continued to purr. Jackman could hear Davies in the kitchen, opening and closing cupboards. His eyes scanned the room for any signs of Richard, although they were quickly disappointed. The photos on the hearth looked as though they belonged to another family. The walls were clear, apart from a couple of Constable prints that hung beside each other at the far end and a mock oil painting of a vase of flowers on the wall behind the sofa.

Davies returned with a steaming mug. She handed it to

Audrey, who looked up at her and took it, reluctantly. She took a sip and grimaced, but said nothing.

"Mrs Garrett, I know this is a huge shock for you," Jackman said. "But we really do need your help. Do you feel up to answering some questions?"

"What happened?" she asked.

"We're still trying to establish the facts," Jackman said in his softest voice. "His body was found in a burnt-out barn. We're pretty sure that he was killed first and his body placed in the barn before the fire started."

"He was killed. You mean murdered?"

Jackman nodded. "I'm so sorry."

Audrey's blank face looked back at him.

"When was the last time you heard from Richard?" Jackman asked.

"I haven't seen or heard from my son in four years."

"Did you have any contact details for him?"

She shook her head. "Last I heard he had gone off to Thailand."

"And when was that?"

"About four years ago. After the... Well, I'm sure you people will know about the trial."

Jackman nodded. "Does he have any other family?"

"Only a sister. Married a Canadian. She lives in Toronto now."

"Would you like us to contact her?" Davies asked.

Audrey shook her head. "I'll tell her myself. He hasn't spoken to her in years."

"What about friends here in Northampton before he went away?" Jackman said.

"Richard never really had many friends. He was a difficult lad from the minute he was born. Always into everything, not placid and helpful like his sister." She cast a sideways glance towards the mantle. "I lost count of the number of times I was called into school when he was a kid and that was only at primary school. He never said much, but he seemed to delight in upsetting people. I couldn't fathom him out. He didn't want to play with toys, or go to the park with friends. He used to hang around on his own, mostly outdoors. He went to work as a builder's apprentice when he was sixteen, moved out shortly afterwards."

"What was the last address you had for him?"

I know he lived in Duston for a while. I'll find you the address, although I can't see how anyone there will remember him now. He shared with a chap named Charlie Truman. He mentioned his name a few times. It stuck in my mind. Never met him though."

"Did he keep in contact after he moved out?"

"He'd come by occasionally. Dee, my daughter was still living at home then. We knew he was mixing with a bad bunch though."

"What do you mean?"

"Visits from the police, searching the house, poking through our drawers. Once they came in the middle of the night. He thought it was funny when we told him, kept saying they had nothing on him, but you don't get that kind of interest without doing something wrong. And then there was the rape charge and the trial. It was all right for him, tucked away in prison." She flinched. "We still had to go out, do our shopping, live in this community. People would stare, shout things in the street. Even after the acquittal, some people around here still don't speak to me. I've lived in this area all my life. Can you imagine what that's like? There's no wonder his sister moved to Canada when she got the chance. She tried to persuade me to join them, but I'm too old to make a new start."

"When did you last see Richard?"

"It would be around four years ago. He came to the house, called in without warning about a month after the trial ended. I remember wondering what the drama was. He rarely came around for nothing. We sat and watched a film together and he left. I was quite surprised, thought that perhaps he'd changed. Then three weeks later I heard he'd flown to Thailand, to work out there. One of my neighbours had heard somebody talking about it in the supermarket and told me. I didn't believe it at first. But when the weeks and months passed and there was no contact... How could he go away like that and not even come and say goodbye? I haven't seen him since."

Jackman could hear Davies' pen scratch against the paper as she wrote all of this down.

"Your son was working on a farm in Stratford-upon-Avon when he died," Jackman said. "Do you know what connection he has with Warwickshire?"

"I've no idea. I didn't even know he was back in the country, let alone in Stratford."

"Has he ever used the name Evan Baker to you?"

Audrey narrowed her eyes. "What do you mean?"

"Your son was living under the assumed identity of Evan Baker. Have you ever heard that name before?"

Audrey snorted. "Always a drama, even in death." She took another sip of her tea.

Jackman leant forward. "Mrs Garrett, have you ever visited Stratford-upon-Avon?"

"Never."

"I'm sorry I have to ask you this, but where were you between the hours of 10pm and 3am last Sunday evening?"

"What are you suggesting?"

"I'm not suggesting anything," Jackman said. "You're not a suspect, but I am obliged to account for everyone's movements."

"I was at the bingo hall on the High Street with Carol next door," Audrey replied. "She drove me home about 11pm."

"Is there anyone we can call, to come and be with you?" Davies asked as they rose to leave.

"No. Carol, my neighbour, will help with anything if I need it. I just want to be left on my own."

Jackman paused by the door and pressed his card into

her hand. "If you think of anything after we've gone, don't hesitate to give us a call."

Audrey glanced at the card and looked back up at Jackman. He walked towards the car and turned at the last minute, just in time to see her swipe a tear from her cheek.

"Something doesn't feel right there," Davies said as she pulled the seatbelt across her chest.

"She said they weren't close."

"He's still her son."

"We'll get the local guys to allocate a family liaison officer to visit and check on her."

They pulled off down the street and turned at the bottom. Jackman was aware of Davies pulling her phone out of her pocket, calling in the name of Richard's friend and requesting background checks, but he wasn't really listening. Meeting Richard's mother hadn't given him the background he'd needed. A name they could look into, but certainly not the wealth of knowledge and local contacts he'd hoped for. He couldn't work out what made Richard Garrett so private. He dropped his foot on the accelerator as they headed towards the ring road and waited for Davies to end her call. "Get hold of Judy Carter in the press office, will you?" he said when she'd finished. "Now that we've told his mother, we'll release the details to the press and put out an appeal for witnesses under the victim's real name."

Davies flicked her finger over the screen. "Got to be worth a try."

# Chapter **Twenty-Five**

Nancy's hands still shook as she later opened the laptop. What she needed now was a diversion from everything. A little piece of normality that would give her time to think and decide what to do next. The Wi-Fi was notoriously poor in the flat and it took an age to connect to the Internet and bring up Facebook. The blue banner appeared on her screen and she logged in. There were numerous comments beside previous posts and she worked her way through, liking and responding. It was an easy way to pass the time and she felt her shoulders relax as she looked at the floral displays they'd made over the past month or so. After she'd loaded the new pictures, she moved onto the several messages outstanding. The first two were thank yous – a wedding and a conference they'd created displays for. The words were kind and personal and made her swell with pride. She hooked up to the printer and printed them out to put up on the noticeboard in the shop.

She didn't recognise the sender of the last message and, assuming it was someone with a new enquiry, she clicked to open. There were no words, just a link to a video. Perplexed, she clicked play. A man in a plain black sweatshirt was standing against a brick wall. The view was from his neck down. Nancy heard a rustling in the background and was just about to turn it off and dismiss it as a prank when the camera raised its level. The man was wearing a loose hood with two slits for his eyes and a gash across the bottom for his mouth.

"This is a message for Nancy Faraday." His words

were muffled and strained, as if he was speaking through a voice box. "Debts pass down the line, Nancy. We want our money. Bring six thousand pounds in used bank notes to the underpass on Shipton Road leading to the recreational ground, at midnight tomorrow. Somebody will meet you there. If you are thinking of going to the police…"

He lifted his hand. She could see he was holding something. Nancy leant in closer, barely believing her eyes when the gun fired. She flinched. The footage ended. Nancy swallowed hard and sat staring at the screen for several minutes. It wasn't until she placed her hands on her face that she realised they were trembling violently.

She checked the date on the message. It was today. But her mother said she didn't have any new debts. Her mind raced.

Her finger hovered over the delete button. She didn't want Becca to see this, or Karen. She couldn't bear to subject them to these problems.

She rushed to the window and peered around the edge of the curtain. A woman across the road was pulling a trolley bag behind her. A teenager strolled past, checking his phone. She couldn't see anybody watching, waiting. Although if the experience of the past few days had taught her anything it was that people like that hovered in the shadows, hoods pulled over their heads, out of sight of the everyday world.

Nancy moved back to her laptop. A part of her felt paranoid. But the man outside the other day was real – she could still feel his breath on the back of her neck.

Ryan's offer of help skipped into her mind. She paused, grabbed her mobile. The call rang once, twice, three times. Nancy held her breath, willing him to pick up.

Finally the phone connected. "Ryan, are you free now? I really need your help."

\*\*\*

A broad-set man with a thick head of salt-and-pepper hair met Jackman and Davies in the entrance foyer of the Northampton Criminal Justice Centre. "DS Tim Hawkins," he said. A rich Irish accent coated his voice. "You found us all right, then?"

Jackman nodded. They'd arrived at the modern glass-fronted building situated in the midst of the sprawling Brackmills Industrial Estate, almost twenty minutes earlier. "Had a job to find a parking space though."

Hawkins shook their hands. "I know. They build a brand spanking new office and don't give us enough parking. Priceless."

He led them through to a small room behind the reception that housed a long rectangular table surrounded by chairs and a whiteboard. "Plenty of meeting rooms though," he said and disappeared with a promise to find refreshments. By the time he returned, Jackman and Davies were seated around the end of the table.

The coffees sloshed about as he placed the mugs down and settled next to them. "We went through the old rape file and tried to contact Alicia Wainwright's family after your phone call this morning," Hawkins said. "When we couldn't reach any of them, we asked the local response team to call at their address. The house is all shut up. The neighbour told them it's her mother's 50th birthday and the family have gone away to the Dominican Republic for two weeks. Due back Friday."

"What about extended family, any close friends she might have had?" Jackman asked.

"We'll continue to make enquiries, but it seems quite a crowd of her family have gone. Alicia's sister, parents, a few aunties and their families."

"Can you tell us anything about them?"

"Not much, I'm afraid. None of them have a record. No intelligence to speak of. They live in a little village just outside of town called Harlestone. It was a very sad affair.

The poor girl went to pieces after the trial by all accounts. Hung herself in the woods nearby."

They sipped their coffees in silence a moment.

"What can you tell us about Richard Garrett?" Jackman said.

"Richard Garrett has been a handful ever since he was a kid," Hawkins said. "I remember picking him up when I worked the beat in my early years. He was a youngster back then, egging cars, throwing stones at windows. His dad died when he was young and his mother couldn't control him so he became the neighbourhood pest. They kicked him out of school as soon as they could. He went to work with a local builder, left home soon after. Last address we had for him was Provence Court, St Giles Park in Duston. That's how he met Alicia Wainwright. She worked behind the bar in the Fox and Hounds between Duston and Harlestone. He used it as his local."

"Do you know much about the case?"

"I didn't work on it directly but I've read the notes. Apparently they'd been seeing each other for four or five months. The main line of defence was consent."

"But he was remanded in custody pending the trial?"

"Yeah, he did eight months on the remand wing at Leicester Gartree. His defence team pressed for bail but he wouldn't leave the girl alone. Poor thing. Sent friends to heckle her at her work. Even used his one phone call in here to reach her. Given his close proximity to her address, the harassment, coupled with the fact that he had no ties, no commitments – I think they thought he'd either threaten her or do a runner."

"Is that enough to change identity?" Davies asked.

Hawkins switched his gaze to her. "Oh, he didn't change identity because of the trial, more because of something that happened afterwards."

"What do you mean?" Jackman asked.

Hawkins took another sip of his coffee. "Richard was one of those crims that, in spite of their habits, it's a job not

167

to like. A man of few words, but enough wit to fill every one. Clever too. We had plenty of intelligence linking him to drugs supply, yet never managed to catch him in the act. He was self-employed, an electrician by trade before he disappeared, which gave him a legitimate business income – but that didn't pay for his BMW, his Ducati and the holidays he went on. But he was different when he came out. I ran into him a few times afterwards and he'd toughened, lost the boyhood charm. He seemed to lay low, didn't feature for a while. When he re-emerged, he'd moved into a new game – house invasions, aggravated burglary, basically robbing other drug dealers. He led a group of lads who broke into cannabis houses and cocaine dealers' homes, stole the money and their stash, whatever they could get. It's not a pretty business. The people in these houses work for top guys, they know they're going to take a beating if they let him get away with it, and don't give in easily. Usually involves violence of some kind. We knew he was pissing a lot of big names off, but our intelligence was sketchy."

"Who was he working with, or for?"

"Interesting question. He shared a cell with Jason Stalwart for a few months at Gartree. Jason's a big name in the Leicestershire drugs scene. He was in for GBH, although he was eventually acquitted. Couldn't make the charge stick. We think Jason was looking to extend his territory. Richard became the pawn in his game."

"What happened?"

"Richard went on a raid one night and got the wrong house. Visited the brother and sister-in-law of Danny Sutton, a well-connected crim serving time for armed robbery. Smashed into their house in the middle of the night, tipped a bucket of cold water over them while they were sleeping and threatened them with a machete. As soon as he realised his mistake he left, but the damage had been done. The word spread that it was Garrett and his crew. We picked up two of the guys he was working with, but he'd done a runner. I think he finally realised that night, the gravity of the situation he'd got himself into. He'd grown overconfident, bitten off more than he could chew and did a midnight flit."

*That explained why Audrey didn't know*, Jackman thought.

Hawkins snorted. "No wonder he changed his identity. There'll be a bounty on his head. He thought he was above it all, could get away with anything with protection from Stalwart."

Jackman explained about the cannabis cultivation beneath the barn.

Hawkins rolled his eyes. "Sounds like Garrett. In all my time in covert intelligence, I've never met such a slippery little character."

"Is there anyone here that he would be likely to contact on his return? His mother mentioned an associate called Charlie Truman?"

Hawkins rested back in his chair and thought for a moment. "I don't know that name, but I doubt it," he said. "We certainly haven't been alerted to anything. We'll put out some feelers though, see if there's been any change in movement or supply recently."

\*\*\*

Jackman passed the sign to Harlestone village and was instantly greeted with views of open, rolling countryside. Davies had fallen asleep next to him, her body rocking gently as they rounded the bends in the road. He turned a corner, slowed past a band of houses, cut the engine and checked his phone. A text from Carmela.

*Thanks for an interesting evening! We must catch a coffee before I leave tomorrow.*

He texted back, *Sure*, and was just pressing the send key when Davies lifted her head and blinked. "Sorry, drifted off for a minute back there."

"I won't tell, if you don't."

She laughed, rubbed the side of her neck. "Where are we?"

Jackman pocketed his phone and gestured towards a brick built house in the middle of the row. "That's where Alicia Wainwright's family live."

Davies followed his eyeline. Long arms of ivy stretched up the front of the house, curling their fingers around the porch. "I read the archive reports on file," Davies said. "She was found in the woods by a young couple on a Sunday afternoon stroll. Her parents thought she was at work." Davies paused, "Must have been awful, for all of them."

The solemn mood lay heavy in the car. Jackman wound down his window. A cow lowed in the distance.

"I'm surprised they stayed here afterwards," Davies said eventually.

"She grew up here," Jackman said. "And they have other children to think of."

Davies shook her head as if to disperse the bad thoughts and glanced at him. "How would you ever recover from something like that?"

Jackman turned the key. The engine roared as it ignited. "You wouldn't."

# Chapter **Twenty-Six**

Jackman had just walked back into his office and switched on his laptop when Keane appeared in the doorway.

"Nancy Faraday is downstairs, sir. She has some information. Wants to speak with you."

Jackman eyed him a moment. "Interesting. Maybe she's suddenly remembered something. Bloody hope so. Get Davies to meet me downstairs, will you?"

Nancy was seated beside a skinny man with dark hair and the shadow of an early beard in the reception area. They both stood as he approached. Jackman looked from one to another, prompting an introduction.

"This is Ryan Hills," Nancy said. "He's a friend of mine."

Jackman nodded at Ryan. "You wanted to see me?" he asked Nancy.

"Is there somewhere more private we could go?" Nancy cast a furtive glance at a man sat close to the desk. He didn't look up, his fingers rippling over the screen of his mobile phone.

"Follow me." Jackman led them both through a set of double doors, down a corridor and into an old interview room. He pushed open the door and switched on the light. It was an internal room with no windows which immediately made it feel cold. Scarcely used these days, other than for storage, the air was thick and musty.

The metal chair legs squeaked across the floor as Jackman pulled it out. "Please, sit down." He sat opposite them, noting the glance they exchanged, the look of anxiety in Ryan's eyes at their surroundings. He was getting tired of games and if Nancy was about to make some kind of revelation he wanted it over with. This had better not be another time-wasting interview. He folded his hands together on the table. "Well, what can I do for you?"

Nancy took a deep breath. "I needed to speak with you about some—"

At that moment the door opened and Davies appeared. She nodded at Jackman and sat beside him, opening up her notebook, clicking the end of her pen loudly.

Jackman looked at his watch. "Yes?"

Nancy looked from Davies to Jackman. She shifted in her chair. "I received a note yesterday morning."

"What kind of note?"

Nancy half stood and rummaged around in the pocket of her jeans for a second. The paper was ruffled. Creases ran through it and it was stuck together with sellotape, but the words were clear nonetheless: *Debts pass to next of kin.*

"Who sent it?"

"I don't know. It was hand delivered."

"Where's the envelope?"

"I threw it away. But there was nothing on it, only my name in capitals. Typed."

Jackman met her gaze. "What do you think it means?"

Nancy looked visibly frightened. "There's more. I went out of the flat yesterday, to put out the rubbish and wandered out into the main street. There was someone behind me. He pulled me back, said that they were watching me."

"Who do you think 'they' are?"

"I don't know."

Jackman listened carefully as she explained the incident and went on to talk about the man in the supermarket. Thoughts of the cannabis cultivation filled his mind and the words of Mike Clarke from the drugs squad, 'someone will be missing a crop'. Since these findings weren't released to

172

the general public, Nancy wouldn't know about this unless she was involved.

"Did you see the man?"

"Not exactly."

"What do you mean?"

"Well, there was a sort of tattoo on his finger. Some letters. Began with a CC – couldn't catch the rest. His breath smelled of old chewing gum."

"You didn't think to call the police?"

"I was scared. I didn't know what to do."

Jackman eased back. "What do you think this all means?" he asked again.

Nancy looked surprised, as if she was expecting answers, not questions. It was Ryan, silent up to this moment, who answered. "We thought it might have something to do with Cheryl, Nancy's mum. She has a drink problem."

"We know she was an alcoholic," Jackman said. "Why would this have anything to do with her?"

"She's borrowed money sometimes. To buy drink and pay bills."

Jackman turned back to Nancy. "So you think that your mother's loan sharks are hounding you to pay off her debt?"

Nancy didn't answer. She pulled her phone out of her pocket, worked the screen. Finally she turned it towards him and he watched the video. As the footage came to an end and the hooded man placed his hands in his pocket and pulled out a gun, Nancy's hand trembled.

"Where did you get this?" Jackman asked.

"It was posted as a private message on the work Facebook page."

"Has anyone else seen it?"

"I don't think Becca or Karen have, no."

"And you didn't tell them?"

"I can't. It's clearly aimed at me and I don't want them to be in danger."

"You no longer think it's linked to your mother?"

"I'm not sure. We've been over there. She's clean, says she has been for almost two months."

"It could be an old debt."

Nancy shook her head vehemently. "I don't know. When I mentioned people following me, asking for money she seemed too surprised."

"What about you, or your friends? Do you owe anybody money?"

"No, nobody."

"Or Evan? You knew him better than anybody, Nancy. Could it have been something he was involved in?"

"No. I would have known."

Jackman was only half listening now. What struck him was the amount – six thousand pounds. That was a steep amount to borrow. "I need you to be completely honest with me now. Are you absolutely sure you have no idea what this money was borrowed for and who used it?"

Nancy gave a single nod. "What happens now?"

"We'll take care of it."

"What do you mean?"

Jackman was silent a moment. "Have you ever heard the name Richard Garrett?" Davies' chair squeaked as she straightened.

"No. Who is that?"

The faint buzz of the light bulb overhead was all that could be heard in the room.

"Did the man you knew as Evan, ever mention that name?" Jackman asked.

He watched Nancy's expression change from confusion to recognition. "That was his real name, wasn't it?" Her voice was barely a whisper. "No, he never mentioned that name."

\*\*\*

"What do you think?" Davies asked.

They were back in Jackman's office, working through

Nancy's account. "I think we need to get someone out to Cheryl Faraday's address, to make sure she is safe. Although given the size of the demands, I'm inclined to think they are more related to the drugs connection. Let's contact Mike Clarke, circulate the details and see if they can come up with anything."

"So you believe her?"

"Don't you?"

Davies tucked a stray curl behind her ear. "I'm not sure. I don't doubt the video, but there's something about her. Something I can't put my finger on."

Jackman pictured Nancy's face as she unravelled her account of events that afternoon. "She's frightened. Perhaps being on the receiving end of so many broken promises over the years has impaired her judgement. She doesn't know how to react. It can't be easy having an alcoholic mother."

"That makes her more sad than guilty."

# Chapter **Twenty-Seven**

They drove home from the station in silence. Ryan seemed to sense that Nancy didn't want to talk. *Richard Garrett*. She'd rolled the name around in her mind.

Cars were parked nose to tail when they arrived outside the shop. Ryan drove past, around the corner and pulled in on the double yellow lines. "Do you want me to come in with you?"

Nancy looked out into the street beyond. Shoppers, tourists, workers milled around, filling the pavement on both sides. "There's no need. You can't leave the car here anyway."

"I'll just walk you back."

Nancy raised a hand. "Really. You've done enough. I'm grateful to you, for coming with me, I mean."

He nodded. "Still, I'd feel better if I saw you in."

"Nothing is going to happen here," she said with as much bravado as she could muster. "I'll go into the shop, get Becca to come up to the flat with me."

"You are going to tell Becca about this, aren't you?" Ryan said. "And Karen?"

"When the time is right." She turned, glared at him. "Don't you say anything, will you? It needs to come from me."

He tossed her an uncertain look. "Text me as soon as you get in. And remember what the detective said – keep your phone with you and don't leave the flat on your own."

Nancy hadn't forgotten those words. In fact, they were branded on her brain. The detective had gone on to talk about a 'safety plan' until they tracked down who was sending those messages. She should stay at home, only go out if absolutely necessary and, if so, take somebody with her; and always keep her phone by her side. Discreet cameras would be rigged up, watching the entrance to the flat, and she'd been given a police alarm, which, if pressed, would immediately alert the control room. A mixture of fear and resentment clung to her. She was a prisoner in her own home.

Nancy climbed out of the car and could feel Ryan's eyes on her as she rounded the corner. A car slowed, flashed its lights to let her cross the road. Just as she reached the curb on the other side of the road she heard a voice: "Nancy, isn't it?"

Nancy blanched. She followed the voice to an attractive woman in a black Fiat who spoke through the open passenger window. "Do I know you?"

"Maybe not. I'm Elise Stenson from the *Stratford Mail*. I'm covering the fire at the barn on Sunday. I'm working on a personal piece from the family's point of view. I was very sorry to hear about Richard. Thought you might like to add something?"

Nancy stepped back and stumbled on the curb. So, the whole world knew who Evan really was. "No. I don't."

"That's okay. If you change your mind..." She leant across, passed her a business card. "I'd be very happy to hear from you." The window closed and the car sped off down the road.

The image of the journalist in the car stayed with Nancy as she climbed the back steps and let herself into the flat, completely forgetting her promise to Ryan that she would speak to Becca first.

Relieved to find the flat empty, Nancy moved into the lounge, sunk into the sofa and chucked the business card aside. Her mind raced. The video footage and the note, the police interview, the journalist. Nothing made any sense.

The sound of a key in a lock turned her head.

"Hello!"

Becca's face appeared around the doorway.

"I thought I heard you come in. Where'd you get off to?"

For a split second, Nancy considered telling her the truth. Coming clean to Becca would lessen the weight pressing on her shoulders. But it would also bring complications. Becca would naturally be worried, not just for Nancy but also about the work's Facebook page. She'd feel obliged to tell Karen. And then there was the note. All these little things were mounting up. *No, best to keep it under wraps for now.* "Just went for a drive with Ryan," she said. The lie slipped out more easily than anticipated.

"Good, glad you guys are speaking," Becca said. "He's been worried about you."

Nancy forced a smile. "How's it going downstairs?"

"Quiet today. Still, at least we've made a start on the displays for Saturday."

Becca chatted on for a while before excusing herself and trudging back down to the shop. After she'd gone, Nancy sat back on the sofa. Her heart was in a vice. She should have been honest with Becca. Told her everything. But these weren't lies. They were hidden truths.

Nancy approached the window and peered around the side of the curtain. A car drove past, but apart from that the street looked quiet beneath her. She moved out into the hallway, checked the lock on the front door. It was firm. Her mobile showed no new messages.

She thought again about the footage sent to her that morning. What if they sent another? She rushed into the bedroom. Her laptop lay on the end of the bed. She sat down next to it, logged onto their Facebook page and scrolled down. There were no new messages added.

Nancy laid back across the bed, her head propped up with her right hand. The name Richard Garrett chimed like a church bells in her mind. She thought about the police interview, how little she knew of Evan's background. Maybe it was time to find out more…

She typed his name into the search engine and pressed enter. A huge list of Richard Garretts came up. A man with a long bushy beard, surrounded by an array of children at varying heights; a silver-haired executive from Glasgow; a biker perched on his Harley Davidson. Curious, she typed in Evan Baker. Again, numerous profiles came up, although none that looked remotely familiar. That wasn't surprising – Evan hadn't made any secret of what he thought about social media. When he'd seen her using Facebook on her phone, he'd teased her, saying it was full of people sharing pictures of fluffy kittens and puppies and talking about what they'd had for tea. They'd laughed about it. At first. But the more she used it in his presence the more she could feel an underlying current of annoyance creeping in. 'Why do you feel the need to share everything on there? Life is about the here and now,' he'd said. As time passed, he'd got so huffy about it, she found herself logging on in private. And somehow she'd used her personal Facebook less and less in her own time too.

Nancy switched to Google and typed Richard Garrett into the search engine. Her eyes flashed past the Facebook and LinkedIn references to the images. Nothing looked familiar. She scrolled down, and paused at a newspaper article from the *Northampton Express* entitled, 'Acquitted At Trial' and clicked.

*After a trial that lasted three days, Richard Garrett, formerly of Provence Court in Duston, Northampton was acquitted of rape at Northampton Crown Court yesterday. Based upon the evidence before them, it took the jury less than eight hours to record a not-guilty verdict.*

*Garrett was charged with the rape of a seventeen-year-old woman last November, following a night out in Northampton. For the past eight months he has been held on remand in custody at HMP Gartree, pending the trial. In a statement his solicitor said, "This has been a gruesome ordeal for both Mr Garrett and his family to endure. He is relieved that it's over and wants to be left at peace to concentrate on rebuilding his life."*

A spokesperson for the alleged victim's family said yesterday, *"We are devastated by the result and will be discussing the verdict with our legal team to see how we can take this forward."*

The date of the article was 2 April 2011. Nancy stared at the screen. Her breath balled in her chest. She reread the statement from his solicitor.

She couldn't quite believe it. Written there in black-and-white. Not her Evan.

As she reread the statement from the family, she shuddered, worked back through their relationship. Evan was certainly adventurous in the bedroom. He was much older than her, more experienced. But she'd liked that – liked that fact that he was stronger than her, dominated her. It made her feel protected. But that didn't make him a rapist. It must have been a misunderstanding. It had to be.

She brushed her hand across the silver bracelet laced around her wrist, an impromptu present on their first month's anniversary. Yes, he was stubborn. Liked things his way. But he was also kind. *There's a big difference.*

Maybe this was why Evan had felt uncomfortable talking about his family. It certainly explained why he'd felt the need to change his identity, have a fresh start in a new area where people didn't know him.

She grabbed her laptop, her fingers working the keys. Evan's mother was called Audrey. She remembered them laughing together because she shared the same name as her gran. She typed Audrey Garrett into the search engine. Immediately a list came up, sandwiched together by a row of images. There were endless Audrey Garretts listed. She added UK to the search box. There were eleven Audrey Garretts in the UK. Nancy knew she lived somewhere in Northampton, but she couldn't remember the exact area. She typed in the town, scrolled down through the directories. Towards the bottom of the page she found the electoral roll website and clicked. Her stomach bounced; here they were listed with full addresses. She scrolled through one in Birmingham, one in South London, another in Manchester. Finally she came to a listing for Northampton. Age 52. Evan was 34, it had to be worth a try.

Nancy followed some more links and found a free phone directory. She typed in the details, more in hope than expectation, and was surprised when the phone number flashed up on the screen.

She reached for her phone. She could maybe just dial, listen to the voice. If it sounded friendly, she could ask. It would be so lovely to find a part of Evan, to talk to someone who knew him like she did.

She bit her lip, grabbed her phone and dialled. What did she have to lose?

# Chapter **Twenty-Eight**

Jackman pulled into his drive and parked up next to the black Fiesta.

He climbed out of the car, grabbed the bottle of Zinfandel rosé he'd picked up on his way home and strode over to his front door. As soon as he was inside, Erik came rushing towards him, his tail beating against everything in his way.

"Hello, mate." Jackman bent down and rubbed his head. "Where's Celia?"

The dog skipped around his legs. Jackman stood and called out to his daughter, but there was no reply. Assuming she'd gone out, he moved into the kitchen, pressed the switch on the kettle and flicked through the post. Swirls of steam were filling the air when he heard a sudden bump upstairs. He placed the letters down.

The low rumble of a growl emitted from the hallway. Jackman crossed the threshold.

Erik cast him a fleeting glance and glared up the stairs. Jackman looked up. A skinny man with dark hair, fitted jeans and a goatee beard was hovering at the top of the stairs. The whites of his eyes were glued to Erik.

"Top marks," Jackman said. "I've never heard him growl at anyone before."

The man switched his gaze between Jackman and the dog. Erik, now bored, slumped down on the floor next to Jackman.

"You must be Adrian," Jackman said.

The man nodded his response. "Hi!" he said feebly.

"Come on down," Jackman said. "He won't hurt you. I think you just spooked him."

Adrian walked down the stairs gingerly, half an eye still on the dog.

Jackman smiled at him. "I'm Will, Celia's dad." He shook his hand. "Where is Celia?"

"In the shower."

"Ah." For a split second Jackman felt sorry for him. He could still remember the first time he'd met Alice's father – a formidable Dane called Elias, one of the few men in his adult life that had towered over him. Elias had never hidden his disapproval of Jackman, making it obvious he didn't think he was good enough for his daughter, especially when they married and decided to make their home in England. "Can I get you a coffee?" he said.

Adrian nodded and followed him through to the kitchen.

"What time did you get here?" Jackman asked.

"About an hour ago."

Jackman busied himself with making another drink and was just handing it over to Adrian when soft footfalls skipped down the stairs and Celia's face appeared in the doorway, beaming from ear to ear. "Dad!" She rushed through and encased him in a bear hug. "I see you've met Adrian," she said pulling back.

"I have."

She pushed her white-blonde hair out of her face, glanced across at the table and smiled. "You bought me rosé."

"Is it still your favourite?"

"It is, although can't afford to have it much at uni. Thanks."

Jackman cocked his head to the side. "There's something different about you."

"Oh, I had a fringe cut in."

"Suits you." She beamed back at him. "Want some dinner?"

"Thought we'd order a takeaway."

Jackman's heart warmed as he leant up against the side and listened to his daughter chatter on about their journey up from Southampton while Adrian sat behind her, barely saying a word. It was good to have Celia back in the house again, her energy was both infectious and intoxicating. Nobody noticed Erik wander in from the garden leaving muddy paw prints all over the floor until...

"Ow!"

All eyes shot to Adrian who pushed Erik off his foot and frowned at the dirty paw print left behind on his pale blue shoes.

"Oh no, he's been digging again." Celia's tone was filled with exasperation. She grabbed an old towel from beside the back door and proceeded to wipe the dog's feet in turn.

"We don't tend to wear light-coloured footwear," Jackman said to Adrian. "There's a cloth underneath the sink. I'll leave you guys to order the food." He wandered out of the room, cuffing Erik's neck as he did so. "Come and sit with me in the lounge. You can't do much damage there."

\*\*\*

Jackman was scraping the last of the rice out of the carton when his phone rang. He jumped up, excused himself and moved out into the hallway to answer.

"Where are you, sir?" Davies didn't bother to introduce herself.

"At home. Dropped in to see Celia. Why?"

"We've finally had word from the Lawtons. They're in Perth."

Jackman felt a stir of excitement. "Great. Get in touch with the local police station and see if we can arrange an interview." His watch read 9.35pm as he ended the call and he couldn't help but wonder what time it was in Perth.

Celia and Adrian had moved from the kitchen into the lounge and were now curled up together on the sofa. "I have to go out again, I'm afraid," Jackman said. He held up his phone. "Work."

"That's a shame," Celia said. "Thought we might watch a film or something."

"Sorry, love."

"Oh well, there's always tomorrow." She stretched her arm out, grabbed his wrist. He felt an urge to lean down, kiss her forehead as usual, but her close proximity to Adrian would have made that feel odd. Instead he gave her a wink. "Nice to meet you," he said to Adrian. "I'll maybe see you later if you're still up."

***

Jackman stared at the bronzed faces that filled the computer screen. Ronnie Lawton had a long face with pointed features and a road map of red-veined cheeks. Seated next to him, Janine was a plump woman with smooth skin that gave the appearance of someone much younger than her fifty-three years, in spite of her red-rimmed eyes.

"Thank you for getting in touch and for speaking to us today," Jackman said. "I realise you've had some bad news."

Ronnie nodded his thanks, "We're a bit shocked." He gave his wife a sideways glance. "Janine hasn't stopped crying since we heard."

"I'm sorry for your loss."

"What happened?"

"The fire service were called to Lowlands Barn in the early hours of Sunday morning. They found Evan's body there."

Janine dabbed her eyes with a tissue. "My daughter said he was killed."

"We are treating it as murder."

Ronnie stretched an arm around his wife's shoulder, pulled her close. Jackman gave them a moment before he continued. "How long have you known Evan?"

Ronnie scratched the back of his ear. "About two years, since he first joined us on the farm."

"How did you meet?"

"We lost one of our permanent guys – he handed in his notice just as we were about to start harvest and we needed some urgent help. He answered the advertisement. To tell you the truth, I was a bit sceptical at first. He'd never done farm work before, all his previous jobs were in the building trade. He was an electrician, but he seemed keen and we were desperate so I gave him a go."

"Can you remember what company he worked for before, where they were based?"

Ronnie shook his head. "Sorry, no."

"Did you get references for him?"

Ronnie looked taken aback at the question. He thought for a moment. "No, as I recall, he brought his own references along. Why do you need to know all of this?"

"We are just trying to build up a profile. It's routine police work. What kind of work did he do for you?"

"To start off with he helped with the harvest, baling and such like. Wasn't long before he was out and about feeding cattle, doing a bit of everything. He was a hard worker, enthusiastic. It's difficult to find people who want to do manual work these days. Workers come and go on farms – people fancy the idea of the rural lifestyle until they realise how demanding it is. Kids want office jobs, Monday to Friday. That's why we ended up keeping him on."

"What about his address? Where did he live?"

"He had a flat in Stratford town. That's all I knew."

"Did he ever talk about family, friends, where he came from?"

Ronnie slid his eyes to his wife, then back to the screen. "Evan never talked much. He was quite a private person. But he turned up for work on time, never missed a day, was a quick learner and worked hard. We've two daughters and neither of them are interested in the farm. I was planning

on asking him to continue to manage it when we got back –
Janine and I aren't getting any younger. We want to do more
travelling, spend time with our grandchildren."

Jackman thought about the cannabis farm. If there
had been an inkling that the arrangement would become
permanent, the investment made all the more sense. He could
have continued with the cultivation and supply, safe in the
knowledge that nobody would upset his arrangement.

"He spoke to me a little." Janine's Lawton's voice was
barely a whisper. "Just snippets from his childhood. He
stopped by for lunch a few times and I remember once I gave
him tomato soup. He said it was his favourite but he'd never
had it homemade before. I think he had to fend for himself
quite a bit as a kid, poor lad."

"Do you know where his family lived?"

"He mentioned a school in Northampton. I think that's
where he grew up."

"When was the last time you communicated with Evan?"

"Must have been about a month ago," Janine said. "We
phoned him when we were in Melbourne. Everything seemed
fine then."

"You don't maintain regular contact?"

"We phoned, every now and then. He had the phone numbers
of both our daughters, just in case. And he could email us, we
would always check our emails when we had signal."

"Okay, tell me about the farm," Jackman said.

Ronnie frowned. "What do you want to know?"

"What was its main produce when you left in January?"

"We have about 500 acres altogether, 200 acres of crops
– maze mainly, but we also grow rapeseed, winter barley,
wheat and fodder beat. The other 300 acres are taken up with
heifers and bullocks, 320 at last count."

"Nothing else?"

Ronnie narrowed his eyes. "No, why?"

Jackman ignored the question. "What was Lowlands Barn
used for?"

"Storing fodder beat and hay for the cattle over the winter mainly. Shame really. It's a lovely brick built barn," his face folded, "or it was. We had the roof repaired a couple of years ago and we even thought about selling it for a residential conversion at one point. But it was my late father's favourite. I couldn't part with it."

"And the generator?"

"What?" He looked at his wife. "What generator?"

"The generator attached to the barn?"

"I don't know what you are talking about. There is no generator at Lowlands Barn. Never has been."

Jackman looked at the faces on the screen. They looked kind, like people whose habits hadn't changed in the past twenty years. Neither of them had seemingly crossed paths with the police and all recent findings pointed towards them not being involved in the cannabis cultivation. He couldn't begin to imagine what they would make of the secret room beneath the barn. Evan wasn't the man they thought he was.

For a short moment, he toyed with telling them the truth about the barn, the secret room below, the cash found at the farmhouse. But Janus had been quite firm that she didn't want anything released to the public yet. And it didn't seem right to add further salt to their wounds at this time.

"Where are you going next?" Jackman asked.

"We're looking for flights home," Ronnie said. "We can't stay here, with all that is going on back there. Stephan and Luca are keeping the farm ticking over, feeding the cattle. But there's more harvesting to be done, and crop to be sown for next year. Besides..." he looked back across at his wife, "Janine wants to go to Evan's funeral. We both do."

"Can I ask you one more question? Did Evan ever go by another name?"

"No, why do you ask?"

"Our enquiries have revealed that he was living under a different identity."

"What was his real name?"

"Richard Garrett."

Ronnie shrugged. "It's not a crime to change your name, is it?"

# Chapter **Twenty-Nine**

The house was bathed in darkness when Jackman returned that evening. He whispered his greeting to Erik, navigated the stairs gently, doing his best not to disturb his sleeping guests.

The spare room at the top of the stairs was lit up by a silvery moonlight through the undrawn curtains. The next door along, leading to Celia's bedroom, was firmly closed. A sense of disquiet wrapped around him. This was the first time Celia had shared her room here with a man. But what did he expect? Celia was twenty. Adrian and her shared a house down in Southampton during term at university. He was almost certain they shared a room there, so why shouldn't they here. But the reality was tinged with a wave of sadness, another milestone to remind him that his daughter was no longer his little girl.

He moved into his own bedroom and sat back on the bed. Ronnie and Janine Lawton's interview had unsettled him. Their words were loaded with sadness and grief at the tragic turn of events. Richard, or Evan as they'd known him, had worked for them for almost two years and they'd clearly grown fond of him. He pictured Richard's mother in his mind. The difference in their reactions to the news was stark.

Nancy's face flashed up in his mind. Her vulnerability had shone through this afternoon. He couldn't help but feel sorry for her. Keane had visited Cheryl on the pretence of a welfare visit and confirmed that the house was clean and tidy, her disposition calm – nothing to suggest she was drinking again. Which supported his theory that there was a more sinister explanation behind the demands.

A single cough emitted from the room next door. He stared at the wall that divided the rooms. Two years ago, Celia left the home she'd been raised in to go to university, full of excitement, leaving the bedroom she'd kept since she was three years old. The décor had changed so many times over the years but the memories remained. After her mother's accident she'd considered giving up her course, moving back to Stratford to be with her dad, but he'd refused to entertain the notion.

Now he realised how unlikely it was that Celia would ever come back home to live again. The room that had once housed all her treasured possessions would become her guest room, whenever she came to stay. The thought induced a pang of sadness.

\*\*\*

Amanda Grayson checked her watch. Almost 10.30pm. It wasn't like Eamonn to be late. She'd been surprised when he'd called and asked to meet, almost half an hour earlier. He sounded desperate on the phone. There was something he wanted to tell her in person. Under normal circumstances, she'd turn him down at that late hour, arrange to meet him the next day. But after all the events of the past few days she'd felt compelled to go, made an excuse about popping out to collect something from a friend, leaving her husband in front of the television, catching up on the rugby highlights from the weekend. She doubted he even noticed she was gone.

She looked around the café, checked her watch again. She could only afford to give him another fifteen minutes.

A pair of headlights passed through the side street, followed closely by another. She craned her neck as they disappeared.

Amanda sipped her coffee, cradled the warm mug in one hand and adjusted the blue silk scarf that hung loosely around her neck with the other. The last time she'd worn it, Eamonn had cupped her chin, told her it brought out the blue in her eyes.

A figure was approaching from the car park in the distance. She squinted, was just about to put on her glasses when she recognised Eamonn's wide gait. She smiled and waved. If he saw her he didn't wave back. He was dressed in a pair of dark jeans and a polo shirt that hung loosely off his chest, accentuating his muscles and making him look ruggedly attractive. The urgency of their meeting felt excitingly clandestine. He strode across the road. She couldn't take her eyes off the contour of his chest, his unbrushed hair, those broad shoulders when she heard the rev of an engine. A pair of headlights cut through the semi-darkness. The car appeared from nowhere. Afterwards, she would be confused as to whether it had revved before it hit him, or afterwards, but at the time it all merged in together. A terrible thumping noise. The screech of tyres.

Amanda jumped up, sending her coffee mug flying to the floor, splashing the window with liquid. A wild shrill scream emitted from her mouth, before she moved forward, bumping tables, pushing chairs aside in her haste to get to him.

# Chapter **Thirty**

Jackman was awoken early the following morning by the sound of footsteps below. He pulled his robe over his shoulders and made his way down the stairs. The French doors in the lounge were slung open wide. Erik came rushing in to meet him.

In the kitchen Jackman found Celia, poring over her laptop, a steaming mug of coffee in hands that were partially covered by her cuffs. Her hair hung messily down to her shoulders.

"Morning," he said. The clock read 6am. "What are you up to?"

"Just checking my emails," she said. "Want some coffee? I've made fresh."

It never ceased to amaze him how sprightly she was first thing in the morning. "Sure." He plonked himself down in a chair and willed his brain to life. By the time she'd handed him a black coffee, he could feel the cogs slowly starting to turn. "What are you up to today?"

"I'm going to give this one a run when I've finished my coffee," Celia said rubbing Erik's head affectionately.

"Adrian not coming with you?"

"He's still asleep."

"Just as well," Jackman replied. "He's probably not got the shoes for it."

"Dad." She pulled stern face, but a smile was playing on her lips. "He's a bit wary of him." Jackman looked across at Erik who lifted a leg and scratched the back of his ear clumsily as she continued. "Adrian isn't used to dogs. They don't have any animals at home."

They sat in silence a moment. "You working today?" Celia asked eventually.

"Afraid so."

"How's it going?"

"Okay." He supped his coffee. Celia went back to her laptop and his mind wandered to the investigation. He needed something, a fresh lead. The description of the tattoo markings on Nancy's stalker had been circulated nationally yesterday evening, and he desperately hoped it rang a bell with somebody. He needed to find out who was harassing Nancy. And fast.

***

Jackman felt the tension as soon as he arrived in the incident room. Keane and Davies were huddled in the corner over a computer screen. He pulled back his sleeve, checked his watch. It wasn't yet 7.30am. "Has something happened?"

Keane looked up. "Eamonn Benwell was killed in a hit-and-run last night."

Jackman stopped in his tracks, letting the words sink beneath the surface. "What happened?"

"He was crossing a side road in Stratford town. A witness said the car tossed him ten feet in the air. Paramedics declared him dead at the scene."

"And the driver?"

"Gone. The detectives working night car last night have checked the CCTV and surrounding police cameras. The car was a black Skoda Octavia, sport version. Reported stolen a couple of weeks ago from the owner's home in Trinity Drive. They drove out of Stratford on the A3400, turned right at the roundabout on to the A46. The Skoda was later found partially burnt-out on the road to Lower Clopton."

"Why weren't we alerted earlier? He's directly linked to our case."

"It's seems somebody forgot to put the markers on the system," Davies said with a sigh. "It wasn't until Keane got in this morning and checked last night's incident logs that we found it.

Jackman pulled out his mobile phone and worked the keys urgently.

Janus answered on the second ring. "Will, I'm glad you called. Isn't Eamonn Benwell linked to your murder enquiry?"

"That's why I'm calling. I've just been informed about the hit-and-run. Who's the SIO dealing?"

"DCI Peverell has taken it at the moment. He was on call. But he's in court today and still seconded to that review team. You're going to have to take it off him."

"No problem. Have him call me and we'll do a handover."

He ended the call and minutes later, Jackman's mobile rang.

"Morning, Will." Peverell sounded tired.

"Morning. I hear you've had a long night?"

"You could say that."

"What do you have?"

"One victim, killed in a hit-and-run on The Waterways at 10.32pm. We've checked the CCTV footage from the town centre and got a few stills of the car, although they're not great. I'll email them across. We've also got a witness who glimpsed a profile of the driver."

"Thanks. Send me everything you've got so far. Has anyone been back out to see the owner of the car?"

"Yes, just now. Usual thing. Didn't lock their front door. Found somebody in the hallway in the middle of the afternoon who claimed they'd got the wrong house. It wasn't until later that they discovered the car keys were missing and the intruder left in their car, which had been parked up the road. One thing that might be of interest though, the car only had one working headlight. The owners were going to take it to the garage that day to have it mended. This is a professional job, the car had cloned plates. We only identified it quickly because the correct number plate was etched onto the windows. It seems unlikely they'd drive through town with one headlight after to going to that much trouble."

"Right. Who called it in?"

"What?"

"The hit-and-run. Who called it in?"

"Er… Amanda Grayson." He said the name slowly, as if he was reading it from his notes. "She was in a café. It happened in front of her."

Jackman pinched the bridge of his nose with his thumb and forefinger and closed his eyes. He could see Amanda Grayson sitting in the Thyme Café on The Waterways waiting for Eamonn. Smoothing her hair, checking her make-up in anticipation. Yet her lasting image of him would be like some terrifying scene from a horror film. He ended the call, turned back to the room. Officers were wandering in now, switching on computers.

Jackman relayed the details to Davies and Keane. Somebody came around gathering mugs to make the morning coffee. A thought struck Jackman. "Get the CSIs examining the car to take out the headlight assembly, will you, and do a search for fingerprints on the surrounding area? Hopefully it won't have been too damaged by the fire."

"Do you think this could be another message from a rival drugs gang?" Davies asked.

"To kill somebody in the centre of Stratford town is a risky strategy." Jackman said. "Let's look at who stands to gain. We've been questioning Eamonn Benwell the past few days, examining his associations, searching his house, his business. We assume that the victim's body was dumped in a barn that housed a cannabis farm below on purpose, and it was set on fire, which means the killers wanted his death to be known, not merely that he was missing. So far, we've found nothing to link Eamonn to the murder, but that doesn't mean he wasn't our man."

Keane looked up. "But if Eamonn wasn't the killer, then it would suit whoever it was to get him out of the way before he talks."

"Amanda Grayson," Davies said, almost to herself. "Wasn't she the girlfriend? Maybe her husband found out about the affair?"

Jackman pictured Amanda Grayson with her neat clothes and expensive perfume, her two children in primary school. Neither Amanda nor her husband featured on the police national computer in any capacity. He couldn't imagine her husband risking losing his job, his family to drive a stolen car, let alone commit murder. "Unlikely," he said. "But I think we need to have a word with him anyway."

\*\*\*

A slim man with dark hair formed around a widow's peak answered the door of the Grayson family home in Tiddington Road that morning. When Jackman and Davies introduced themselves he extended his hand. "Robert Grayson. Thanks for coming around." He spoke with authority, his voice calm and composed, although his grey pallor betrayed a weariness beneath the surface. "Amanda is in the sitting room. I've taken the children to her mother's."

"Thank you," Jackman said. He waited for Davies to follow Robert into the kitchen to take down his account of events, and pushed the door open into a large front room. It was furnished in quite an old-fashioned way: floor-to-ceiling bookcases lined the end wall opposite the window, a rocking chair sat in the corner beside an Indian rug. Amanda was seated on one of three sofas arranged around the television at the other end. She stood as he entered and indicated for him to sit. "Thanks for coming, Inspector. Can I get you a drink?"

"No, thanks. I understand you've had quite a shock."

She looked up at him through puffy eyes and gave a solemn nod.

"I'm sorry."

His words induced more tears. She pressed a tissue to her face. Jackman gave her a moment, recalling how composed she was at their last meeting. They'd met in the same café where she'd been waiting for Eamonn last night. It was the perfect central location, mainly frequented by travelling business people and tourists, tucked away from the main road, cars parked out of sight at the rear. He couldn't help but wonder how many times they'd met there over the past months.

"I want to be a witness," she said quietly. "I'll give evidence in court if that's what's needed."

Jackman cast a fleeting glance towards the kitchen.

"It's all right, he knows everything," Amanda said. "I can't hide anymore. I owe it to Eamonn. He was a good man, he didn't deserve this." Her words trailed off and she swallowed.

"What were you doing in the café?" Jackman asked.

"Eamonn contacted me and asked to meet. It sounded important." She went on to explain what had happened. When she reached the collision, her words splintered and she shuddered.

Jackman sat quietly as she dabbed her eyes. "I understand you saw the driver?" he said eventually.

She nodded. "It happened quickly, but the light flashed across his face."

"Do you feel up to coming down to the station, to do a formal photo identification? Shouldn't take too long."

"Of course." She looked down, flicked a loose thread from her trousers. It was a moment before she spoke again. "People think of affairs as sordid, dirty little secrets;

clandestine meetings in secret hotel rooms. But it wasn't like that for me. The only time my husband and I talk these days is if we are entertaining guests, to synchronise our diaries, or if there's a problem with the children. He buys me roses for my birthday because that's what he bought me when we first met fifteen years ago. But my favourite flowers are orchids. Always have been. Eamonn and I talked about books, films, places we'd like to visit. The real world. It was just nice to be me again." Her lip quivered. "For a while."

# Chapter **Thirty-One**

"Are you sure about this?"

Nancy looked at her reflection in the full-length mirror. She twisted side to side, held out her arms wide. "What do you think? Too casual?"

A pile of clothes littered the bed behind her. In the end she'd opted for loose denims and a black T-shirt, tied her hair back in a ponytail.

"You look fine," Becca said.

Nancy faced her reflection. "I'm not sure…"

"Don't you think you might be better leaving it for a while? You've both had a huge shock."

Nancy leant in closer to the mirror, stroked her brow. The bruise above her eye was barely visible now, under a layer of foundation. She pulled back, crossed to the dressing table and rummaged through the top drawer until she found a black-and-white silk scarf, then moved back to the mirror and tied it loosely around her neck. "I think that's better. Less casual."

"Are you listening to me?"

Nancy rounded on her friend. "Audrey sounded all right on the phone. I'm sure she'd have said if she didn't want me to go. Anyway, it might be good for both of us."

"How do you mean?"

"We were both close to Evan. We could help each other."

Becca took a deep breath, spoke through her exhalation. "I'm not sure."

Nancy stared at her friend, imploringly. She couldn't ask

Ryan to come with her after the detective had told her to stay at home yesterday. But she needed to do this. Today. "I'm sure it'll be all right. I've a good feeling about it."

Becca stood. "Okay, if you're sure. Just be careful. I'll meet you downstairs."

Nancy waited for her to leave and scooted across to the window. She couldn't see anyone lurking around outside. Apart from a single car parked up the road, it was empty. Another glance in the mirror. Audrey sounded like a nice, kind name. It conjured up images of a smartly dressed woman, with a beautiful house full of matching handmade soft furnishings and freshly baked Victoria sponge, just like Nancy's grandmother.

She gave a fleeting thought to her own mother. Cheryl couldn't heat up a ready meal without burning it, let alone bake a cake. And as for sewing... The only thing the sofa and curtains had in common were the nicotine stains.

Nancy checked her watch. It was just after 9.30am. She pushed the clothes aside, perched on the edge of the bed and pulled on her shoes. This moment should have been so different. She imagined Evan and her arriving at the home he'd grown up in, walking up a pathway, knocking on a shiny white front door. He'd give her a smile, place a reassuring hand on the small of her back. His mother would come out to meet them, welcome her with open arms. Invite them inside to a tea she'd specially prepared for the occasion. They'd sit around the table talking, laughing while she recalled memories of Evan's childhood.

She swallowed back the tears before they had a chance to smudge her mascara. Maybe Evan's mum would still welcome her with open arms. Maybe she would find it comforting to talk with her. They could chat about his obsession with engines, how he liked to take things apart to see how they worked. Evan was her only son. His father had died when he was young. She and Audrey could help each other. This comforted Nancy as she checked her watch again. They ought to get going. They would be early, but Becca was always telling her that people liked early. Early made a good impression and that was exactly what she intended to make today.

***

Jackman's phone rang as he pulled back into the station car park. The rain had started, drumming the windscreen and creating wide puddles on the tarmac that splashed up against the side of the car. "Damn rain," Davies said. "Feels more like April than August." She pressed answer.

"Morning!" Hawkins' warm Irish accent rushed into the car.

"Morning," Jackman said. "Have you got something for me?"

"Not sure. It's a bit tenuous, but I thought I'd pass it on anyway. We've received some intelligence about a disagreement between Northants and Warwickshire drugs gangs. We were aware of an abundance of cannabis in supply recently, bringing the prices down, but couldn't work out where it was coming from. In light of your case, we've done some work around Truman, Richard Garrett's associate, gaining fresh intelligence. It seems he's been moving considerable amounts of cannabis of late, rivalling our local suppliers. The guys here caught wind of where it was coming from and linked it to a Nick Anderson. Do you know that name?"

"I do – a local gang leader here, although like most he's got his legitimate businesses and keeps it well under wraps. Our drugs guys have been tracking him recently."

"Well, it seems he upset them down here, so they sent a message."

"Anderson's garage was burnt down, about three weeks ago. Suspected arson by local kids. Could have been that."

"Sounds about right. Whatever happened, the new supply

has dried up so it worked. Seems they are bracing themselves for a response though."

Jackman recalled how Mike Clarke had reported Nick Anderson's car in the vicinity of the farmhouse on the night of the burglary. The empty gun cupboard. "So we've got a turf war on our hands?"

"Possibly. It might mean that Anderson is connected to your murder, or at least the cannabis farm. It seems, even after his death, Richard Garrett is creating debts to settle."

"What about Charlie Truman?"

"Disappeared off the face of the earth. Not surprising really."

They rushed across the car park, through the shower. Davies had filled Jackman in on her discussion with Amanda Grayson's husband during the car journey back, but raised it again as they climbed the back steps. "He really had no idea about the affair," she said. "He's away a lot and his life seems pretty much filled with his work by all accounts. I bet he doesn't even know what his kids like to eat for dinner." She paused at the top of the stairs, rounded on Jackman. "Could you really keep a secret like that from someone so close?"

Jackman shrugged. "Loads do, it seems."

Keane stood as Jackman and Davies entered the incident room. "DS Clarke's trying to get hold of you," he said to Jackman. "Says it's urgent."

Jackman made his way into his office, wrestled the wet jacket off his shoulders and called Mike Clarke back.

"We circulated the description you sent over to us yesterday to all our source handlers." Mike said. "I think we've got an identification for you. His name is Luke Denton. Small time guy. He's been mentioned in connection with a few assaults, was arrested a couple of times, although nobody pressed charges. He officially works as a bouncer, but we're under the impression he mostly enforces unofficial debts."

"For Anderson?"

"That's what we're thinking. We've seen him at Anderson's snooker hall. They use the same gym, although you rarely see them together. There's a tattoo on the side of his forefinger – CCFC – for Coventry City Football Club, looks like it's a recent job because it doesn't show up on any custody records."

Jackman scratched the back of his neck. "Strange choice of job for a man with such an obvious tattoo."

"We are not dealing with the brightest button here, he's a muscle head. Walks around in designer gear, rubs shoulders with the big guys. He's got a very high opinion of himself, but certainly doesn't have the brains to carry anything big off. My guess is that Anderson sold him a debt – the cost of rebuilding his garage after it was wrecked. Maybe that was why Evan was killed, he either refused to pay, or couldn't afford to. Afterwards he leant on Nancy. 'Debts pass to next of kin' – that's what the note said, isn't it? Well, as far as these guys are concerned, next of kin stretches to anyone that constitutes their nearest and dearest."

"Six thousand pounds doesn't sound much for rebuilding a garage."

"This will only be the first instalment," Mike said. "It's how these people work. Part of their 'policy'. Start low, induces less of a panic, less chance of the target contacting the authorities, then come back for more later. If you can't pay, for whatever reason, they move down the line. That includes girlfriends, wives, anything apart from kids – attracts too much attention. He probably thought Nancy was involved, had access to Evan's ill-gotten profits and got a bit carried away with his own sense of self-importance. He's watched too many movies – the note, the video footage. I'm sure if Anderson had been around, he'd have reigned him in a bit."

"Where can we find him?"

"I'll email you the address, but our intelligence suggests he plays pool with a group of mates on a Friday afternoon at The Squirrel pub on Drayton Avenue."

"Great, we'll try there first."

"A word to the wise. Watch him," Mike said. "There's no mention of firearms on our intel, but he's a tricky customer."

# Chapter **Thirty-Two**

Becca rounded the corner of Cosgrove Way, pulled up and cut the engine. "There you go. It's just up there on the left-hand side.

Nancy fixed her gaze up the road at a line of terrace houses, set back from the road. Her mouth felt dry. "Do I look okay?"

"You look fine. Really." She felt Becca's hand on her arm and turned to meet her gaze. "Sure you don't want me to come in with you?"

For a moment she was sorely tempted. But she hadn't mentioned to Evan's mother anything about bringing a friend along. She shook her head, swallowed. "No, I'll be fine."

"Okay, well, call me when you are finished. I'm going to drive around the corner and listen to some music. I can be back here in a couple of minutes."

Nancy climbed out of the car, adjusted her scarf and pulled her bag over her shoulder. The road was empty that morning. She looked at the front gardens as she passed. One had a pristine lawn, another was block paved; another was covered in bright-coloured shingle that formed the base for a caravan. She hesitated outside a house decorated with an array of hanging baskets bursting with pansies and a front garden laid to lawn. She glanced up at the number: 112. The house next door wasn't numbered; the front garden was fully paved. Some of the slabs were broken and a few dandelions and tufts of grass had pushed their way through the gaps. Nancy paused. The view through the bay window was obscured by net curtains. She switched to the next one along – a black wrought-iron sign clearly read number 116.

Nancy wandered down the drive of the house with the paved front. A brown wooden door was situated on the side with a single gold letterbox in the middle and a bell on the frame. She pressed the bell and waited. After a couple of seconds she pressed again. When there was still no answer she checked her watch. Maybe being early wasn't such a good idea. She fisted her hand and knocked the door a couple of times, slightly louder than she'd intended.

A thud sounded from inside, followed by footsteps.

The door was pulled open to reveal a short woman with a bush of grey hair wearing a navy cardigan over a cream T-shirt. A gathered light blue skirt hung loosely over her ample hips. The woman frowned. "Yes?"

Nancy looked past her. "Oh, I'm sorry. I'm looking for Audrey Garrett?"

The woman folded her arms across her chest. "That's me."

No smiles. No open-armed welcome. Just a pair of hard milky-grey eyes. Nancy fought to hide the disappointment in her face. "I'm Nancy."

"Oh." Her mouth formed a thin smile that didn't reach her eyes. "You're early."

"Yes, sorry." She felt Audrey look her up and down.

"No problem." Her eyes rested on Nancy's shoes. "You'll have to take those off."

Audrey turned and led Nancy into a dark hallway and waited while she kicked off her heels. A single gilt-edged mirror hung on the wall. The air was tainted with the floral scent of an air freshener.

To Nancy's relief, the front room was brighter and more colourful. Cream curtains were tied back at each end of the long net that covered the front window. A grey sofa and armchair positioned around a modern electric fire were stuffed with peach floral cushions overlapping each other in a triangular pattern. Glass doors revealed a dining room beyond. A cat was curled up on the end of the sofa. It raised its head and glared at her.

Audrey sat on the armchair and gestured for Nancy to sit. She lowered herself onto the far edge of the sofa, away from the cat, not daring to mess up the pretty cushions.

"Thanks for letting me come around," Nancy said. "It's good to finally meet you." She beamed at Audrey.

Audrey nodded, but didn't smile back.

Nancy wound her feet around each other.

Suddenly, Audrey stood. "I guess you'll be a tea drinker if you knew Richard. He grew up on the stuff. Do you take sugar?"

"No, thank you." Nancy winced inwardly at the name, Richard. It didn't feel right to call him that, he'd always be Evan to her. She sunk into the chair as the door closed behind Audrey. The cat's unwavering stare made her uneasy. Maybe Becca was right. It was too soon.

Nancy looked through the glass doors to the long wooden table that was so polished it looked like it had never been used. They should have been sitting around there, eating sandwiches and freshly made cake, drinking tea, talking and laughing together. Nancy could tell tales from the shop, offer to do her garden for her. She glanced back around the room. The walls were an off-white colour, and bare apart from a few printed paintings. A collection of photos littered the mantle above the fire, but she didn't recognise any of them.

The door pushed open and Audrey walked back in carrying a small round tray containing two mugs of tea.

Nancy smiled as she passed across a mug. "Thanks."

They sat in silence cradling their mugs for a moment, until Nancy could bear it no more. "It's such a shame that we have to meet… like this."

Audrey looked up, ignored the statement and gave a nod towards the bruise on her forehead. "The police said you took a blow to the head. That looks sore."

Nancy flicked the wisps of fringe that veiled the cut above her eye with her free hand. "It's a lot better now, thanks. Only, I know he was planning for us all to meet together."

A strange expression flickered across Audrey's face. "He was?"

Nancy tilted her head. "Yes... He said so." Her stomach felt queasy.

Audrey blinked a few times, averted her gaze. "The police told me it was likely quick. That's a godsend I suppose." She raised her mug, sipped her tea.

"What was he like? As a boy, I mean?"

Audrey looked towards the window. "Stubborn, determined."

Nancy tried a different tack. She thought about his working on the farm. He'd told her that he used to work as an electrician. "Has he always been a practical person?"

"He never knew what he wanted to do."

Nancy sat forward, placed her feet flat on the floor. "I'm sorry, maybe this isn't a good time. I just thought it would be nice to talk."

"Why?"

Nancy's lip quivered. "Because you were his mum and I was his girlfriend."

"Was he nice to you?"

The question, out of the blue as it was, made Nancy start. She hesitated before she answered. "He was a lovely, caring man." Her tone sounded guarded, careful, as if she wasn't sure of her own words.

"Good."

More silence. Nancy twisted in her seat. "Do you have any photos of him when he was younger? I'd love to see them."

Audrey visibly bristled. "Why would I keep photos of a son that disowned me?" she said.

"What?"

"Oh, he never told you that?" She snorted. "He hasn't spoken to me in four years."

# Chapter **Thirty-Three**

The door to The Squirrel pub juddered as Jackman pushed it open. A knot of people crowded the bar, some drinking and chatting, others waving notes waiting to be served. A man and woman in suits raised wine glasses together in the corner; a large table at the side was filled with people in warehouse overalls, enjoying a drink after an early Friday afternoon finish from work. Jackman moved into the room. Almost immediately his head was drawn to raised voices. He followed the sound to a gap at the end of the bar showing a room beyond. The corner of a pool table jutted out from behind a cluster of bodies.

The warning from Mike Clarke entered his mind. It could just be an overreaction, but he wasn't about to take any chances. He turned to Davies. "Give me a couple of minutes, will you?"

She turned towards him. "You must be joking."

"I'm not. Any trouble, call for back up."

He didn't look back as he walked out of the room, crossed a corridor and into another area. The group had their backs to him and dispersed slightly as he approached. One of the men was leant across the pool table and they appeared to be moving position to watch the shot. The chatter quietened. Jackman paused. The potted ball was immediately followed by a low-bellied roar and swells of laughter. The man taking the shot stood back, a grin stretching across his face as he took a swig from his pint.

Jackman immediately recognised him from the photos Mike Clarke had emailed across.

He waited for the furore to die down before he spoke. "Luke Denton."

Heads turned.

Denton's eyes were on him. "Depends who's asking." he said.

Jackman introduced himself. Denton took another swig of his drink. "And?"

"I need you to come to the station to answer some questions."

Denton placed his pint down and stepped forward, snooker cue still in hand. "What did you say?"

"I said, I need you to come to the station. Now." He could feel the heat of the bodies as they encircled him.

"I'll just finish my game." Denton edged forward. Their faces were inches apart.

Jackman stood tall, eyes fixed on his. He could smell the beer on his breath. "I don't think so."

Several seconds passed. The whole pub hushed. Jackman could hear feet fidgeting around him, but didn't flinch. Denton chewed twice on his gum. Jackman could see the tattoo on his forefinger out of his peripheral vision. He thought of him grabbing Nancy, frightening her. He must have been twice her size.

Suddenly Denton broke away, grinned and placed down his cue. "You can keep the balls on the table, guys. We'll finish it later."

"I doubt it," Davies said pushing through the bodies behind and removing cuffs from her pocket.

\*\*\*

Nancy didn't hear the sound of her heels tapping the pavement, the thrum of cars engines passing, even the helicopter that passed overhead. All she could hear was the

211

sound of her own blood rushing through her ears as she pounded the streets that afternoon. She moved quickly, in an effort to get as far away from the icy atmosphere at Audrey's as possible.

Her body was trembling as she climbed into Becca's car. As soon as she saw her friend's face, the tears that she had held so bravely at bay sprung to her eyes.

Apart from a few soothing words, Becca hugged her friend, stroked her hair and said nothing. The tears became sobs, that eventually quietened and, as Nancy's breathing regulated, Becca spoke up. "Was it really that bad?"

Nancy pulled a tissue from her bag, blew her nose and sat back in her chair. "She was so cold, so detached. I couldn't have felt more unwelcome."

"Maybe she is still in shock?" Becca asked, hopefully.

"Maybe." Nancy opened her window, gulped the fresh air into her lungs. Meeting Audrey had only served to widen the void she felt inside. "Can we go home, please?"

Becca turned over the engine, pushed the car into gear and paused. She glanced in her wing mirror. "That's weird," she said.

Nancy was only half listening, her mind still running over her time with Audrey, desperately searching for something positive to draw from it. "What?"

"That blue Fiat." Becca turned, nodded towards a car parked down the road. "It was in our street this morning. I remember looking at the number plate, NN9, and thinking it was similar to Mum's. And it was parked on double yellow lines."

Nancy recalled the inspector's words the day before. Her cheeks reddened. She'd been so wrapped in the notion of meeting Evan's mum that she'd pushed the detective's advice to the back of her mind. "Oh, God…"

Becca didn't listen. Before Nancy could grab her arm, she'd climbed out of the car and was marching towards the Fiat. Bile rose in Nancy's throat. By the time she'd caught up with her friend, Becca had reached the passenger door window. She instantly gasped, "Darryl!" she said. "What are you doing here?"

Darryl looked sheepish, an expression which made him look younger than his years. A childhood friend of Ryan's, he'd always been shy, especially in the company of girls. "Ryan asked me to watch over Nancy today. He's been worried about her." He looked at his dashboard. "Wasn't expecting you guys to come out here though. I'm almost out of petrol."

Becca turned to Nancy.

"There's something I need to tell you," Nancy said. She smiled gratefully at Darryl and guided Becca back to their car. Nancy took a deep breath before she emptied out the events of the last few days: the note; the man stalking her; the video footage. They sounded even more sinister as she relayed them, especially after the time lapse, but she worked through the details meticulously and in chronological order, giving as much detail as she could. By the time she was finished she felt like a used balloon, every ounce of air squeezed from its insides.

Becca sat quietly, her face aghast. When Nancy explained about the police interview, she rounded on her. "Jesus, Nancy. Why didn't you tell me?"

"I couldn't put this on you. You've done so much for me already."

"Where's the guy now?"

"Who?"

"The man that's been following you?"

Nancy shrugged.

"And you still don't know why he wants all that money?" She shook her head.

"That explains all the texts from Ryan," Becca said. "I knew he was worried about you, but he's sent me several today, asking if you're okay."

Nancy looked across at her friend. "I'm so sorry, Becca."

"It's not your fault. Let's just find some money for Darryl so that he can fuel-up and we can get home. We'll all feel better once we're there."

*** 

"Don't you ever do that again," Davies said as they marched up the steps to the incident room. The journey back to the station had been a sour one. Davies insisted on sitting with the handcuffed Denton in the back.

It wasn't until they'd booked him into the custody suite that Jackman was able to account for his actions. And now he was starting to feel irritated. "I told you what Mike Clarke said. Liable to show off to his mates. And there's no point in us both being involved in a disturbance. Imagine all the paperwork." His attempt at a joke fell flat.

"What about you?" she said.

"I don't have a young kid."

"We should have taken someone else with us."

"There wasn't anyone else. They were all committed. I didn't think we'd need uniform, otherwise I would have called them. And I was right." The tight atmosphere was broken by Keane bursting out of the men's toilets in front of them, tucking his shirt into his trousers. He grinned, oblivious to their argument. "I was just coming to find you. Do you want the good news or the bad news?"

Jackman gave Davies a swift glance. "Make it good," he said.

"We've had some information about Anderson." Keane checked his watch. "He's on a flight home right about now. Due to land in less than an hour."

"He must think he's in the clear, coming back at a time like this," Davies said. "Somebody's bound to have got word to him."

"There's more," Keane said as he guided them down the corridor. "Forensics have matched sets of fingerprints on the

214

generator with those of Nick Anderson and Eamonn Benwell, as well as Richard Garrett."

"That's interesting," Jackman said. They'd reached the entrance door to the incident room now. "What's the bad news?"

"Janus has been here almost an hour. Asking for you. She's not happy."

Jackman felt his mobile vibrate and hung back as they entered the incident room. A text from Carmela:

*I'm free for the rest of the afternoon if you fancy that coffee.*

The door to the incident room flapped open. "She's in your office," whispered Davies. "Waiting."

"I'll just be a minute." He typed back a swift response:

*Sorry, can't do today. Something's come up with the case.*

Jackman walked into the incident room and joined Keane and Davies. He immediately spotted Janus sitting in his office in the far corner, tapping away at her computer. She looked up, closed her laptop and marched out to meet them.

"I think we need an impromptu meeting," she said. "Let's get up to date, see where we are." Chairs squeaked and tables were shoved aside, as everyone gathered around the front of the room. "Maybe you could start," she said to Jackman.

"We've picked up Denton, arrested him for demanding money with menaces from Nancy. He's with his solicitor at the moment. We have the CCTV stills from the supermarket, plus Nancy's description of his tattoo. Be interesting to see whether we can get any links to Anderson out of him during the interview."

"Anderson's on a plane now," added Keane. "Due to arrive at 5pm."

"Great," Janus said. "Get onto DI Warren at Birmingham CID, see if they can pick him up. Give my name if you have to. We'll cover their transport if they can bring him here. I want his phone seized as soon as he leaves the plane, before he has a chance to talk to anyone. We know his car was in the vicinity of the farm and barn on Sunday; his fingerprints confirm he's been there. Intelligence from Northampton gives him a motive. Let's get a warrant to search his house – see what else we can find."

"What about the drugs squad and their budget?" Davies asked.

"I'm not being pushed around by the drugs squad. This is a murder enquiry." A roar gathered momentum as it passed around through the room. Janus smiled. "All right, that's enough." She waited for the mumblings to die down. "Let's get everything organised. I want this done by the book." A fresh murmur of voices grew. Janus turned to face Jackman. "Can I have a word?"

Jackman followed her to his office and closed the door behind him. "What's up?"

"I need you to join us for a meeting upstairs in a quarter of an hour. The assistant chief constable is here, along with representatives from two other forces for a meeting. There's a new regional focus on drugs crime and they've shown a keen interest in the cannabis cultivation in your murder investigation."

"What about Mike Clarke? He's the drugs man."

"Oh, he's here with his flipchart and handouts. But we could do with your input on the reality of how it all fits into the case you're working on."

"I can't do this right now. We are just on the cusp of—"

"Yes, you can." Janus interrupted. "We'll get a POLSA-led team in to search Anderson's house, cars and businesses. Birmingham CID will pick him up at the airport."

"What about Denton?"

"Delegate. Get one of your team to interview him. Keane seems pretty well-versed in the evidence against him."

"Surely we can do this another time?"

Janus didn't attempt to hide her frustration. "No. Look, Will, you might as well get used to this. As a SIO your job is to set the strategy, update the policy log, allocate the budgets. Manage. Christ, I don't know any force where the inspectors are as hands-on as you are. If you want to make DCI and progress into management you need to be directing events, not picking up suspects and interviewing. And Justin Campbell is here from the Thames Valley's Serious Crime Unit. He'd be a good contact for you."

Jackman stared at her aghast. He wasn't interested in allocating budgets. The only reason he'd applied for promotion was so that he could run his own investigations without the likes of senior officers like Reilly breathing police politics down his neck at every opportunity. And meeting new contacts, discussing policing strategy and budgets was just about last thing he needed right now.

# Chapter **Thirty-Four**

Jackman felt oddly out of place seated around the table in the conference room later that afternoon. He was the only one in an open-necked shirt, although he had donned a jacket upon Janus' insistence.

A graph covered the screen at the end of the room and Justin Campbell from Thames Valley, a spindly-looking man who looked like he'd never left his office without a laptop tucked beneath his arm, was working through the trends in their crime figures. Jackman glanced across at a table at the far end of the room, loaded with cups, saucers and biscuits. Mike Clarke had enthusiastically opened the meeting and said there would be plenty of time to chat and 'share ideas' afterwards. Jackman cursed inwardly. Mike would be far better suited to the upcoming interview board than he ever would be.

His mind drifted back to the case. He wondered whether Keane had managed to get Denton to open up in interview; whether they'd gathered together any more evidence. The search team would be working their way through the snooker hall and Anderson's home on Saturn Way.

Jackman surreptitiously checked his watch. Anderson's plane had landed almost ten minutes earlier.

"Will, perhaps you'll fill us in on the cannabis cultivation at Upton Grange Farm?" Janus' voice snapped him back to the present. He sat forward, looked at the impassive faces around the table, and explained how the cannabis was stored, how they had discovered it, and how it was linked to cross-border supply.

Mike Clarke picked up where Jackman finished in his usual adept manner, with a PowerPoint presentation on what to look out for with cannabis farms, how to spot them early, what was involved. Jackman glanced at his watch again. Almost an hour had passed.

When Mike sat down, the assistant chief constable gave a long audible sigh. "It will be interesting to see how we get on with the alleged leader, a…" He looked down at his notes.

"Anderson, sir. Nick Anderson," Jackman said. He made a play of looking at his watch. "He should be arriving for interview at any moment. He'll be crucial in deciding how to take this forward."

Janus frowned at Jackman, but her superior surveyed him a moment over the top of his glasses before he spoke to the room. "Yes, I can see that. Let's see how we get on with Anderson. I don't want anything released in the media about the discovery at Upton Grange Farm until we know how far reaching the ramifications are. We'll put it all together as a new PR package, the introduction to our crack-down on Warwickshire's drug crime." It seemed nobody apart from Jackman recognised the pun, and if they did they certainly didn't show it. "Make sure you put your best officers on this one," he said to Jackman. "When did you say he was due to be interviewed?"

"He's due at the station any time now. If you don't mind, sir, I'd really like to get down there to keep an eye on things."

"Of course. Keep us updated."

Jackman didn't dare glance at Janus, battling to keep his composure, as he rose and left the room. As soon as he closed the door behind him he raced along the corridor and down the stairs.

The first person Jackman saw as he entered the incident room was Keane. "How did the interview go?" he asked.

"You didn't miss much. He's gone no comment throughout. Won't talk about his links to Nancy or Nick Anderson."

Jackman swiped a hand across his forehead. "Which solicitor does he have?"

"Miranda Holmes."

"She must think he's pretty damned if she's not even allowing him to give an alibi."

"The tattoo links him to Nancy. Russell has been through the town centre CCTV footage from the supermarket and we've found him on there, accosting her on Thursday. Can't link him to the video yet, but our techies are going through his phone. Even if he deleted it, it should still show."

"Good."

"There's more," Keane said. "We got the fingerprints back on the headlight assembly from the car used in Eamonn Benwell's hit-and-run. Since they're on the inside, they weren't damaged. It's a direct match with Denton's. And his phone pinged the signals in Stratford town centre between 10.18 and 10.37 last night. What with that and the photofit and possible ID from Amanda Grayson, we're pretty close to a charge for Eamonn Benwell's murder as well."

"Excellent. Get him arrested for the murder too, so that we are prepared. What about links to Garrett and Anderson?"

"Nothing more there yet, but Anderson's back and with his solicitor."

Jackman felt a presence behind him and turned to find Davies hovering. "Sir, I think there's something you might want to see."

They made their way down the stairs and into the back office of police reception. Jackman peered around the corner into the waiting area. An attractive blonde was sat, with a young girl beside her who shared the same blue eyes and was plaiting strands of her mother's hair. A boy was knelt on the floor, fiddling with his phone. He recognised them as the Anderson family from Mike Clarke's slides. "How long has she been here?" he asked Davies.

"Since the troops descended on her home to search. Refused to let them in at first. She seemed to know that her husband was being brought here, refuses to leave without him."

"She might have a long wait then," Jackman said as he withdrew his head. He thought for a moment. "She looks vaguely familiar – any record?"

Davies shook her head. "Nothing on her. Anderson's been cautioned for possession of cannabis, but apart from intelligence as long as your arm connected to drugs supply, he remains pretty clean himself. Probably gets someone else to do his dirty work."

Jackman thought about the tracker from the drugs squad placing his car at the farmhouse last Sunday. *It must have been something important to take him out there himself.* "Anything from the searches?"

"Nothing as yet. Not surprising, really. Whatever involvement he'll have had, he's bound to have covered his tracks well. He'd never have come home otherwise."

"Check with the electoral role, will you? See if there are any other properties registered under his name. We're searching the obvious – his house, the businesses. It's a long shot, but got to be worth a try. Those guns have to be somewhere."

She nodded.

"What did he have on him when he was arrested?"

"Just his phone really. We've sent it off to be examined, requested call records. Nothing significant in the rest of his luggage."

"See if you can get his phone sited for last Sunday evening too."

***

"Have you ever heard the name Luke Denton?" A line of sunlight streamed through the window of the flat, giving the appearance of a white sash across the detective's dark shirt.

Becca reached across, grabbed hold of Nancy's hand as she shook her head.

"We believe he was the man who sent the note, the video footage, and waited for you outside your flat," Russell said.

Nancy swallowed. "Who is he?"

"He's a local man, works in security. Mostly watches doors at the town's clubs. Occasionally he also enforces unofficial debts."

Nancy slid her eyes to Becca. "I don't understand."

"Our investigation is still ongoing," Russell said. "We are looking into everything, including any possible links with Upton Grange Farm."

Nancy screwed up her forehead. "You mean Evan?"

"We're not sure at this stage."

"But the note said that debts passed to next of kin.

"Next of kin, in their eyes, may mean anybody close to the debtor. Including girlfriends."

"What happens now?" Becca asked.

"Mr Denton has been charged with demanding money with menaces which he denied. He'll be kept at the station over the weekend and appear at the magistrate's court on Monday. We are also looking at him for some other offences. In view of the nature of the charge, there's a good chance he'll be remanded in custody."

"Thank goodness." The relief in Becca's voice was palpable.

Nancy stared at the detective, bewildered. "Are you saying that Evan borrowed money?"

"No. I'm saying that we have to look into every possibility to establish exactly what happened. We are not ruling anything out at the moment."

Nancy pushed her back into the sofa. She wasn't sure how many more surprises she could handle.

The detective stood. "Anyway, I wanted to let you know that we have somebody in custody."

"We're really thankful. Aren't we, Nancy?"

Nancy looked up at them both and gave a feeble smile.

Becca went downstairs to see her mother after the detective left, leaving Nancy on the sofa, picking through the detective's words.

Perhaps Evan was struggling for money. She knew the farm didn't pay well, he'd mentioned it a couple of times. The detective had been cagey, careful not to share more details. But six thousand pounds seemed a hefty amount to borrow. And for what? Surely he would have told her?

Although… Evan wasn't completely truthful. He'd lied about who he was.

Her mind raced. What did the real Evan Baker even look like anyway? Did he know that somebody was using the same identity as him? Was that even possible?

The newspaper article about the rape trial pushed into her mind. Her meeting with Audrey.

Her life was like a tangled ball of wool, and she couldn't work out how she was ever going to unravel it.

She grabbed her phone. She needed to get out of there.

# Chapter **Thirty-Five**

Jackman switched off the screen in front of him. After spending the last hour watching Keane carry out the initial interview with Nick Anderson, he felt tired and worn. Anderson knew the score, even better than the smug solicitor he had beside him. They had nothing, no evidence to link him with the murder apart from that they knew he was in the area, and a few fingerprints at the barn to link him to the cannabis cultivation. No proof whatsoever.

Jackman rubbed the heels of his hands into his eyes and inadvertently caught sight of the clock out of the corner of his eye: 7.30pm. He sighed, grabbed his mobile and called home. Celia answered almost immediately. "Hi, Dad."

"Hey. How was your day?"

"I gave Adrian his first taste of Stratford. We were proper tourists – went to Mary Arden's Farm and Anne Hathaway's Cottage. He even wanted to see if we could get late tickets to the theatre, but luckily there were none left."

Jackman laughed. Celia certainly didn't share her mother's love of Shakespeare.

"What time are you back?" she asked. "We were just thinking about dinner."

"I'm not sure, could be late. We've a suspect in custody. House searches." The line went quiet. "You still there?"

"Yes. It's just… I was hoping to see a bit more of you."

"I'm sorry, love. I'll make it up to you both tomorrow evening, I promise. We'll all go out for dinner somewhere together. My treat."

"Okay," she said. Her voice was laced with disappointment. "Better make it somewhere really good, it's my last night."

For some time after she'd rang off, Jackman pondered her reaction. Clearly it was important to her that he spend more time at home because Adrian was here. *She must be very keen on him*, Jackman thought. He scratched the back of his neck uncomfortably.

Russell knocked on his door. He beckoned her in. "I hope you've got some good news for me," he said. "Or failing that, a takeaway. I'm starving."

She laughed. "Nothing from any of the search teams, I'm afraid. They're both calling it a night. And no other properties registered to Anderson, apart from his wife's business. The phone companies can't get us call records until the morning, but his mobile phone pinged the masts in the vicinity of the farmhouse on Sunday night, which places him there at between 10.51 and 11.06pm."

"Thank goodness," Jackman said. "At least that gives us a reason to keep him. Tell Keane to let his solicitor know." She turned to go as another thought nudged him. "Is Mrs Anderson still here?" he asked.

"As far as I know. It seems she's staging a sit-in."

Jackman took the stairs down to reception two at a time. He could hear Davies' heavy breaths behind him, labouring to keep up. "Why do you want to speak to her?" she asked.

"I'm not sure exactly," Jackman said.

She rolled her eyes at him as they reached the bottom, but said nothing.

The reception area was almost empty as Jackman opened the back entrance. The woman immediately looked up. Jackman strode across the tiled flooring, introduced himself and Davies.

"When are you going to let my husband go?" she asked. She tilted her head towards the kids. "It's already past their bedtime."

"He's just helping us with some enquiries," Jackman said. "You should go home. He'll be in touch soon."

"I'm not budging."

"I want to go to the toilet." The young girl was pulling on her mother's forearm.

Mrs Anderson sighed. "All right." She looked across at her son. "Come on, Kyle."

He didn't look up. "I'm not going in the girl's toilets."

"Oh, for Christ's sake!"

"I'll stay here with him," Jackman said. "Until you get back."

She eyed him warily, looked back at her son. "Come and sit down on a chair and wait for us, Kyle. We'll only be a few minutes."

The boy moved across, took the chair next to Jackman, gave him a quick glance from beneath his fringe and continued to play a game on his phone. He looked no more than nine years old. Motorbikes raced around the screen.

"You like bikes?" Jackman asked.

The boy nodded, but didn't look up.

"Me too," Jackman continued. "I used to have a Ducati."

"What colour?"

"Red."

The boy looked up at him, his eyes wide. "My dad's got a yellow one."

"Has he? Nice. You ever been on it?"

The boy nodded warily, glanced back at the toilets before he spoke. "Only outside the garage. He's got a Harley Davidson too."

"Wow!" Jackman said. He exchanged a quick glance with Davies. There'd been no mention of motorbikes by the search teams. "Have you been on that?"

He nodded. His eyes were like saucers. "It goes really fast."

"Does it? You did well to get the speed up on your driveway."

"Not on our driveway."

"Oh?"

Another quick glance at the toilets. "In the blue garages behind the big road. Dad's got two." He nodded, as if he was sharing a special secret. "Mummy doesn't know about them."

The door to the toilets banged against the wall as it opened. Mrs Anderson was dragging her daughter by the hand, clearly agitated. "When are you going to let my husband out?" she said. "She's wet herself, she's so upset."

"I needed the toilet!" the girl said, but her pleading words were ignored.

"I really can't say," Jackman said. "He's with his solicitor now. Can we get you anything?"

Mrs Anderson huffed, her face taut.

"Look, why don't you go home?" Davies said. "We'll call you as soon as he is able to be released."

A wail rose in the background. "He pinched me," cried the girl.

Carly Anderson reddened as the girl threw herself on her mother. Davies put on her gentlest tone, worked on her some more and finally Carly Anderson agreed and walked out into the night, flatly refusing the offer of transport home.

As soon as the door was closed, Jackman hiked up the stairs, closely followed by Davies. They approached the map in the incident room, worked their way through possible locations. "Anyone know where there are banks of garages in town, with blue doors, close to a main road?" Jackman asked the room.

"I keep my camper in one off the Birmingham Road," Keane said. "Not ideal because it's tucked away and the kids ride their motorbikes up and down, but they're council owned and the rent is low. All the doors are blue."

"Find out if any of them are rented by either Anderson or his wife. Try her maiden name too." He grabbed his mobile. "I'll get another search team to stand by."

# Chapter **Thirty-Six**

Nancy wandered underneath the arrangement of clock faces that decorated the entrance to The Fish public house, through the restaurant and into the bar area. This was the first time she'd been here since losing Evan. The familiarity of the surroundings made her uneasy.

Ryan had sounded relieved to hear from her earlier. He was pleased that the police had apprehended a man for harassing her, keen to go out for a drink somewhere 'to celebrate'. He'd hesitated when she'd suggested The Fish, although hadn't argued against it. 'If it makes you feel better,' was all he'd said.

The bartender gave a smile as Nancy approached. "We were so sorry to hear the news, Nancy," she said. "How are you?"

It struck Nancy that she didn't know the bartender's name. She'd been so wrapped up with Evan, she'd never taken the trouble to find out. "I'm okay, thanks."

"What can I get you?"

"I'll have a vodka and coke," Nancy said. She looked back at Ryan.

"Lager top, please," he said.

Nancy allowed herself a furtive glance along the bar. Her eyes rested on Evan's seat at the end. Part of her expected to see him there, supping at his drink. Her eyes dropped to the scrapes on the tiles beneath where she used to pull the next stool across so they sat together, enveloped in their own little world.

"You all right, Nance?"

The sound of Ryan's voice snapped her back to the present. "Sure." He passed her a drink, stepped back to move away. "Wait." She grabbed his forearm. "Let's sit beside the bar. We can see what's going on from here."

Ryan turned his head to view the pub. In contrast to the tables in the restaurant around the other side, teeming with families enjoying a meal together, the bar area was sleepy for a Friday evening: a table of lads sat in the far corner, a couple on a round table at the side, an older couple leant against the old fireplace. When he looked back at her he was frowning. "There's not much going on in here tonight," he said.

Nancy ignored him and seated herself on the nearest bar stool, clearing the condensation on her glass.

Ryan hovered awkwardly next to her. "How are you feeling now?"

"I'm all right." She didn't look up. "Thanks for... you know. Looking out for me."

"I did it for my own peace of mind. Would have followed you myself if I could have got away from work. Must be good to put it behind you though," Ryan said. "To feel safe again." They sipped their drinks a moment. Nancy was suddenly aware of music playing in the background. She recognised Katy Perry's voice, although couldn't place the song. It blurred into the background, swimming around her head with the rest of the events of the last week.

"Explains one thing though," Ryan said, placing his glass down.

"What's that?"

"Why Cheryl was so upset. Maybe she was telling the truth."

Nancy pondered this a moment. She hadn't properly spoken with her mum since accusing her of drinking again. Perhaps she should call her. She reached down for her bag, moved her hand inside for her phone. Although... She couldn't be absolutely sure the man harassing her wasn't connected to Cheryl. The detective said they were still looking into things, trying to establish what had happened. And it wouldn't be the first time Cheryl had reneged on her promises. She let go of her phone and pulled back.

Nancy glugged the vodka back, banged the glass on the bar. It was loud, too loud.

"Nance, you okay?" Ryan said.

"Sure. I'll have another please. Make it a double."

Ryan had barely touched his drink. He ordered another, handed it over. She pressed it straight to her lips. "Take it easy, Nance. You know what you are like with drink."

She pulled the glass from her lips, angled her head. "And what is that?"

"You know what I mean." Ryan glanced about awkwardly.

"What, that I can't take my drink? Not like my mother?"

"Come on. You know I didn't mean that."

"Well, don't say it then," she snapped. The anger was raging through her so hard, so fast that all she needed, all she wanted right now, was another drink.

The barman switched the CD and the soft sounds of the Cranberries filled the bar area. Nancy and Ryan drank in silence.

She finished her glass, placed it down on the bar. "I'm just going to the loo." Her voice had raised a decibel, almost on its own.

Nancy could feel the heat in her cheeks. Eyes boring into her. She looked around, just in time for two men in the corner to avert their gaze. A couple at the end of the bar were deep in conversation. They flicked a quick glance at Nancy and continued. She turned on her stool to find a sea of eyes look away awkwardly. The bar area had hushed. People weren't staring. They were consciously looking away. It couldn't have been more obvious.

A single notion pushed through the hazy fog that now wrapped itself around her mind. Did these people think she'd filled Evan's place? She could imagine their sordid little conversations in the car on the way home, 'He's not even cold and she's out with someone new.' Her blood boiled. How quick people were to judge. It was the same for Evan with his background. How dare they?

Nancy stood. The room blurred slightly. She wavered, realising she hadn't eaten since breakfast. Becca had stopped at the motorway services on the way back and ordered a sandwich, but Nancy had settled for a latte. Her insides had been far too chewed up with meeting Audrey to be able to negotiate food.

"Hey," Ryan placed his arm around her. "Careful."

She pushed him away. "I'm fine. Just need to get something to eat."

"Okay, let's go and get something."

Nancy gave a single nod. "I'll just go to the ladies, first."

The walk around the edge of the bar to the ladies' room was one she had done numerous times in the past, but never with such great concentration. She battled to keep straight, pressing one foot carefully in front of another, kept her head high.

As soon as she was through the door she rushed to the sink and splashed her face with cold water, then pressed her forehead to the cold marble. When she stood she felt calmer.

But one thing was clearer in her mind than ever before. Evan might have taken someone else's name, their identity, but he was no fraud. The Evan she knew was a kind, considerate man, he would never have hurt anyone, and she was sick to death of people making judgements about him. She reached into her bag, searched around the side pocket, pulling out a pack of gum and a blister pack of paracetamol. She pressed out a couple of tablets, holding her hair back so that she could drink from the tap to swallow them down, then placed a minty stick of gum on her tongue. As she replaced the packet, her fingers caught the edge of something. It slipped out of her bag and fell to the floor. Nancy reached down and curled a nail underneath the business card from the journalist. She rose and stared at it for several moments, before grabbing her phone and punching out the numbers. It was about time people found out who *her* Evan Baker was.

***

"You asked to see me?" Jackman faced Miranda Holmes as he spoke. The fact that she was representing both Luke Denton and Nick Anderson wasn't lost on him.

"You have arrested my client for murder, yet you have no evidence to link him to the crime."

Jackman leant back and watched her irritably scratch the point of a manicured nail down the side of her neck. She was well-known in the station, with her expensive suits and her abrasive manner. Strangely, even though it showed them as well-connected criminals, suspects supported by Miranda Holmes wore her representation like a badge of honour, as if they'd really made it. He wondered how she managed to sleep at night. "Are we talking about Mr Anderson?"

"We are."

"I have a number of other matters to put to him."

"Come on, Inspector. You and I both know it's all circumstantial."

"How much is he paying you to stay here this long?"

"I really don't think that's relevant." She started gathering her papers together. "He's tired after his flight. I suggest you let him go home to his family."

There was a knock at the door and Russell's head appeared. She widened her eyes as she asked to speak to him. Jackman excused himself.

"They've located the garages," Russell said when they were safely out of earshot. "They're rented in Carly Anderson's maiden name which is why they didn't flag up before. There's a false back on one of them. The search team missed it at first, it's a professional job. Behind it they found some firearms and an array of different mobile phones."

"Are any of the firearms linked to Upton Grange?"

"We've linked the serial numbers of three firearms with those registered to Mr Lawton at Upton Grange Farm. We've sent a mobile fingerprint machine down there to see if we can lift anything."

"Brilliant." Jackman let out a relieved sigh. "We finally have something to go on."

"Shall we prepare the suspect for another interview?"

Jackman glanced back at the door behind him. "No, not tonight." He gave her a wink and let himself back into the room.

Anderson's solicitor pursed her lips as he approached. "Well?"

"You are right, of course, Mr Anderson would be tired after his flight." She raised her eyebrows. "He can bed down here for the night as I now have a lot more questions for him."

# Chapter **Thirty-Seven**

Nick Anderson stared defiantly at Jackman. He looked fresh, despite spending the night in a police cell, the shadow across his chin the only clue that he'd been denied his home comforts.

In contrast, Jackman was running on adrenalin. He'd stayed late last night, assisted by one of the intelligence officers they'd called in especially to help, and ploughed through the contacts and text messages on the mobile phones found in the garage. The hours passed by. He was almost ready to quit for the night when they placed a loose SIM card into one of the phones and a string of messages came up to another party named 'Evan'. Texts such as: *The debts are coming out of your share*, and *Do as you are told*. They'd have to wait for billing from the mobile phone company to identify any further details and that would be after the weekend. There was nothing on Evan's mobile phone that they'd found at the farmhouse, but knowing that it was usual for dealers to use different phones and SIM cards to lessen the chance of detection, Jackman really felt they were onto something. He'd arrived home just after 3am, his head buzzing, making for a fitful few hours of sleep before he stepped back into the station at 7.30 that morning.

Miranda Holmes leant forward. "Inspector, we've been in here for almost half an hour and according to my watch you only have another five hours to hold my client. Do you have something new? Because, if not, I suggest it's time to consider release."

Jackman ignored her. He focused on Anderson. "We know you were at the farm on Sunday evening."

"No, you traced my phone there," Anderson said. "And I told you, I lost it."

"So you weren't there at all?"

"I was at home. My car was parked on the drive. I'm sure my wife will vouch for that. You have spoken to her?" He slung himself back over the chair, a bored expression spreading like a stain across his face.

"We have. But your car wasn't on the drive, was it? It was at the barn."

Miranda sat upright. "Do you have some proof of this, Inspector?"

Jackman looked from one to another. Protocol meant that he couldn't release details of the tracker.

Anderson scoffed. Said nothing.

Jackman surveyed him a moment. "How long have you rented the garages off the Birmingham Road?"

A muscle flexed in Nick Anderson's jawline.

Jackman made a play of looking at his notes. "Numbers 34 and 35, I believe."

"I don't know what you are talking about."

"It's where you and your son ride on your motorbikes, isn't it?"

"Who told you that?"

"There's a camera rigged up on one of the garages opposite yours. Barely visible."

Anderson turned away.

"It's also where you stored the guns you stole from the farmhouse."

"I've never seen any guns."

"Strange," Jackman said. "Because they have your prints all over them. Along with the collection of mobile phones and SIM cards we found there."

Anderson glowered at Jackman.

"Are you sure you don't want to say anything about the

phones? Their text messages certainly make for interesting reading."

Anderson gave his solicitor a single sideways glance. "No comment."

*\*\*\**

An hour later, Jackman took a deep breath and placed his plastic cup on the table in front. "Something doesn't feel right."

They were seated in a spare meeting room waiting for the custody sergeant to call them through to formally charge Anderson. Janus had called in on her day off, keen to be a part of the action.

Davies glared at him. "What do you mean?"

He averted his gaze, deep in thought. "Let's work it back. What was Denton's motive?"

"We know he killed Eamonn Benwell," Davies said. "It's on CCTV."

"I'm not denying that, but why?"

"To frame him for the murder in the barn. Probably thought he was doing Anderson a favour. Eamonn was linked to the barn through his cars."

"Anderson could have killed Evan in any number of ways. Why would he burn down and ruin a cannabis farm that he could take over and reap the rewards from?"

"To send a message to Northampton? Put an end to their fight?"

Jackman scratched the corner of his temple. "Why take the guns, then?"

Davies shrugged. "Maybe they were his security policy."

"It seems soft to me."

"You think too much," Janus said. "We've got him in custody. His fingerprints were at the barn. We can place him near the scene on Sunday. Some of the SIM cards contain suspect messages to Evan. He has means and motive."

236

"We know the victim had a bang to the head. How did he transport the body from the farmhouse to the barn?"

"We still need to establish that. It's likely he had help."

"Doesn't explain why he would burn down the barn."

Janus sighed. "The CPS have agreed a murder charge, pending further enquiries."

"We won't get the phone billing until Monday," Davies said. "And there's a wealth of text messages and numbers to work through."

"But for today, it's over," Janus said. "And it's a great result. Send everyone home to get some rest. Issue a brief announcement to the press and we'll follow it up after the weekend. You need to be fresh for Monday. We're releasing the news of the cannabis farm next week, part of Warwickshire's new campaign against drugs. The chief constable will be coming over himself to launch it."

Jackman cringed. It was extraordinary how Janus could spin this case around so that it represented a result for the police, a PR exercise. The two men who'd lost their lives would pale into the background. He'd often thought her hard-nosed approach would be better suited to a manufacturing plant than a people-based service.

The custody sergeant's face appeared around the doorframe. "Okay, you're up," he said. "He's at the front desk."

\*\*\*

Jackman dragged his feet on their way back up to the incident room after they'd made the formal charge, still trying to work through Anderson's motivation in his mind. He recalled the text message: *The debts are coming out of your share*. Why would Anderson burn down Evan's only source of income to pay back the debt? It didn't make sense.

The cheer that rose as he entered the room took him by surprise, forcing him to push the questions to the back of his mind. He held up a hand. "Well done, everyone. Brilliant work." He dug his hand into his pocket, pulled out a few notes. "Pop out and get a round of pizzas, will you?" he said to Davies.

"You're not coming?"

He shook his head. "Take Keane with you. He's the resident pizza expert." He turned and collected his keys off the table. "There's something I need to do. Won't be long."

# Chapter **Thirty-Eight**

As Nancy woke she was immediately assaulted by a slice of daylight seeping in through the gap in the top of her curtains. She turned away, jammed her eyes closed. The movement induced a surge of bile to her throat, causing her to rush to the bathroom and hang her head over the toilet. She retched, hard. Several times. Only to vomit a small amount of liquid.

The heat in her head cooled as she sat back on her heels. She recalled leaving the toilets at the pub last night, feeling the weight of eyes follow her back to the bar. Bickering with Ryan over a request for another drink, the cool air of the car park. Then nothing. Last Sunday she'd experienced a similar memory blank. The night Evan died. Fear curled its long fingers around her shoulders. Was the memory loss last Sunday really a result of the concussion or was alcohol masking her senses, blocking her mind. Just like it did with her mother.

Ryan used to laugh at her when they were together. He called her a cheap date because she only ever drank a single glass of wine. She placed a hand over her eyes. He wouldn't be calling her that this morning. Nancy stood, padded into the kitchen, grabbed the washing-up bowl and took it back to bed.

The pain in her head eased slightly, pushed aside by a barrage of thoughts teeming around her mind. For as long as she could remember, she'd avoided drinking alcohol.

Never once had she come home drunk, been ill and forgotten herself, although she'd nursed Becca through a hangover many a time. Ryan had indulged her sobriety; she drove his car when they went out. In contrast, Evan always drove and encouraged her to sample different shorts and enjoy the experience. 'Drinking a few glasses doesn't make you an addict,' he'd said. She cursed. But if only she hadn't drunk last week, she'd be able to remember what happened.

She looked at his photo on the bedside table. The man accused, arrested and charged with rape. The very thought wrenched her heart into her mouth every time it crept into her mind. Rape was such a heinous, violent crime. Her Evan wasn't perfect – obsessive in his tidiness, and he liked things done a certain way. But she couldn't believe he was capable of such a twisted act.

Detective Russell's visit rang out in her mind. They were looking into links with the farm and the man harassing her for money. Was Evan killed because he was involved in something illegal? Or was history repeating itself with misguided judgements? She wouldn't let that happen again. She couldn't.

Nancy hauled herself up and into the shower. The tepid water slowly calmed her nerves. As she climbed out and got dressed, she could hear the door open in the shop below. Becca and Karen had returned from setting up the weekend's event flowers and were preparing for the Saturday morning rush. She checked her watch and just had time to pull a brush through her hair before the doorbell sounded.

The door was opened to reveal an elegantly dressed woman in a trouser suit and matching dark rimmed glasses. She clutched a briefcase in her right hand. Elise Stenson's dark hair was smoothed back into a bun this morning, accentuating her prominent cheekbones. "Where would you like me?" she said.

\*\*\*

Dark rainclouds were rapidly gathering overhead by the time Jackman entered Tiddington Road. He could see the twinkling lights of a modern chandelier illuminating the front room as he left the car and crossed the driveway. His knocks at the door were followed by a trampling of feet pounding the stairs. Music was switched on, a heavy beat thumped from the room above.

He waited a moment, knocked again. Finally the door pulled open to reveal Amanda Grayson. She was dressed casually in a pair of black jeans and long white top, her hair tied back loosely. The light dusting of make-up she wore did little to hide the dark shadows that hung beneath her eyes.

"Sorry about that," she said, raising her eyes skyward as she let Jackman in. "They've got the devil in them today. I guess it's understandable. Their dad moved out this morning."

Jackman gave a sombre nod and followed her into a long kitchen. An oversized work station dominated the middle of the room, surrounded by matching cupboards; a table at the far end overlooked a long garden.

"Can I get you a drink?"

"No, thank you. I have some news. We've arrested a man for Eamonn's murder."

Amanda stood very still. "Who is it?"

"His name is Luke Denton, he's a local Stratford man. He was charged yesterday and will be remanded in custody, pending trial."

"Do you know why?"

"Not at the moment. Our investigations are still ongoing."

A sense of disquiet hovered in the room. Amanda Grayson reached for a nearby stool, manoeuvred herself onto it. "It's such an unnecessary tragedy," she said.

Jackman thought back to his initial meetings with Eamonn Benwell when he'd expressed what appeared to be genuine concern that the body in the barn might be Evan. Yes, there

241

were question marks over his bank accounts, his income, but perhaps he was fiddling the books, not putting jobs through to keep them from his wife. That would explain the cash under the floor in his flat. His fingerprints on the generator placed him at the barn, but he'd never denied he'd spent time there. He was a man who thought he'd found a safe place to store his cars and unknowingly become involved in a drugs ring. A ring that ultimately led to his own murder. Perhaps his only sin was not cooperating with the police, or giving them an explanation for his movements on Sunday. The idea, unpalatable as it was, wedged itself in the back of Jackman's mind.

Amanda lifted her gaze. "Thank you. For coming here to tell me." She took a deep breath. "I'd like to be alone now."

# Chapter **Thirty-Nine**

The rain had burst through the clouds and was hammering the windscreen by the time Jackman pulled into the Rother Street station car park. He had to drive around to find a space and finally squeezed in at the far end. In the short time it took him to cross to the staff entrance, his shirt was soaked and his hair flattened, pressing down onto his forehead.

As soon as he passed through the door he shook his shoulders, sending a spray of water droplets kicking back at the glass doors. It wasn't until he looked up that he saw a figure hovering at the bottom of the stairs.

"Carmela. I wasn't expecting to see you."

She stepped forward. The jeans and raincoat did nothing to tone down her natural glamour. Her sleek hair was tied back from her face. A plastic folder tucked underneath her right arm. "Only just arrived. Tried your home. When there was no answer, I guessed you'd be here." She smiled. "You can sack the guard dog, he didn't make a sound."

Jackman laughed. "He isn't there. My neighbour looks after him when I'm at work."

"Not the neighbour with the damaged door, I hope?"

He laughed. "No, different one."

"Any news on that incident?"

"The woman's still away. Uniform reached her on holiday in Wales. The door's secure and she doesn't seem in any hurry to come back."

"Good job we were nearby."

Jackman smiled and pushed a hand through his hair, loosening yet more water droplets. "Didn't think you were working today."

"I'm not." She cleared her throat. "But I found some more stuff for you on protecting vulnerable people. It's a current priority for Thames Valley Police. Thought it might come in useful." She stepped forward, proffered the folder.

"Thanks." Jackman reached out and nodded gratefully as he took it.

"How's your case doing?"

"We charged this morning."

"That's wonderful news."

"I'm just here to tie up a few loose ends."

"Right. I could hang around, if you've time for a quick coffee that is?"

Jackman checked his watch, pulled a face. "Sorry, I can't. I'm meant to be meeting my daughter in an hour. I really don't mean to keep turning you down."

"Not to worry." Her face brightened, but her eyes looked disappointed.

At that moment, Keane and Davies crashed through the doors, a tumble of chatter and laughter, as if they'd just shared a joke. They stopped short when they saw Carmela.

"Hello again," Davies said.

Carmela nodded at her.

Davies turned to Jackman. "Ready to celebrate?" Keane held up four pizza boxes. "Are you joining us?" Davies said to Carmela.

"Not today, thanks."

"You're welcome to," Jackman said awkwardly.

"Another time, maybe."

"Okay." Davies turned to Jackman. "See you in a minute. Don't leave it too long, otherwise there will be none left." They bounded upstairs, still chuckling.

Jackman looked across at Carmela. "Sorry about that. You'll be missing out though, sure you don't want to join us?"

Carmela shook her head and smiled. "Congratulations on the result." She moved forward. A brief touch on his forearm. "Let me know how it goes on Monday."

He drew a heavy breath as he watched her walk out into the car park, scratched the back of his neck. Problem was he liked Carmela. A little too much. The heavy rain had stopped now, leaving a soft shower in its wake. He waited until she'd reached her car, turned and climbed the stairs.

A roar rippled around the incident room as he entered, followed by a couple of wolf whistles. Jackman gave a rueful smile, crossed to his office and changed into a dry shirt. By the time he emerged, bodies were standing around, sprawled across chairs, perched on the edge of desks, tucking into pizza.

Davies passed him a box of a half-eaten cheese pizza. "Didn't know the training department was working weekends," she said with a wink. "Must have plenty of money left in their budget."

Jackman ignored her, leant back against the filing cabinets and shoved a slice of pizza into his mouth. He hadn't eaten since breakfast and it tasted almost as good as it smelled. The second slice went down easier. Jackman loved this part of the force. After a week of long hours, pulling together, supporting each other, often at the expense of their personal lives and families, it was good to see so many smiles. Time passed by without notice. He gave a brief speech thanking every one of his team for their input this past week. Even Janus called in to offer her congratulations, relieved at clearing two high-profile crimes from her lists. The hard graft would start again on Monday: securing a charge was one thing, building a convincing case for the Crown Prosecution Service to take to trial quite another. But for now, celebrations prevailed. The youngsters were talking about moving on to the pubs to extend the frivolities. The mature staff were starting to peel off, to spend what was left of the weekend with their families.

Jackman glanced around idly, his eyes searching the room

for Davies. He moved through the bodies and finally caught sight of her in his office. She was combing her fingers through the loose curls that had come detached from her hair tie and fell across her face, poring over some paperwork on his desk.

"You okay?" he asked as he walked in.

She looked up, but her eyes were lost in thought. "Think so. Just had a thought and came to look at a call that came into the incident room this morning."

"What is it?"

"A woman in North London. Saw the national appeal and called in. Said she had some information on the victim that might be useful."

"What kind of information?"

"Don't know. It was given a low priority after the charge, but something about it has nagged at me all day. The name was unusual, so I looked it up." She passed an A4 printed sheet to Jackman. It was a copy of a newspaper article reporting a trial. "Her daughter was raped as well."

Jackman pulled himself from the article, looked at Davies. "Not by Garrett?" Davies shook her head. "No, but I remember it in the press at the time. The case didn't secure a conviction at trial. Just like Garrett's." She shook her head, as if to dismiss the thoughts inside. "Oh, I don't know. Something about it feels odd. Why call in now?"

"We'll bump up the priority. Follow it up first thing Monday."

She grabbed the sheet of paper from him and placed it in a tray with a nest of other notes of phone calls still to be followed up from the public appeal. "Better get back to see if my baby boy has cut that tooth yet. What about you? Any plans with your new friend?" She raised a teasing brow.

Jackman shook his head.

"Oh, come on. You'd be mad not to see that she's taken rather a shine to you."

"She's just been helping me out with something."

"So you said."

Jackman ushered her out of his office and back into the incident room where he bade her and the final few officers goodbye. He smiled to himself as he cleared away the last of the pizza boxes. Nothing like a group of cops to devour a takeaway.

His mobile buzzed and he was surprised to see Janus' name flash up on the screen.

"Will, have you seen the *Stratford Mail*'s latest report?" Her voice was tight.

"Not just yet, I—"

"You'd better take a look. Now."

\*\*\*

"Oh, look Nance. Your article is up." Becca sat at the table picking at a warm sausage roll while checking her iPad with her free hand.

Nancy placed the last mug on the drainer, emptied the washing-up bowl and wiped her hands. "That was quick."

"Well, I guess she needed to process it," Becca said through a mouthful of food. "Otherwise it'd probably have to wait until Monday."

Nancy leant into the screen.

*The Man Behind the Fire*

*In the early hours of Monday 10th August, a man's body was found in a burnt-out barn in the Warwickshire countryside, between the villages of Ardens Grafton and Exhall. Police treated the death as suspicious and launched a murder enquiry. Evan Baker, from nearby Upton Grange Farm, was reported missing and police appealed for witnesses that might have seen him on the night of the murder to come forward.*

*Last Thursday, police confirmed the identity of the body in the fire as Richard Garrett, although he has been living under the name of Evan Baker for some time.*

*Richard Garrett, originally from Northampton, was*

*charged with rape four years ago. He was remanded in custody pending trial, but later acquitted of all charges.*

*Evan – also known as Richard – was out with his girlfriend, Nancy Faraday, on Sunday night to celebrate their three-month anniversary. Nancy, who is currently grieving the loss of her boyfriend, said, "This is a tragedy. Evan was a kind and loving man who will be sadly missed."*

*When questioned about his change of identity, Nancy said, "People were out to out get him. Irrespective of the truth, they made judgements. Richard changed his name to Evan due to people's prejudices."*

*The police have been examining the farm since Monday, using diggers and excavation machinery.*

*A spokesperson for Warwickshire Police declined to comment on the use of diggers. They simply answered, "The police investigation is ongoing. If you have any information about the incident, please contact Warwickshire Police…"*

The accompanying photograph was one of Evan taken off Nancy's phone and slightly blurred.

"God, it's awful," Nancy said. "What about all the stuff I told her about him? She hasn't put any of that in. Just concentrated on the trial and change of identity."

Becca placed a hand on her shoulder. "I'm sorry, Nance. You knew the real Evan. That's all that matters. Should I cancel tonight? Only with everything that's happened…"

Nancy looked across at her friend. She'd completely forgotten that it was the anniversary of Becca's father's death. Becca and her mother had planned to go to the theatre in London. They marked the date every year, just the two of them, and it seemed awful for Nancy to ask them to cancel. "Of course not," she said. "How many years is it now?"

"Seven," Becca said. "I can't believe how quickly it's passed."

"No, you go," Nancy said. "I'll be fine here. Just have a quiet night in."

"Okay, well, maybe Ryan will come over?"

"Maybe."

Becca checked the clock. "Right, I have to go back to work. We'll never be going anywhere tonight if we don't get today out of the way."

\*\*\*

The phone was ringing as Jackman wandered wearily back into his office later that afternoon. He grabbed the receiver, introduced himself.

"Where is everyone?" Janus' voice snapped down the end of the phone.

"You gave them a pass for the rest of the weekend, after the charges this morning."

A single tut clicked down the end of the phone. "I've just heard your statement on the news."

Jackman sat down heavily in his chair. After the speculation in the newspaper article, he'd been forced to make an impromptu statement to the press. He'd kept it suitably vague, avoiding any mention of the work at the barn, concentrating on the arrests they'd made, the progress with the murder investigation. "Hopefully the promise of a full statement next week will keep the beast at bay," he said.

"I'm not sure anything will keep Elise Stenson down. The sooner we release details of the cannabis cultivation the better. Enjoy the rest of the weekend and let me know if you hear anything in the meantime."

He replaced the receiver, grabbed his coat and headed for the door. At the last minute, he remembered his wet shirt from earlier, doubled back to his office and peeled it from the back of the chair. His eyes simultaneously rested on the notes of the phone call Davies had been talking about. Against his better judgement, he picked up the woman's contact details and the printouts, placed them in the back of the plastic folder Carmela had given him earlier and strode out of his office, pulling the door closed behind him.

# Chapter **Forty**

Celia was brushing her mother's hair when Jackman entered Alice's room at Broom Hills later that afternoon.

"Hi, Dad." She smiled.

He bent down and kissed her forehead before doing the same to his wife. "What time did you get here?" he asked.

"An hour ago. Thought we'd wait for you."

"I got held up." He gave an apologetic shrug.

Adrian wandered through with a couple of coffees and smiled a greeting. "Can I get you one?" he said, holding up a cardboard cup.

Jackman shook his head. "No, thanks."

"How long have you got?" Celia asked.

"I'm finished for the weekend now."

She beamed back at him. "That's great. Adrian and I have something special planned for all of us tonight."

Her obvious pleasure warmed Jackman. He listened as Celia chatted away to her mother about college. Adrian chipped in at intervals. Jackman watched him, impressed. Many of their friends and family were awkward in Alice's presence, not sure of what to say or how to act. Yet Adrian appeared unfazed.

Jackman decided to stay on awhile after they left and read the highlights from the day's newspaper to his wife. He flicked through, giving her one-line snippets on each article, then turned to the sports section. Alice loved sports. He was in the middle of an article on women's football when he recalled that Adrian played basketball at college. He looked across at his wife, about to share the joke about Erik messing up Adrian's shoes when he paused. She looked tired, the pallor of her skin tinged with grey. Now wasn't the right time.

Jackman folded the newspaper, leant forward and pressed the button of the bed to lay her flat. The drone of the electrics filled the room. As he sat back, his mobile hummed in his pocket. It was a message from Carmela:

*Hope the information is useful. Make sure you read the piece at chapter two.*

The folder in his inside pocket pressed against his chest. He pulled it out and leafed through the pages to chapter two. It was headed 'Protecting Vulnerable People'. He pictured Carmela's face that morning. She'd gone out of her way to drive across with the information on her day off. Idly, he flicked back through her previous text messages. Memories of the other evening brought a smile to his lips.

He raised his eyes longingly at Alice. Her head rested to the side, her eyelids drooped. He looked at his wife for several minutes before his shoulders slumped. He shut down his phone, stuffed the pages back into the folder, tucked it back into his inside pocket, bid her farewell and left the room.

\*\*\*

The knock at the door woke Nancy with a start. The book, balanced precariously on her lap, fell to the floor. She blinked, checked the clock. It was almost a quarter to seven. She retrieved the book from the floor, flicked through to find her place. Only a few pages into the chapter. She must have fallen asleep almost immediately after Becca had left. The door banged again. She jumped, cursed her frayed nerves and moved out to the hallway. A shadow was visible behind the glass. "Who is it?"

"Nance, it's me. Open up."

Ryan grinned as she pulled the door open, holding his hands out wide. He grasped a bottle of Pinot Grigio in one hand, a box of Cadbury's Milk Tray in the other – her favourites. "Thought you might like some company."

"I'm sorry about last night," she said.

"It's forgotten." He raised his hands, winked. "Well?"

The gesture was so touching, she couldn't resist. "I'm not in the mood for drinking, but I'll take the chocolates."

"Knew you would."

She stood aside for him to enter, locked the door firmly behind him. "Do you want a glass for that?" she said, nodding at the bottle.

"I'd rather have a cup of tea," he said. "No fun drinking on your own."

As she moved into the kitchen he jumped in front of her. She caught a waft of his aftershave. "I'll make it. You go and sit down."

Nancy didn't need telling twice. Every tendon in her body cried out with fatigue. She returned to the lounge, rested back on the sofa and flicked through the television channels. By the time Ryan had returned with two mugs of tea, an old episode of *Friends* was playing.

"Great," he said. "Love this." He pushed himself into the gap next to her. His skin felt soft and warm.

Nancy's eyelids grew heavy. "I'm not sure I'm going to be up to much Ryan. I might have to go to bed soon."

"No problem. Kick me out whenever you are ready." He peeled the cellophane off the chocolates, pulled back the lid and placed them on her lap. "They'll wake you up."

They watched the screen for a while, tucking into the chocolates, drinking their tea. Time passed by easily.

"I'm going to open that wine," Ryan said eventually. "Are you sure you won't join me?"

She looked up at him. "Well, maybe a small one."

Ryan retreated to the kitchen and returned almost immediately with the open bottle and two glasses. He passed one across. Sharp and citrusy, it went down easily. The theme tune to another episode flashed up on the screen. She held her glass up for a refill.

"You sure?" he said, and chuckled.

Nancy hesitated. Thoughts of her mother entered her mind. Drinking last night, the hazy recollections... "No, actually I'll have a water. Clear my head."

Ryan's eyes glistened in the half-light of the corner lamp when he returned with her water. He poured himself another wine.

A party atmosphere filled the screen. Bodies were squashed into a tiny space, talking, laughing. Ryan turned to Nancy. "Do you remember when we had that party at my house, when my parents went away?"

Nancy laughed. "It made us the most popular kids at school. For a week."

"Only because you announced it on Facebook."

She nudged him with her shoulder. "Your parents came home early. I'll never forget your mum's face – I thought they were going to kill us."

They both chuckled. The water sloshed about in her glass and Nancy wavered to avoid a spillage. Her head felt warm and heavy. "Was worth it though, wasn't it? The beer we hid kept you going for ages afterwards." They both laughed again. Ryan tipped his head to the side, knocking it gently on hers. She could smell his shampoo, sporty and sweet. Closed her eyes. His lips touched hers, soft and inviting.

Nancy pulled back quickly. Too quickly. "What are you doing?"

"I... I don't know." He looked genuinely surprised.

Nancy shook her head. "I think you'd better leave."

Ryan stood. "Nance, I'm so sorry. I don't know what came over me. I think it was talking about..."

Nancy stood as well. "You should go, Ryan."

He followed her out into the hallway. "I'm really sorry, Nance."

After she'd closed the door behind him and checked the locks, she retrieved the glasses from the lounge and washed them up, her eyes burning. It had been lovely to sit with Ryan, comfortable. Just like old times. But it was all too soon. What about Evan?

Sleep evaded Nancy for some time that night, in spite of fatigue to the point of exhaustion cocooning her body. When it finally did take a hold it was errant and divisive, filled with broken dreams, old memories morphing into new. She woke several times. It wasn't until the daylight splintered through the gaps in her curtains that she finally fell into a deep all-encompassing slumber.

***

The smell of barbequed meat wafted through the air as Jackman got out of the car later that evening. He walked past the front door and entered at the side gate, shouting his greeting.

An ever-keen Erik bounded around to meet him, his tail circling. Jackman gave him a pat and edged past him into the back garden.

"Hi!" Celia waved a pair of tongs at him from behind the BBQ. With her fair hair tied messily behind her back and her slender figure, she looked just like her mother. Alice had loved to cook too and from a young age, Celia had felt compelled to join her.

"Hey," he called. "I was going to take us all out for dinner since it's your last night."

"I've got burgers," Celia said. "Homemade. Hungry?"

"Am now." He crossed the lawn to the patio and planted a kiss on his daughter's cheek. "Where's the soft lad?"

"Dad, stop it," she said, although her voice melted into a chuckle. "He's just getting us some beers."

Almost on cue, Adrian emerged from the back of the house carrying two bottles. He raised one of them to Jackman. "Hi. Didn't realise you were back. Want one?"

"There's some mineral water at the bottom of the fridge for Dad," Celia said.

Adrian placed the beers on the table. "I'll just get you one."

"I've made some extra spicy chilli burgers, just for you," Celia said as Adrian disappeared.

"Great." He settled himself into a chair.

"Well, I did say we had something special planned."

"Thanks. What else have you guys been up to today?" he asked as Celia started placing the food into buns.

"We had lunch with Sam and Mikey."

"Sounds good."

Adrian emerged with Jackman's mineral water. Dinner was served. They chatted away as they ate, Adrian even made a joke about shoes which made them all laugh.

Erik sat underneath the table patiently waiting for any scraps to fall, then flitted off and returned with a tennis ball, dropping it at the end of the patio. Adrian grabbed it and threw it down the garden. The dog immediately retrieved it.

"Think you've made a new friend there," Jackman said.

Celia shot him a thankful smile and Jackman relaxed back in his chair. The burgers had gone down easily and as the time passed, he could feel his eyes growing heavy.

"You look tired," Celia said. "Late night?"

"You could say that." He stood, stretched his arms out. "Think I'll turn in."

"Sure you're okay for the airport run tomorrow?"

"Of course," he said, suppressing the sadness in his voice.

# Chapter **Forty-One**

A taxi pulled up behind Jackman as he pulled the last case out of the car and closed the boot. "Are you sure you've got everything?" he asked Celia.

She looked down at the luggage. "Think so. But they do have shops in Sweden too, Dad, so it's not the end of the world."

He encased her in a tight hug. It would be at least six weeks before he saw her again and although he'd grown accustomed to her long absences at university, the thought of her being in another country held a finality about it that was strangely disconcerting.

Jackman pulled back and shook Adrian's hand. "Sure you're okay here?" He wanted to see Celia to her plane, but it wouldn't be fair. Adrian was going to miss her too and they needed time together. Alone.

"Yeah, I'll get the train after Celia's plane leaves."

Jackman nodded and watched as they rolled the cases towards the entrance. The doors swung open. Celia suddenly stopped, rushed back and flung her arms around him. The single moment folded back the years and brought a knot to Jackman's chest. "I'm going to miss you," she said, reached up and kissed his cheek. "Look after Mum for me."

Jackman waved until the doors slid closed behind them. Back at his car, he sat for a moment, staring into space when a thought pushed into his mind. He opened the glovebox. Carmela's folder was still in there, tucked away from the day before. He leafed through the papers until he found the details of the woman who'd phoned the incident room. He checked the clock on the dashboard. Almost 12.30pm. He pulled out his phone and dialled.

\*\*\*

Jackman turned off the M1 and made his way through the outskirts of North London. Victorian terraces were interspersed with modern eclectic-looking buildings and ancient churches. Shops lined the streets, punctuated by lines of residential housing. So many years had passed since he'd lived here. He'd forgotten what it was like to live in the midst of a hub, traffic and chatter constantly in the background. As he drove through Hampstead the houses became larger, detached with shiny Porches and BMWs on the drive, then back into the terraces, packed tightly together utilising every ounce of space. He slowed at the traffic lights and smiled to himself as a red Ferrari pulled up next to him – that wasn't something he saw on Stratford High Street.

The lights changed and he continued on for another ten minutes, winding in and out of the traffic until he turned off the main road into Holloway. Tufnell Park Road was a line of terraces that overlooked parkland surrounded by metal railings. He pulled in on the left, climbed out of the car. Hanging baskets filled with red geraniums swayed in the afternoon breeze as he approached a white front door. There were two bells in the small porch and he rang the top one marked 822a.

Footsteps descended stairs. A woman with short brown hair opened the door. She wore a loose cream top over black denims; a single gold locket hung around her neck. Gold flip-flops clad her feet.

Jackman held up his card. "I'm looking for Mrs Kerry Shaw. I phoned earlier."

The woman gave a kind smile. Her eyes were surrounded

by more lines than Jackman would have expected at her age. "Kerry, please," she said. "Come on in."

She moved aside for Jackman to enter and waved him up the steep stairs. "The kitchen is straight ahead."

Jackman padded across the laminated flooring and into a square kitchen that was neatly fitted with pine cupboards.

"Do sit down." She gestured towards a small table at the end beneath the sash window. "Tea, coffee, or something cold?"

"Tea would be lovely, thank you. Milk, no sugar."

As Kerry busied herself with the drinks, Jackman glanced out of the window at the garden below. It was laid to lawn, the borders well-maintained and planted with a mixture of perennial bushes and summer impatiens creating a merry splash of colour.

Kerry placed a teapot on a mat and proceeded to pour it into the cups. It reminded Jackman of his visits to his grandma as a kid.

"You said you have some information about Evan Baker?" he said. The name made Kerry pause. The lid of the teapot rattled slightly. "Or should I say Richard Garrett?" he added.

Kerry waited until she had finished making the tea and sat in the seat opposite Jackman. Her face tensed as she spoke. "I'm guessing you know our history?"

Jackman nodded. "I know that your daughter reported rape and her alleged attacker was acquitted at trial."

Kerry swallowed and shut her eyes momentarily. "Jason Anders. That man's face will be for ever etched on my brain." Kerry took a deep breath, opened her eyes. "You're probably wondering why I called you. It might be nothing, but... about a month after the trial I was surfing the net when I found a local support group for families whose daughters had been attacked. It was run by a woman called Nicola Wallis from Rugby. Her daughter had been attacked and her assailant was acquitted in 2011. I was still living in Warwickshire at the time."

258

Jackman gave a single nod.

"I was having a bad day so I emailed her and she sent me the details of their next meeting." She paused and took a sip of tea. "But when she emailed back I went off the idea. My daughter, Sammy, was a mess and I didn't have the energy or the capacity to think about anything else so I declined. But then as the months folded past, and Sammy didn't seem to improve…" Kerry's voice cracked slightly. "I don't know, I was at my wits end. We had doctors and counsellors coming out of the woodwork, but it didn't seem to make a difference."

She stared out of the window.

Jackman pressed his lips together. "Take your time."

"Do you know what's it's like to watch somebody you love fall apart bit by bit? She stopped going to work, wouldn't go out on her own and eventually wouldn't go out at all. I was frightened to death I was going to lose her. That I'd come home one day and she'd have…" She cleared her throat. "The counsellors said she would work through it, that it was temporary, but when I couldn't see any improvement I started to look further afield. And then I remembered the email from Nicola. There was a telephone number at the bottom of it. I called her up and she was nice and supportive. She listened to me for over an hour on that first phone call and I agreed to go to one of their meetings.

"It wasn't easy, I had to arrange for Mark, Sammy's brother to come and stay. He was the only other person she felt safe with. And I still wasn't sure. Anyway we met at Nicola's house. There were four of us altogether, all family of women who'd been attacked. I found the first meeting very hard, listening to their stories. I wasn't sure I'd go back, but the second meeting was more helpful. They suggested things to help with Sammy, little strategies like taking her to the park, just for a few minutes at a time. It took a while, but I did start to see some improvement. So I carried on for a bit."

"Why did you stop?" Jackman asked.

"A number of things really. Sammy was improving, getting

some of her confidence back. Except she wouldn't go out alone. She was always worried that she might see him, bump into him, that he'd hurt her again. We took a holiday, went to stay with my brother in Barcelona. She was different there, more confident, more like her old self. When we came back I could see a change in her. She was somehow happier there, where nobody knew what had happened to her. Anyway, eventually she moved out there. She still lives with my brother's family but she is working now and seems to have regained some independence. I go out to visit two or three times a year, when I can get a cheap flight. And I came here to look after my mother. Decided to keep the flat on after she died."

"And the support group?"

"I stopped around March last year. It had certainly helped, but there was also a dark side to it."

"What do you mean?"

"A kind of bitterness. I suppose it's understandable with what we've all been through but instead of discussing strategies on how to help each other cope, the talk switched to injustice and how the law had let them down. I came home from the last meeting feeling a bit tainted by all the negativity."

"What sort of negativity?"

"Oh, you know. If they could take justice into their own hands, what they would do. Daydreams really. I just couldn't see how it could help."

They sat in silence for a moment before Jackman eventually spoke up. "Where were the others from?"

"Angie was from Coventry and Joni from somewhere in Stratford I think. Nicola was the only one from Rugby, like me."

"And you haven't heard anything from them since?"

"Nicola contacted me when I didn't attend the next meeting. I said I was busy. I never really gave them a reason why I left, I suppose I didn't want to hurt anyone's feelings. It just petered out."

"So why contact us now?"

Kerry scratched the side of her nose. "It's probably nothing. I've been away in Spain this past month with Sammy. My son still lives in Warwickshire. He phoned me when I arrived back on Thursday evening and was telling me about the fire and the body in the barn. The name Richard Garrett sounded familiar. It reminded me of the support group. I can't be sure, but I've a feeling he might have been mentioned."

Jackman remembered that Alicia Wainwright's family lived in Northampton. He hadn't been made aware of any links to Warwickshire.

"Then when he told me Angie was found dead..."

"Sorry, what?"

"Angie Fraser. She killed herself, jumped off the Erskine Bridge four weeks ago. Had been missing for a few days beforehand, according to the news." Kerry's eyes filled with tears. "Such a sweet woman. She used to come to the meetings with Joni. Angie was the gentler one of the three. It was such a coincidence, that I thought I should tell somebody."

"Can you remember Joni's surname?" Jackman asked.

Kerry stared at the table for some time before she raised her eyes. "No, I'm sorry. I only learnt of Angie's because it came up in conversation once – both our mothers grew up in Glasgow. Nicola would know. She was the one who contacted people, organised the meetings."

# Chapter **Forty-Two**

Jackman climbed back into his car and sat motionless for a moment, pondering the situation. Russell had been out and visited Alicia Wainwright's family after they'd returned from their holiday on the Saturday morning. All of them had alibis for the night of Richard Garrett's murder. He'd asked her to take it wide and check with any extended family they were in contact with, but nothing had come to light.

He reached for his phone and tried Russell's mobile. When it switched to voicemail, he tried Davies. She answered almost immediately and listened while Jackman relayed Kerry's story to her.

"That explains why I couldn't find the papers," she replied.

"What?"

"I'm at work. Left John and the baby having an afternoon nap and thought I'd come in and look at that London lead. You beat me to it."

"Have either of these names been mentioned as part of Alicia's extended family?"

He heard a rustle of papers in the background. A brief hesitation. "Not that I can see," Davies said. "Not mentioned in Russell's report or the details sent across from Northampton."

"There's something odd about this," he said. "We've an address for Nicola Wallis. Get uniform out to see her, will you? To check her movements for last Sunday evening. Is there anything on the system about Angie Fraser?"

He heard Davies heave forward, the tapping of keys. "She was reported as a missing person in Rugby just over a month ago. Her body was recovered from the banks of the River Clyde a few days later. Recorded as suicide. Looks like she jumped off the Erskine Bridge."

"Right. They must have interviewed friends, family close to her. See what you can dig up. And we'll also need full contact details for this Joni woman. I'll be there as soon as I can."

\*\*\*

Nancy was surprised when she woke and stared at the red digits on the clock beside her. It was 3pm. She reached for her phone, pulled up a text from Becca:

*Thinking of you. Text me when you're awake.*

She punched out a quick reply and scrolled down to read a text from Ryan:

*Sorry about last night. Hope you're okay. x*

Memories of the evening before flooded her brain, merging with the broken dreams that disturbed her night. Her head was brimming, but there was something she needed to do.

Nancy hesitated. Something told her to call Cheryl, sort things out. But she stopped short of pressing the call button.

Nancy had just made it through to the sitting room, the steam still rising from her mug of coffee, when the doorbell sounded. She rested her head against the back of the sofa, ignored it. It rang again. She clenched her teeth. When it sounded for the third time she marched out to the hallway and wrenched it open.

The woman that faced her made her start. She cleared her throat. "Oh, I'm sorry. I was expecting someone else." She looked up as the woman that towered over her gave a smile that didn't reach her eyes.

When she spoke her voice was surprisingly low. "I was

an acquaintance of one of Richard Garrett's girlfriends. I saw your piece in the newspaper."

"Oh." An awkward silence followed. Visitors were the last thing Nancy fancied at the moment, strangers even less so. But she stood aside. "Would you like to come in, Mrs…?"

The woman ignored the question and marched into the flat. The door to the sitting room was open and she made straight for it, as if she was an old friend visiting. Nancy followed her. By the time she had reached the sitting room, the woman was ensconced in her seat on the sofa.

Nancy gaped at her a moment. "Er… Can I get you some tea?"

"White, two sugars. Don't stir."

There was something about her that made Nancy nervous and she felt strangely calmer when she'd retreated to the kitchen. Her phone was on the side and as the kettle was boiling she picked it up and texted Becca:

*Hope you are having a lovely time.*

Her finger hovered for a split second, as she mulled over whether or not to share the news of her visitor, but she decided against it. It wouldn't do any good anyway. Only make Becca call. And she didn't want to do anything to spoil her time away. She glanced fleetingly at the police alarm and picked up the mug.

By the time Nancy was back in the sitting room, the woman was standing, looking at the photos on the hearth. She passed over the tea. "So, what can you tell me about him?"

The woman shot her a look. "What?"

"You said you were a friend of one of Richard's girlfriends. You must have met him at some stage. I assume that's why you're here?"

The woman didn't answer. She turned and for a split second Nancy thought she was looking at her own reflection in the mirror. An uncomfortable silence filled the room. Before she quickly turned back.

The blow that hit the side of Nancy's head knocked her

264

sideways and sent a shower of steaming tea over the sofa. She felt the nylon of carpet on her cheek. It was a moment before she realised what had happened. Just when her brain was starting to register, another blow came – this time low, from a foot. And the world turned black.

***

Water on her face. Cold. Nancy squinted, flinching. More drops of water. They were running diagonally across her cheeks, into her ears, down her neckline.

She opened her mouth to shout and felt loose threads of material on her tongue. Nancy opened one eyelid to a tiny slit – just as a deluge of icy water hit her right in the eyes. She blinked, shaking her head to the side. She made to haul herself forward. Tried to lift her hands. And failed. They were secured tightly behind her back.

Fear pulsed through her.

She scanned the room. She was laid out on the sofa. Her hands were bound behind her back, her legs strapped together at the ankles. The cable ties pinched into her skin.

The woman towered over her, a look of contempt fixed upon her face.

Nancy opened her mouth, tried to plead, but the gag turned her words into muffled squeaks.

"Do you know who I am?" the woman snarled.

Nancy jolted her head from side to side.

"My name's Sheila Buckton. Your boyfriend raped my granddaughter." The whites of her eyes showed as she bent forward. "Don't you realise what you've done?"

Nancy shook her head again, but it was more of a tremble than a shake.

"You wouldn't give up, would you? Had to speak to the newspapers about how he'd been cast in a bad light. 'People were out to get him.' Wasn't that the line you used? You have no idea…" She gritted her teeth. "Five months." She snorted. "Five months he was with our Alicia. Of course he was nice to her at first. Bought her things, made her feel special. Then, when she was in too deep, he started pushing the knife in. Slowly grinding her down. Taking everything from her until she had no friends, barely saw her family. He raped her that night, I'm sure of it. He knew that, even if she had the strength to get away, to go to the police, she'd never be able to stand up and prove it to a jury. That's why he played along with it. Because he knew she couldn't. They were together about three months before he changed, started to show his true colours." She paused, squeezed her eyes together. "You don't get it, do you? I was saving you. My granddaughter never recovered after he attacked her. Hung herself at nineteen. Such a waste. I watched him with you. And I couldn't bear to let history repeat itself." She hissed the words out, showering Nancy with her spittle.

"But you couldn't let it go, could you? You had to go to the papers, to make him out to be the knight in shining armour. The only armour he had was in here." She pointed at her chest. "How dare you!"

Nancy could feel her limbs trembling. Taste acid in her mouth.

There was a knock at the door.

Sheila's head darted up.

Nancy seized the moment, took as deep a breath as she could from behind the gag and called out. Even behind the muffled material it was impressive.

Sheila glanced back towards the door. The banging became louder, more urgent. She shot a look back at Nancy and made out into the hallway.

Nancy heard a familiar voice. It was Ryan. He'd come to check on her. His head appeared around the doorframe. Nancy looked into his eyes. He'd battled through. Come to save her.

Until his head jolted awkwardly and his body crumpled forward.

Nancy tried to let out another scream, but her voice was muted in panic. She watched Sheila Buckton kick his legs aside, an action that made his whole body rest awkwardly beside the armchair. Then she reached into her pocket and pulled out a small box.

As realisation set in, Nancy's body began to squirm.

Sheila stared at her, right into her eyes, as she struck the match and lay it in the chair beside the fire, then struck another. She tossed that one at the rug. Two more and Nancy could see the chair had ignited, tiny flames expanding.

And with that, Sheila retreated, slamming the door shut behind her.

Wisps of smoke were rising into the air around her. In desperation, Nancy shifted and wriggled until she tipped off the sofa. The phone rang in the distance. The juxtaposition of Becca's voice on the answerphone mingling with the flames felt surreal, as if she were watching fireworks on New Year's. She pushed forward until her movements weakened. Her vision was blurring until slowly, almost peacefully, the lights went out and all became quiet.

# Chapter **Forty-Three**

A growing sense of foreboding encircled Jackman as he crossed the county border into Warwickshire. Something about the interview with Kerry made him uneasy. He dialled Davies again and didn't waste time with pleasantries. "How did uniform get on?"

"They've interviewed Nicola Wallis. Claims she was at home with her husband last Sunday night. The support group wound up not long after Kerry left. She maintains the contact dwindled. She hasn't heard from the others in months and didn't seem to know about Angie Fraser's suicide."

"I've gone through the statements and case files. Angie was registered with the community mental health team and being treated for depression. She disappeared a few days before. It's thought she drove up to Scotland to her birthplace, her car was found nearby. Left two children, the daughter that was attacked and a son. Both were devastated it seems. Nothing to suggest it wasn't suicide."

He heard a phone ringing in the distance. "Excuse me a moment, sir," Davies said. The line went quiet. He could hear a rustle of papers in the background, excited chatter, but couldn't make out what was being said. It was a several moments before Davies returned to the phone. "That's interesting. Joni is the nickname of Sheila Buckton, apparently she was obsessed with Joni Mitchell when she was young."

"The same Sheila Buckton that reported the fire?"

He could hear Davies clicking away at her computer as he spoke. "I can only assume so. Looks like there is only one Sheila Buckton registered as living in the Stratford area. Can't find any links with the Wainwright family though and she wasn't mentioned in the list Northampton sent over of family contacts, although she does share the maternal surname of Alicia's mother. It's possible she could be extended family. I'm going to get over there, see what she's got to say."

Jackman thought about Sheila Buckton, how close she lived to the barn, her interest in the case. If she was linked to Alicia in any way she had motive and means. "Make sure you take somebody with you. Have we heard from Nancy, at all?"

"I've phoned and texted her," Davies said, echoing his thoughts, "and left a message on the landline. She's not picking up. Want me to get uniform out there?"

"No, I'm not far away. I'll call by myself."

Jackman eased his foot off the accelerator as he reached the outskirts of Stratford and headed for Nancy's flat. It wasn't until he got out of the car and glanced up that he noticed the edge of a flame lick the window in the flat above the florists.

He ran through the side entrance and around the back. Smoke was seeping out of the open gaps in the upstairs windows. His feet bounced off the metal steps as he climbed two at a time.

"Nancy!"

All was silent, apart from the crackle of flames inside. Jackman didn't hesitate, thrusting his shoulder into the door – repeating the action several times. He tumbled forward as the lock gave way and immediately became drenched in the smoke that billowed out of the open space, exacerbated by the additional oxygen.

Jackman lifted his shirt to cover his mouth and made his way in. He kicked open the kitchen door, each of the bedrooms, then pushed the lounge door.

Flames instantly lashed out at him, forcing him back. He protected his face with his free hand and saw the body of a woman through the flames. He pushed forward through the thick heat, trying to shield his face.

Nancy was unconscious, her body curled into a foetal position on the floor beside the sofa, its low position sheltering her slightly from the flames eating through the room. Jackman bent down and hauled her up. But that meant taking a hand from his nose.

A lungful of smoke immediately sent him into a coughing fit. He forced himself to hold his breath, grabbed her, lifting her into his arms. It wasn't until he was into the hallway that he saw the other body folded awkwardly beside the armchair. The face obscured. He carried Nancy out, placing her down on the small balcony and looked back. The fire was stronger now, the hallway full of smoke. He grabbed a cotton sheet that was hanging over the edge of the balcony. It felt damp against his skin. He wrapped it around himself and ran back into the fire.

Jackman's vision blurred. He had to feel his way through the lounge doorway and across to the other body. He tugged at it. There was no sign of life. Using all his might he pulled it, hauling it up and made for the exit.

Jackman didn't remember the retreat out onto the balcony, brushing the flames from his arm, falling to his knees. He didn't even hear the distant sound of sirens as he collapsed, the heat overpowering him, until he could breathe no more.

\*\*\*

The sound of heels clicking the linoleum flooring made Davies look up. Janus offered a vague smile, brushed past and sat next to her. "Any news?"

Davies shook her head. "They're assessing him now. Nothing on the others yet either." She fixed her gaze ahead, not daring to close her eyes. Because every time she did, she could see the scene in Nancy's street when she'd arrived earlier. Fire fighters crawling around like an army of ants. Paramedics lifting bodies in ambulances. Her stomach dipped. "I should have been there."

Janus pushed her glasses up her nose. "You couldn't have known—"

"I should have made him wait, until I was there with him."

Nurses moved passed them, porters pulled trolleys, their wheels rattling against the floor. Neither of them spoke for a while. "He knew something was wrong with the Anderson murder charge," Davies said. "And he was right."

"We used the evidence we had before us," Janus said.

The sound of Davies' mobile phone ringing filled the corridor. She pulled it out of her pocket, listened for a moment before she said, "I'll be right there."

Janus looked up at her as she stood. "I asked uniform to drive by Sheila Buckton's house at regular intervals and report back if there was any sign of a presence," Davies said. "They've just spotted a car parked outside that wasn't there earlier. Call me as soon as there is any news."

\*\*\*

A dishevelled-looking man with sallow cheeks and heavy eyes that looked like he hadn't slept in a week answered the door of Sheila Buckton's home later that afternoon.

Davies held up her ID, introduced herself and the plain clothes officer she had purloined from the CID shift to accompany her. "I was looking for Sheila Buckton," she said.

He hung his head. "You'd better come in."

By the time Mark Buckton had introduced himself as Sheila's son they'd reached the kitchen. The same room Davies had been in almost a week ago with Sheila relating her account of the fire. "Do you know where your mother is?" Davies asked.

Mark Buckton sat at the table and pulled his hands down

his face, tugging at the skin as he did so. When he spoke, his voice was husky. "I know what you are here for."

"Do you?"

He nodded. "I was there last Sunday night, out walking near the farm."

Davies looked at the officer next to her. He retrieved a notebook from his inside pocket.

"Do you live here?"

"No, I have a flat in Stratford near my work. But I shoot over here occasionally, and come and stay over when I do, to keep Mum company."

"Were you out walking on your own last Sunday?" Davies said.

Mark nodded.

"Do you often go for walks over the fields late at night?"

"When I can't sleep, yes."

"Did you walk up to the farm?"

"No, I went on foot up the side of the field opposite. I used to walk my dog over there when Mum first moved here. He's passed away now. There's a gap in the hedge where you can get into the farmhouse garden."

"What about their dogs?"

"The kennel is around the back, on the other side of the main house. They don't generally stir, if you are quiet. They were barking that night though. The sound of an engine started them off. I watched a car come up the driveway to Upton Grange Farm. Couldn't see the make in the dark, but it definitely wasn't the farm Land Rover. Two men got out. I heard the sound of breaking glass. A while later, they left. They were carrying something."

"Did you see what it was?"

"No, it was pitch black," he replied. "There were no lights anywhere. I gathered it was a break-in of some sort and stayed hidden in the bushes at the side. I was planning to leave, as soon as the coast was clear, but it was only a minute or so before I heard another engine and recognised the Land

Rover. I heard them cross the gravel towards the door. Even above the barks of the dogs I heard her gasp. They waited a moment. I could just about make out the conversation. She wanted to call the police, he wouldn't let her. When they went inside it was quiet for a moment, I guess he was checking the house. The barking subsided. That's when I heard the argument. They were shouting at each other. Then a thump. I moved to the side of the house and saw her on the floor."

"What happened next?"

"I felt like I had to intervene. She was still on the floor when I went inside. Alone. I was trying to help the girl when I heard him coming through from the lounge. He was angry, shouting. I grabbed a pan off the rack, one of those heavy, copper-bottomed ones. I hid behind the door, lashed out as he walked through – just to protect myself. He turned, stared at me a moment before his knees buckled. That's when I saw it. The resemblance. My mother was right. He was the man who raped my niece."

"Do you have any idea where your mother is now? We really need to speak to her."

He ran his hands through his hair, leaving his elbows suspended. "I think there's only one place she will be."

\*\*\*

The churchyard gate creaked as the officer pushed it back. He scanned the area, desperately picking through the gravestones. A shrill wail emitted in the distance, splitting the air in two.

He followed the voice, ran around the back of the church, sidestepping the gravestones in his haste. By the time he caught a glimpse of her in the half-light, he was out of breath. "Mrs Buckton."

She was kneeling down in front of a grave.

She turned. Her hair was wild and ragged, her eyes fixed wide. He saw the knife, the end pointing to the pit of her stomach. He waved a hand behind his back at his colleague racing to catch up and immediately heard her footsteps slow. "Mrs Buckton, please. Put down the knife."

For a moment nothing happened. A light breeze whistled down the side of the church. He heard his colleague step forward, felt her arm brush his side. Her voice was soft. "Mrs Buckton?"

Sheila Buckton raised her gaze to the female officer. But the expression on her face folded. She lifted the knife with both hands high into the air.

He raced forward just in time to watch the knife be driven into the ground before her.

# Chapter **Forty-Four**

"The glass was already broken when I arrived. It seems I wasn't the only one who wanted him to suffer that night."

Davies stared into the eyes of Sheila Buckton. For the past hour they'd been seated in the interview room listening to her account of what happened on Sunday evening. The officer that had picked her up had reported a woman with a knife, sprawled across a gravestone. Her wails had subsided into confused sobs, berating herself for lacking the strength to join her beloved granddaughter. But the drive to Warwickshire appeared to have calmed her. The doctor that examined her cleared her for interview. And as soon as Davies opened the introductions, Sheila started to speak and couldn't seem to stop. Keane scribbled away next to her, barely able to keep up.

"Are you saying somebody else had already broken into the farmhouse before you got there?" Davies said.

"Yes." Sheila cast a sideways glance at her solicitor. "The back door was ajar. There'd been some kind of fight. Richard and the girl were both lying on the kitchen floor. They looked like they'd been knocked out or something. He stirred as I let myself in, but was dazed."

Davies narrowed her eyes. "Rather convenient."

"What?"

"Somebody else knocking them out when you arrived. What was your plan?"

"I've been watching his movements for a while. I heard

his truck pass that night, guessed he'd come home from the pub. After about twenty minutes I drove to the farmhouse. His truck was parked outside. The kitchen light was on. I was expecting him to be at home alone."

"How did you propose to get him to come with you?"

"I'd acquired..." She cleared her throat. "A gun, two bullets just in case."

"Where did you get it from?"

Sheila looked down at her clenched hands. "I was given it."

"By whom?"

"I'm not prepared to say."

"What happened next?"

"I made him drive."

"I thought you said he was dazed."

"He seemed to manage okay."

Davies paused a moment. She was accustomed to suspects being evasive, making up stories. But what surprised her about Sheila was that she delivered it with such sincerity. And not an ounce of remorse. "I've been looking for him from the moment Alicia died. I swore if he ever came back..."

"Why the barn?" Davies said.

Sheila looked up at her. "I didn't want him to have an easy death. He didn't deserve that after what he did to Alicia. I wanted him to suffer."

"But why call the fire service?"

"Why not? He would have been dead by then."

Davies let the silence linger for a while. Keane's pen scratched away on the paper beside her. "It must have been difficult to manoeuvre him into the barn," she said eventually.

"What do you mean?"

"You're in your early sixties. Do you expect me to believe—"

Sheila snorted. "I'm stronger than I look."

"But you did have help, didn't you?"

Sheila's face hardened.

276

"Somebody very close to you helped, didn't they? Somebody with a vested interest in the suspect, just like you."

"I did it on my own. I managed."

"Oh, come on. You don't expect me to believe that he didn't struggle. At all?" Davies sat forward. "You see we know that the victim was knocked unconscious when he was left at the barn, before the fire was started. And we know your son, Mark, was there with you that night. He helped you lift the victim into the car, take him to the barn."

"You can't prove anything." Sheila hissed.

"We already have Mark's admission. You can't protect him anymore."

There was a deafening silence. "Do you have kids, Detective?" Shelia asked.

Davies stared at her, said nothing.

Sheila turned to the side, momentarily lost in her own little world. "My husband wasn't a good man. Oh, he was lovely in front of my parents, the perfect gentleman, but when we were on our own... He wanted to take what he believed was rightfully his, before I was ready to give it. I fell pregnant, we got married. My parents were old-fashioned. That's the way it was then."

"Can we—"

"My daughter, Christine, was a daddy's girl from the moment she was born," Sheila continued, cutting through the interruption. "Never content unless she was sitting on his knee, beside him on the sofa, watching at the window for him to arrive home. Even through her early teenage years when most girls turned to their mothers..." She shook her head. "Never her. Always her father. And when he left he took her with him. She was fifteen." Sheila met Davies' gaze. "I'll never forget the look on his face. He had his beautiful girl. I rarely saw her after that, he continued to turn her against me, blame me for our separation, until she wouldn't have anything to do with me. He lavished attention on her. My son, the only other time he'd showed any interest in me,

277

was always pushed aside for that girl." The chair beside her squeaked as Keane shifted about, but Davies ignored him, willing her to continue.

"I wasn't invited to my daughter's wedding, but I did hear that she moved into his house in Harlestone Village, Northamptonshire after her dad died. Only an hour away from here. I used to drive across there, walk around the village and sit in the churchyard in the hope of seeing her children when they were young. Sad when I think of it. Skulking around behind sunglasses. Not that she ever recognised me when I did catch a glimpse. Alicia got in contact with me, just after her eighteenth birthday. Apparently she traced me online. Tried loads of Bucktons in the Warwickshire area until she found the right one."

"How did she contact you?" Davies asked.

"By phone at first. I'll never forget the day I met her. She didn't look anything like Christine, apart from the brown corkscrew curls. She was small, petite, with soft brown eyes and a pretty face. And there was a sensitivity about her that she certainly didn't get from her mother. It was awkward at first. She came armed with a million questions – why her mother and I didn't see each other, why I hadn't tried to find her, what had happened between us. In fact, it was my son that really brought us together. Her uncle. He was here, the second time she visited. They were so similar, shared an interest in animals. He brought his terrier over and they really hit it off. After that she'd drive across to see us in Warwickshire every month or so. None of us mentioned her parents. Our relationship was new, fragile, and we didn't want to sour it. I did ask once about her sister, but she didn't want to talk about her. We used to have horses sometimes, in the field across the road, and she'd always go across and see them. I think that's what she wanted to do really, work with horses. She was on a gap year, supposedly looking at university courses." Sheila's face darkened. "We didn't see her after the incident. In fact, we didn't know anything about it until a while afterwards. She cancelled. Twice. Ignored my texts. Mark was distraught. He's never married, saw her almost as a daughter. Then one day she turned up, out of the blue, and told me what had happened. It was awful." Her eyes flooded with tears. "She sat at my kitchen table and shivered the whole time. She was like an empty shell, every ounce of life sucked from her."

Sheila swiped a tear from her cheek. "We helped her, as much as we could, to prepare for the trial. Of course, we couldn't be there. I sent messages every day, little texts to let her know we were thinking of her. He was in custody. I thought the trial was a formality. I followed it online." She closed her eyes. "When the not guilty verdict came out, I was floored. I couldn't believe it.

"We didn't see her for a while after that, about four months, I think. Mark was frantic, we both were, but in a way I guessed she needed some time. Her family were around her. When she did come she looked ill, ghost-like. That was the last time we saw her. I never heard about the suicide until…" Her face hardened. "So you see, I had to do something? None of us expect to bury our children, but our grandchildren? It's inconceivable. Mark wanted to hunt him down, there and then, tear him apart. But it was only the shock talking. What good would that do?

"I'm not sure exactly when I changed my mind," she continued. "As time passed by, I couldn't bear the idea of him out there, laughing, living, while Alicia was… It ate away at me, but I wanted to plan it out, make him suffer. Just like we had. Just like Alicia did. So I decided to find out as much as I could about him. I researched his name online, found out where he'd lived; went to visit his mother, although she refused to see me. I copied all the photos I could find of him from Facebook, Twitter, Instagram onto my hard drive and spent hours looking through them. I went to Northampton, sat outside cafés to see if I could spot him, watched his movements online. He still had the audacity to drink in the same pub!" She looked up, incredulous. "I was getting close to him. Then suddenly, almost overnight, everything stopped. No more social media. I went across to Northampton, visited the pub, asked after him. And that's when I heard he'd gone away. Abroad somewhere, that's all they knew.

"Part of me was relieved, the other side distraught. What if he attacked another innocent girl, one as sweet and young as our Alicia? I couldn't bear the idea he would ruin someone else's life. As much as I tried to move on, it sat there, niggling away at the back of my mind. He'd ruined her life, wrecked those of her family and friends, yet he was free to do it all again. I even joined a support group of other women in similar situations. Thought it might help my son, although he wouldn't go. They were really nice. It helped for a while."

"When did you find out he was back?" Davies asked.

Sheila met her gaze for a split second. "I remember the first day I spotted him. I was driving back from Stratford town on the A46. It was like déjà vu, even though I'd never seen him in person before, I'd studied so many pictures of him. I remember coming home, searching through them, convincing myself that I must be wrong. A few weeks later I saw him climbing out of a tractor outside the entrance to Upton Grange. He was with another man. I heard him speak and straight away the accent drove into me. Alicia said he had a Northamptonian accent, he dragged some of his words. I wasn't really sure what she meant until I heard it. I remember driving up to the farmhouse to see Janine, pretending I was out of milk, to find out more about him. She was happy to talk to me, told me he'd joined them over a year ago, was surprised I hadn't seen him before. It was her who told me his name was Evan Baker. Then she mentioned he'd been abroad.

"I raced home, googled Evan Baker. Nothing of any significance came up in the Stratford area. I thought my eyes were playing tricks on me, that I was going mad.

"It was the next time I saw him, a month or so later, that

I really knew. He was closing a gate to a cattle field and the furtive way he looked at me, those shifty eyes. It had to be him.

"I could hardly believe he was working locally. He wouldn't have known about my relationship to Alicia. I was estranged from her mother so we'd never met. I bet he thought he was safely away from the prying eyes of her Northampton family, where people might recognise him. The world's a small place, isn't it?"

Davies ignored the question. "What did you do next?"

"I watched him for a while. It's not easy on these quiet country roads, I had to be careful. He seemed to spend a lot of time at the barn, so I thought that's where he should die." Sheila looked directly at Davies. "He raped my granddaughter, took away her life. He deserved to die."

"He was acquitted." Davies said.

"Doesn't mean he wasn't guilty."

"What about his girlfriend?"

"I felt sorry for her at first. In some ways I thought I'd done her a favour, she could have been his next victim. Just like Alicia. But when she gave that newspaper interview, talking about him as if he was some kind of saint who'd been wronged, I couldn't let her get away with that."

"So you went to her flat."

Sheila nodded.

"What about her friend?"

"I didn't ask him to come by."

"A police inspector was injured, trying to save them."

"I did what I had to do. For Alicia," Sheila replied. "Just wish I'd had the guts to join her when I had the chance."

# Chapter **Forty-Five**

Jackman reached his arm out to the bedside table. He felt the dressing on his tricep catch the end of the wood and winced. Extending the arm again, he grasped his watch and pulled it. 10.30am. Monday 17th August. Right now he should be sitting in front of an interview panel, facing grilling questions on his ability to manage, his views on current policing policy, his ideas for taking the organisation forward. Instead he was laid up in a hospital bed. He clenched his teeth. *All that preparation, for nothing.*

He checked his messages – one from Celia saying she'd arrived, another from Carmela wishing him the best of luck for his interview, sent yesterday. She obviously hadn't heard about the fire.

Jackman remembered very little of the last twenty-four hours. His last recollection was of flames around his right arm, a burning sensation, falling to his knees. Nancy. He'd gone into the building to rescue Nancy. He recalled her limp body. Had he been too late?

He remembered the visit to London, the revelation of the support group. Maybe he should have sent a team straight around to check on Nancy. Maybe he shouldn't have waited to check out the links. If he'd done that, if the police had arrived minutes earlier...

The door opened and a nurse wandered in, a smile lighting up her face as she made eye contact. "Lovely to see you're awake," she said, exposing a row of perfectly white teeth.

Jackman pulled himself to a seated position. "How long have I been here?" His voice was husky when he spoke, his mouth dry.

"You don't remember? You were brought in last night, with a man and a woman. Nasty burn to the top of your arm and smoke inhalation, but you'll be fine."

"What about the others?" He was sitting up now, staring at her anxiously.

"The man, Ryan, has been moved to the burns unit. He's stable now."

A flashback: emerging from the flat. The weight of the body he was carrying pulling him down. Heat. He couldn't see anything through the smoke…

Jackman felt something wrap around his good arm, snapping him back to the present. The nurse pressed a button, checked her watch.

Jackman coughed. His throat was raw. "What about the woman?"

"I'm not sure, to be honest." She was only half listening, watching the monitor in front of her. "Blood pressure's fine," she said. The Velcro made a loud ripping noise as she removed it from his arm.

"Could you find out for me?" Jackman asked. "It's important. Her name is Nancy Faraday."

"Nancy," she repeated. "Okay, I'll go and ask."

Jackman massaged his temples. He could see Nancy's pleading eyes in the incident room on Thursday, feel her frail body flopped over his arms.

The door pulled open and the young nurse's face appeared. "Nancy has been transferred to a ward," she said. "Some minor burns to her legs, knocks and bruises, but she is going to be fine." She smiled again at the clear relief in his face. "We're a bit short of ward beds at the moment, I'm afraid. As soon as one becomes available we'll get you transferred too. Shouldn't be too much longer. Your colleague's been here nearly all morning.

She's gone now, but I promised to call her when you woke up. Is that okay?"

"Don't worry, I'll ring her myself." He plastered a smile on his face and waited for her to retreat.

Jackman sat there for a moment, listening to his own breaths. *Thank goodness Nancy was alive.* A huge weight lifted from his torso. He swung his feet around, hung them off the edge of the bed and stood. He only wavered slightly. Good start. If he was still in A&E, it wasn't too far to the exit and there were bound to be taxis nearby. There were always taxis at hospitals. The last thing he wanted to do was to wait around to be put in a ward filled with patients.

*** 

Nancy pushed open the door and froze. Ryan's eyes were closed, his left arm and leg wrapped in bandages and elevated. An intravenous drip fed a clear liquid into his right arm. Low breaths of a ventilator filled the room. She could feel the air seeping out of her lungs as she scanned his body, gripping on to the edge of life.

Her eyes eventually locked with Margaret's, Ryan's mother, who was seated at his bedside. His father, John, stood behind her, resting a soothing hand on his wife's shoulder. "I'm so sorry." Nancy said to her. The inadequacy of her brittle words stuck in her throat.

Margaret shook her head. "It's not your fault."

Nancy had known Ryan's parents for almost six years, since she and Ryan had met in secondary school, two young kids going out together. Margaret had ferried them to the cinema in the early days, dropped them in town, at the swimming pool, invited Nancy into their home. She was a young mother, only late thirties herself, although she'd aged ten years over the past twenty-four hours and today she looked pallid and drawn as her saddened eyes stared at her only son.

The last thing Nancy remembered was Ryan's shocked face in the doorway of the flat, watching him stagger forward, collapse beside the armchair where he'd laid awkwardly. The old woman lighting the match.

It should have been her, lying here, like this.

When Nancy had woken up in hospital, Detective Russell had come to see her and explained that her colleague had rescued her, how he'd gone back in for Ryan. The fire had taken a hold by then. The flames had caught them. For Ryan, this meant second-degree burns to his left arm and leg. He was unconscious; his body went into shock on arrival at the hospital.

A tear dripped off the edge of her chin.

"Come on, love. He's going to be okay," Margaret said. "They're just keeping him in an induced coma while they control the pain."

Nancy nodded gratefully, unable to speak. Her eyes flitted back to the bed. A thought struck her. Ryan was left-handed. The burns affected the left side of his body. It was going to take him a long time to recover from this, to be able to go back to work, drive, function like he had before. And there would be scars...

A nurse entered the room. "I'm sorry, but we can only have two people in here at once," she said. Her tone was soft, accustomed to dealing with tearful relatives and families in difficult circumstances.

"I'll—" Ryan's father moved towards the door.

"No, don't please." Nancy stepped back. "I'll come back later."

The walls closed in on Nancy as she wandered down to the waiting area. Everything was a blur. She didn't know how this had happened. She'd thought she was safe.

She grabbed a tissue from the box on the table, dabbed at her eyes as she recalled the woman's story. Her granddaughter had died. Committed suicide. Because of the rape charge. Nancy worked her way through the past three months,

285

searching for clues, little signs that might indicate a violent tendency. She had immediately assumed Evan to be wrongly accused, but perhaps it was more a case of wrongly acquitted.

The door opened and Karen and Becca entered. Becca rushed to her side.

Within seconds she was enveloped in hugs from both of them. It was a while before they pulled away.

"I'm so sorry about the fire," Nancy said. "Is there much damage to the shop?"

"Shops can be mended," Karen said dismissively. "You're both still here. That's what matters."

"It's your business."

"It's not your fault that some mad woman has gone on a rampage, Nancy," Becca said. "The insurance will sort it out."

"Needed a bit of a makeover anyway," Karen said, smiling. "Hasn't been redecorated in years."

Nancy was overwhelmed by their kindness. And at that moment she realised she'd never really know the truth about Evan. She could only make judgements based on what she knew – he was acquitted at trial, he rented out the barn; he was nice to her. Maybe she was wrong and he had brought all of this on himself and risked her life and others along the way. But he was gone now and she would never know. It wouldn't do any good to torture herself. Right now she needed to concentrate on what was important. The people around her. Ryan. He was there when she really needed him and had ended up in this state because of his loyalty to their friendship. She had to find a way to repay that somehow, make sure that she was a part of his recuperation. Because she knew it would be long and difficult.

"You look exhausted," Becca said. "We're taking you home."

Nancy thought about the beautiful town centre shop with the mock-Tudor frontage. The flat above that had been their home for almost three years. She felt a stab of sadness. "We haven't got a home."

"You've always got a home with me," Karen said.

Nancy followed them towards the exit. As she passed through the door, a figure was waiting on the other side, pushing to come through. They collided. Nancy smelled the nicotine before she pulled back.

"Hello," Cheryl said. "I heard about the fire. Came to see how you were."

"We'll meet you downstairs," Karen said. She patted Cheryl's arm, trotted down the stairs. Becca looked back twice as she followed.

Nancy stared into the eyes of her mother. It was time to make amends. She knew they would never have a conventional mother/daughter relationship. There were far too many absent memories for that. But if the events of the past few days had taught Nancy anything it was to accept people for what you know about them and move forward.

# Chapter **Forty-Six**

Jackman was awoken by the sound of knocking, followed by a gruff bark. He jerked forward, momentarily disorientated, and scanned the room. He was on the sofa in his front room. Erik was sitting by the door. He pushed his hair off his forehead, blinked a few times and glanced at the clock. 4.10pm. He could vaguely remember a taxi drive home from the hospital, a brief exchange with his neighbour as he collected Erik. He must have crashed out right here, slept through.

He swallowed, flinched. His throat felt as though he'd swallowed a mouthful of sand as he slid off the sofa and stood. Ignoring the door he wandered through into the kitchen, filled a glass of water and glugged it down, followed by another.

Knocking again. This time fist on glass. He wandered back into the lounge to find Davies' face at the window.

A pain shot through his right arm as he moved into the hallway and pulled open the door.

"Evening," Davies said, walking past him and into the house, before he'd had a chance to open his mouth. She was greeted by an enthusiastic Erik who burst through from the lounge, bouncing around the small area. "Evening to you too!" Davies said, chuckling as she bent down to pat his back. She looked back at Jackman. "How are you feeling today?"

"All right," he said, although his movements felt heavy and laboured as he pushed past her and guided Erik out of the hallway.

"You look bloody awful," she said, following him into the kitchen.

"Thanks."

She grimaced at the bandage on his arm. A mixture of blood and water were seeping through the wadding. "That needs re-dressing."

"I'll sort it out. What are you doing here?"

"I've come for a coffee," she said. "Then I'm taking you back up to A&E, to get your dressing changed."

He gave a raspy cough. "God, you're bossy."

"Well, if you will discharge yourself from hospital, what do you expect?"

"I'm fine. Aren't you meant to be at work?"

"They can cope." She busied herself with filling the kettle, crashing through the cupboards, one at a time.

Every knock and bang reverberated around his head. "The mugs are in that cupboard," Jackman said eventually, pointing at the other side of the kitchen. He watched her move around. "How are things?"

At that moment his phone buzzed on the table. "Looks like you're needed," Davies said.

Jackman grabbed his mobile. It was a text from Carmela: *How'd it go today? Was thinking of you.*

He stared at it a moment, trying to think of something to say when it buzzed again:

*Shall I put the champagne on ice?*

A smiley face sat next to it. Jackman let out a long sigh and placed it face down on the table.

The phone danced on the surface of the table as another message came through. Davies passed him his coffee. "They're persistent," she said.

"It's Celia," he lied.

"Ah. Does she know about the fire, your injury?"

He shook his head. "No, and she isn't going to. I don't want anything messing up her trip. Now are you going to tell me what's happening back at the station?"

"All right, but you are signed off sick. Janus'll do her nut if she finds out I'm here."

"She'll be tied up with her new campaign against drugs. Go on."

"Okay, well, the CPS have agreed for us to charge both the Bucktons with murder. We're still awaiting the full forensic report from the barn. We've reopened Angie Fraser's file too and are looking at her associations with Sheila Buckton. It seems unlikely that there were suspicious circumstances to her death, but the techies have found a wealth of emails exchanges between the two, right up to the moment Angie disappeared."

"And Anderson?"

"That's an interesting one. We've had more intelligence through that suggests Anderson was keeping guns at his garage that was torched, and dirty cash too."

"They wouldn't be covered on his insurance."

"Quite. There's also been a suggestion that the victim was short-changing him on supply, claiming the plants weren't doing so well."

"That would explain how he managed to send some of it to Northampton."

"Exactly. It also explains why he broke into the farmhouse too. The texts suggest Evan and him were arguing. He wanted the guns away from Evan and into his possession, for protection from him and the Northampton dealers. Anyway, they've downgraded his charge to possession of firearms, conspiracy to burgle and handling stolen goods. We've shared the details with the drugs squad, to look into his role in the supply, but they've gone bananas, accusing us of wasting two weeks of surveillance for meagre charges. Even threatened to send Janus the bill."

Jackman scoffed. "I bet that received short shrift."

Davies laughed. "So it's case building now. Making sure everything sticks. We're winding down the incident room, moving everything back to Leamington."

"Any news from the hospital?"

"Nancy's been discharged. She has some minor superficial

burns. They're talking about bringing Ryan out of the induced coma in the morning."

"Poor kids. Has anyone been out to see Nancy and told her about the cannabis cultivation at the barn? It's bound to come out with all this fanfare. Be much better if she heard it from us first."

Davies nodded. "Russell had that pleasure."

Jackman rubbed his forehead. Slowly the dust motes in his head started to settle. "How's the little one?"

"Looking at another nursery tomorrow. " She sucked an audible breath. "We'll see how that goes."

They sat in comfortable silence, drinking their coffees. Jackman felt the caffeine seeping into his system, awakening his senses. The pain in his arm intensified.

"Oh, almost forgot," Davies said. "Did you know that Thames Valley are looking for DCIs?"

Jackman looked up at her. "What?"

"They're running a board and advertising. Desperate apparently." Davies shot him a lot. "Must be because they're taking DCI Reilly."

"What do you mean?"

"Apparently it's closer to his home, less travelling. He leaves in a month. So, he'll ride the wave of the new drive against drugs campaign as his passing shot to Warwickshire."

"Sounds about right." Jackman allowed himself a relieved smile. If he'd have passed the board, he would have not only lost his team, but he would have taken DCI Reilly to Thames Valley with him. He wouldn't have wished the fire on anyone, but right now he couldn't be more thankful for the distraction. He grabbed his phone, worked through the messages from Carmela. Part of him longed to respond. But he just couldn't find the words right now.

Davies stood and placed her mug on the side. "Right, come on. Let's go and get that dressing changed," she said. Jackman gave one more glance at his phone, stood and followed her out of the door.

# Acknowledgements

Warwickshire readers will quickly spot that Cherwell Hamlet is a fictional place invented for the purposes of this novel. However, Ardens Grafton and Exhall village are very real and if you find yourself in this vicinity do call in at The Fish pub at Wixford and have a drink beside the river; I'm sure you'll receive a warm welcome. My thanks go to the people of Warwickshire for allowing me to take liberties with their beautiful countryside, with a special mention to Joyce Dooley whose local knowledge and assistance with finding different locations in and around Stratford-upon-Avon was indispensable.

I'm grateful to Northamptonshire firefighters, Mike Rodden and Dave Billing, who were extremely generous with sharing their knowledge on the effects of fire. Any deviations from reality or errors in the book are purely my own.

I'd also like to thank all the detectives and retired detectives who've helped with procedural research in this novel, most notably Ian Patrick and Glyn Timmins.

Gratitude goes to Lauren Parsons, Lucy Chamberlain and Tom Chalmers at Legend Press for continuing to have faith in my work and believing in the DI Jackman series. I really enjoy working with you!

Thanks also go to Mary Knight who gave me great insight into working farms.

Since I started my writing journey I have received

wonderful support from some lovely book clubs including Book Connectors, Shell Baker and Llainy Swanson at Crime Book Club, Tracy Fenton and The Book Club (TBC) on Facebook, David Gilchrist and UK Crime Book Club, Fran Osborne and all at Broughton Book Club, Lizzie Hayes and Mystery People, and the lovely Clare at Marvellous Readers, which was the first book club I was ever invited to as an author – an evening that will always be a special memory for me.

So many friends have helped and supported me along the way with *Beneath the Ashes*: Rebecca Bradley, Ian Patrick and Louise Voss were wonderful early readers and gave valuable feedback. Colin Williams very kindly carried out the first proof read. Also, Derek Archer, Emma Thompson, Stephanie Daniels, Philip Bouch and far too many more to mention – you know who you are. Finally, Dad and Lynne – I've dedicated this one to you both to thank you for your unrelenting support through all the ups and downs with my writing and there have been plenty!

And of course, David and Ella, my nearest and dearest who make it possible for me to write. I really appreciate you guys.

We hope you enjoyed *Beneath the Ashes*, the third Legend Press novel from Jane Isaac, and the second in the DI Will Jackman series.

Jane's Legend debut, *The Truth Will Out*, was described by best-selling crime author, Phil Rickman, as 'tense and cop-savvy'. Following this gripping police procedural was *Before It's Too Late*, described as 'a dark, tense and pacy thriller' by SJI Holliday.

*The Lies Within* is Jane's forthcoming novel, and tells the story of Grace Bannister, whose daughter's body is discovered in a Leicestershire country lane. With her family falling apart and the investigation going nowhere, Grace's only solace is the re-emergence of an old friend who seems to understand her loss. But when the police discover another victim, the spotlight falls on Grace. Can DI Will Jackman find the killer, before she is convicted of a crime she didn't commit?

If you can't wait to read more, here's a sample of *Before It's Too Late*, available online and from all good bookshops:

# Chapter **One**

*A rumble in the background woke me. I could feel something rolling, somewhere nearby. Gently, side to side, like a baby rocking in a crib.*

*I swallowed, slowly opened my eyes. The images were unclear; bleary dark shadows flickered about in the distance.*

*The rocking continued, and I suddenly became aware that it was my own body moving. A wave of panic caught me. As much as I tried, I couldn't keep it still. I had no control over my limbs.*

*Rivulets of sweat trickled down my neck. More blurred images. The sound of an engine.*

*Darkness. I was travelling in a vehicle with no windows.*

*I tried to recall earlier: the thump of music, the babble of conversation punctuated by bouts of laughter. Hanging my head over a toilet pan. Pressing my cheek to the cold tiles in the cubicle. Worming my way through sweaty bodies jammed together, moving to the beat, drinks sloshing everywhere. I needed air, and quick. Tom's face contorted in anger, the muscle in his jaw flexing as he spoke through tight teeth. The slam of the pub door behind me. The relief at emerging into the silvery darkness. Alone. The throb of an engine as it revved behind me.*

*My thoughts fragmented and faded. Little pieces of the jigsaw were missing. I reached for them in the semi-darkness, but they danced about on the periphery.*

*My head grew heavy, a thick smog began to descend on my brain.*

*The van stopped abruptly, snapping me back to the present. I was shunted forward. A pain speared through my foot and up into my calf. I couldn't move, yet I still felt the sharp ache.*

*The engine cut. The grate of a door as it swung open. A soft breeze reached in and tickled my hair.*

*Footsteps shuffled around me. Hands reached beneath my armpits. Warm breaths on my neck. Dragging.*

*I mustered every ounce of energy to turn my head and let out a gentle moan.*

*The breathing instantly halted. The grip released.*

*A cloth was pressed down on my nose and mouth. A sickly-sweet smell. I desperately wanted to struggle, I tried to, but my limbs felt like they were immersed in a puddle of glue. The world spun around me. Slower and slower. Gradually fading. Until my brain became an empty well of darkness.*

# Chapter **Two**

Detective Inspector Will Jackman lowered the window and sucked in a wave of crisp air. Stars peeped down at him through the dark blanket of sky above. A moth flew into the car and fluttered about on the dashboard but he ignored it, relishing the breeze that rushed through his hair as he pressed on.

The sweet scent of grass mingled with wild honeysuckle wafted into the car. The smells were always stronger in the dark hours, especially that gap between 2 and 5am when the roads were quiet and the people of Stratford rested in their slumber. It reminded Jackman of his early years in the police, working instant response on a rolling shift pattern around the clock. The whole atmosphere changed at night. Jobs were more sporadic but intense. Colleagues rallied around in support. Emotions were heightened. Back at the station things took on a much lighter feel, practical jokes came to the fore in an effort to lighten the load and stave off the fog of fatigue.

Jackman cast the memories aside and pushed on, leaving the town behind him, through a tunnel of trees that cast hazy shadows on the road ahead. By day, Warwick Road Lands was a haven for riverside wildlife, walkers, families sharing their picnics with the ducks in the balmy sunshine. As the sun subsided and the birds roosted it grew peaceful once more, haunted only by the occasional footfall of a passing fisherman, the call of an owl or the swoop of bats, hunting their prey.

He grew closer, turned into the empty car park and stopped the car. Gravel scratched beneath his feet, the sound elevated in the darkness, as he crossed the tarmac and made for the river bank.

He glanced at his watch. It was 2am. Right here. This was where Ellen's body had floated just over a week ago, huddled amongst the bulrushes on the water's edge.

On Saturday 3rd May, Ellen Readman had packed her suitcase into the boot of her black Ford Ka and climbed into the driver's seat. Her face had stretched into a wide grin as she had lifted her hand to wave at her housemate, revved the engine and disappeared down the road. She was off to visit her Aunt in Corfu for a week's break. A missing persons' enquiry later revealed that she'd never even reached the airport.

Media appeals followed, asking for witnesses to come forward, desperately trying to trace Ellen's movements. Her car was last spotted by police cameras leaving Stratford on the A46. But, apart from the usual crank calls and the odd sighting earlier in the week, nothing to reveal what happened next. Until her body surfaced in the River Avon.

If Jackman closed his eyes he could still see her lying there, tossed aside like a rag doll. Her face was concealed beneath a mop of long dark hair, thickly matted with Japanese knotweed. The t-shirt she wore was pulled tight across her bloated body, a short denim skirt clung to her thighs, her feet bare. Jackman let out a ragged sigh. Her parents came across from nearby Nottinghamshire to identify her body. Tissues pressed to tear-stained faces, distraught over the death of their youngest daughter. Twenty-two years old. Barely a couple of years older than his own daughter, Celia.

Jackman sunk his hands into his pockets and glanced across the water. It was calm and still. The pathologist's report indicated her body had been immersed in water for some time. Grazing on the backs of her thighs suggested she may have been lodged somewhere, freed up by the increased flow of the river due to the barrage of heavy rainfall the weekend before.

As soon as the incident room was established, police computers had identified a link with the case of a woman found in the River Nene in rural Northamptonshire, two months earlier. Twenty-two-year-old Katie Sharp's neck bore similar ligature marks, her body no sign of sexual intervention. Just like Ellen. She'd also been immersed in water for some time before a dog walker had stumbled across her.

Jackman massaged his temples. Despite there being separate incident rooms in two counties, less than an hour's drive from each other, neither were close to finding a motive, let alone a suspect. Forensics worked hard on the clothing, the bodies, the surrounding area, and yet any clues were likely flushed away.

The investigation had been code-named Operation Sky and now it felt like the clouds were rolling in, blocking out any gaps of possible light as the lines of enquiry began to dry and shrivel. The irony was not lost on him.

Jackman picked up a stone, skimmed it across the water and watched it plop twice and disappear, before turning on his heels back to the car.

Come and visit us at
**www.legendpress.co.uk**

Follow us
**@legend_press**